Dear Reader,

Imagine a dyed-in-the-wool Yankee married to a drop-dead-gorgeous Oklahoma cowboy (an Oklahoma State University cowboy, that is). Yep, that's me. After my husband and I hung up our air force uniforms for the last time, we settled in his native Oklahoma and I immediately became fascinated by the history of my adopted state.

In our rambles, Al and I have visited the prehistoric Spiro Indian Mounds; Heavner State Park with its mysterious rune stones; many of the Native American tribal headquarters; working cattle ranches along the Chisholm Trail; Forts Gibson, Reno and Sill, where Geronimo was imprisoned; historic Guthrie, start of the Great Land Run of '89; Robbers' Cave, once refuge to Jesse James and Belle Star; and many of the oil-baron mansions that rival any castle in Europe.

The tapestry woven from these different strands utterly intrigues me. So much so, I jumped at the chance to do a series of novels that begins when a United States Army expedition chartered to explore the southern reaches of the newly acquired Louisiana Territory enters the splendid, untamed wilderness that ultimately becomes Oklahoma.

So snuggle in, put your feet up and travel back in time with me to the formative years of a great state!

Merline Lovelace

**ALL ROADS EVENTUALLY
LEAD BACK TO THE TRUTH**

SUZANN LEDBETTER

After the brutal murder of her husband, police officer Liz Rivas entered the witness protection program to save her young son. Today, twenty years later, she's Jenna MacArthur, shop owner in Pfister, Missouri. Jenna and her son, Sam, a rookie cop, have built new lives in a small town where everybody knows everybody's business. Or at least think they do.

Then a stranger arrives in Pfister, a man who remembers Liz Rivas. He is Paul Haggerty, a fellow cop from her past. There are memories here, sure…and a fierce attraction. But is he a connection to her former life—or a threat to the life Jenna has sacrificed so much to build?

In Hot Pursuit

Available the first week of September 2003,
wherever paperbacks are sold!

MIRA®

Merline Lovelace

66649	THE CAPTAIN'S WOMAN	___ $6.50 U.S.	___ $7.99 CAN.
66871	THE COLONEL'S DAUGHTER	___ $6.50 U.S.	___ $7.99 CAN.
66784	THE HORSE SOLDIER	___ $5.99 U.S.	___ $6.99 CAN.

(limited quantities available)

TOTAL AMOUNT	$_____
POSTAGE & HANDLING	$_____
($1.00 for 1 book, 50¢ for each additional)	
APPLICABLE TAXES*	$_____
<u>TOTAL PAYABLE</u>	$_____

(check or money order—please do not send cash)

To order, complete this form and send it, along with a check or money order for the total above, payable to MIRA Books®, to: **In the U.S.:** 3010 Walden Avenue, P.O. Box 9077, Buffalo, NY 14269-9077; **In Canada:** P.O. Box 636, Fort Erie, Ontario L2A 5X3.

Name:_____
Address:_____ City:_____
State/Prov.:_____ Zip/Postal Code:_____
Account Number (if applicable):_____
075 CSAS

*New York residents remit applicable sales taxes.
  Canadian residents remit applicable GST and provincial taxes.

MIRA®

MERLINE LOVELACE

A Savage Beauty

MIRA®

ISBN 1-55166-707-X

A SAVAGE BEAUTY

Copyright © 2003 by Merline Lovelace.

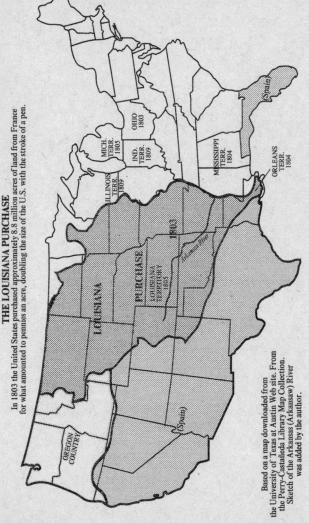

THE LOUISIANA PURCHASE

In 1803 the United States purchased approximately 8.8 million acres of land from France for what amounted to pennies an acre, doubling the size of the U.S. with the stroke of a pen.

LOUISIANA

PURCHASE

1803

LOUISIANA TERRITORY 1805

Arkansas River

ILLINOIS TERR. 1809

MICH. TERR. 1805

IND. TERR. 1809

OHIO 1803

MISSISSIPPI TERR. 1804

ORLEANS TERR. 1804

OREGON COUNTRY

(Spain)

(Spain)

Based on a map downloaded from the University of Texas at Austin Web site. From the Perry-Castañeda Library Map Collection. Sketch of the Arkansaw (Arkansaw) River was added by the author.

Legend of the Blue-Eyed Maiden

The first pale-skins came up the Great River so long ago, they are remembered only in legend. Their canoe had strange carvings on its prow and was rowed by many oars.

They were big men, some with beards that flamed like fire, others with hair that gleamed like the full moon at harvest time. And their eyes! Such strange eyes. Not dark as night like those of the People, but blue. As blue as the summer sky.

These strange-looking warriors left the Great River and navigated its tributaries, until the banks narrowed and they could row no farther. There they encountered the Mound Builders, shrewd traders who bartered for conch shells from the south and turquoise stones from the west and constructed great ceremonial chambers covered by towering piles of packed earth.

The pale-skins stayed with the Mound Builders for only one winter. They cut strange symbols in stone to mark their presence. A muscled giant with a scar on his right cheek—called Bjorn Strongarm by his companions—placed several of these stones at the entrance to a small valley and vowed he would return someday to claim the land he'd marked as his.

He never returned, but the woman who'd warmed his bed that winter swelled with child. The babe was born with the copper skin and black hair of the People, but with the eyes of her father. On the day of her birth, a great storm blew up and rained hail as large as a man's fist, flattening the crops all around. The Mound Builders were forced to barter their precious shell earrings and bracelets for corn to survive the winter.

The next spring, no rain fell at all. Streams and rivers crept away from their banks. Crops withered. Animals fled the forests. Then, on the very day the blue-eyed babe marked her first year, another storm arose. The sky darkened. The winds shrieked. A twisting black cloud destroyed a great ceremonial mound that had taken many lifetimes to construct. The priests read the omens and declared the Mound Builders must cast out the strange-eyed child. Her mother took her away and, after months of foraging for food and shelter in the forests, found a home with the Cave Dwellers in the mountains to the north.

Many, many summers passed before pale-skins came again. These men, too, rowed up the Great River. Girded in iron helmets and breastplates, they searched for gold and treated those they encountered with great cruelty. One iron-hat captured a young maiden with eyes like wildflowers in bloom. Legend has it she was descended from the daughter of Bjorn.

This pale-skin used his captive brutally. Bruised and bleeding, she plunged a dagger into his throat and escaped to the mountains. The headman of the iron-hats, called de Soto by his men, took revenge for her act. Villages were burned, men put to the sword, women savaged. Once again, a blue-eyed child had brought death and destruction to the People.

The People fought back. They took to the rivers and the woods, harassing the iron-hats until they were forced to retreat. So desperate was their flight that when their captain sickened and died, they placed him in a hollow log, weighted him with his armor and sank him in Great River so the People couldn't mutilate his body and thus destroy his spirit.

The legend of the blue-eyed child was told and retold over countless fires. So often, its origins became lost in the mists of time. So often, the People began to believe the disasters she'd wrought were merely myths, greatly exaggerated with each telling.

Then French trappers paddled up the Great River, and men calling themselves Americans soon followed....

1

December 19, 1806
Six months' trek out of St. Louis,
along a bend of the Arkansaw River

Rifle Sergeant Daniel Morgan stopped dead. Wrenching his gaze from the deer tracks he'd been following, he raised his head and sniffed the frosty air.

He smelled coffee. Real coffee. Either that or his senses had gone addled from the boiled tree bark he and his small troop had been gulping down for weeks now in a futile attempt to keep their insides from freezing as stiff and hard as their fingers and noses.

His nostrils quivering, Daniel drew in another whiff. No, he'd pegged it right. That *was* coffee. Chicory flavored and strong smelling as a bull moose. The scent set his mouth to watering and his empty stomach to dancing a jig with his spine.

He gave the deer tracks another, frowning glance.

They went west, through a copse of bare-branched oak trees. The breeze carrying the tantalizing scent blew in from the east. Cradling his rifle in the crook of his arm, Daniel pondered his choices.

He'd left seven men hunkered down under a hastily erected shelter—a nervous lieutenant, four frostbitten privates and two Osage guides. They had departed St. Louis in July, part of a twenty-eight man expedition led by Lieutenant Zebulon Pike. Like the Lewis and Clark expedition that had set out two years before and had yet to return, Pike's group had been formed to explore the immense territory recently acquired by the United States in the Louisiana Purchase. Where Lewis and Clark had gone north, following the Missouri River, Pike and his band had headed west across the plains toward the mountains.

Daniel's small band had broken off from the main expedition near the end of October. With orders to chart the course and the navigability of the river called the Arkansaw by those living along its banks, they'd carved a dugout, constructed another boat of bent branches and tight-stretched hide, and paddled south.

In the two months since, the eight-man detachment had suffered just about every disaster that could befall a weary band of travelers. Within hours of leaving Pike, their boats had grounded in shallow water, requiring long, exhausting portages overland. Hostile Pawnees had raided twice. A submerged tree trunk had ripped through the canoe and caused the loss of most of their supplies—including much of their precious powder and shot. Luckily, a chance encounter with a hunting party of friendly Osage had provided a fresh supply of meat and enabled them to press on.

As winter closed in, the temperature had fallen below freezing. Snow made travel slow and hazardous. Frostbite and chilblains had become their constant companions. Ice blocked the river and forced the men out of their canoes and into the water. Using axes and bare fists, Daniel's small detachment chopped and hacked their way down the waterway they'd been sent to chart.

Two of his men, he suspected, were within a hair of deserting and finding their own way back through the wilderness to St. Louis. The others were fast losing what little remained of their determination to complete their assigned mission. Half starved and near frozen, they were all in a sorry state. Daniel had promised to bring back fresh meat to revive their flagging spirits and fill their empty bellies. He'd do just that, he decided, and maybe surprise them with a handful of coffee beans, as well.

Veering left, he followed the enticing scent. Some minutes later he spied a curl of smoke lifting above a stand of spruce. His boots crunching on the crusted snow, he approached cautiously. The camp was a temporary one, he saw, with only a single blanket draped teepee-like from a low-hanging branch. Snowshoes and a bulging haversack lay propped against the tree's trunk. A tightly bound bundle of beaver pelts rested beside the haversack.

Daniel took a moment to study the figure hunched

on a fallen log, warming his hands at the campfire. A Frenchman, judging by the tasseled, red knit stocking cap pulled down over his ears. Strands of sparse gray hair wisped out from under the cap and over the folds of his bearskin coat.

His companion was hunkered down beside a small, ice-encrusted stream some twenty or so yards away, skinning beaver and pegging the pelts out on the bank to dry. Daniel eyed both for some moments before stepping out from behind the screen of spruce.

"Good day to you, sir."

Springing to his feet, the grizzled trapper snatched up his musket and rattled off a rapid stream of French. Daniel didn't understand the words, but knew he was being asked to stand and identify himself as friend or foe.

"I'm Rifle Sergeant Daniel Morgan. Second United States Regiment of Infantry."

The trapper's musket lowered. A grin split his seamed face. "*Bienvenue,* Sergeant. Come in. Come in. Share my fire."

Only too willing, Daniel crossed the small clearing. The Frenchman thrust out a horny paw.

"I am Chartier. Henri Chartier. And this—" With a jerk of his chin, he indicated his companion. "This is my little Louis."

Daniel gave the figure by the stream another glance. Small and slight, the boy was almost lost under his wolfskin cap and buffalo robe. The bloody knife in his hand and the dozen or so fresh-skinned beaver attested to his industriousness. The copper hue of his cheeks and the glossy, blue-black hair straggling out from under his shaggy cap attested to his Indian blood.

Briefly, Daniel wondered about his relationship to Chartier. Hired assistant? Purchased slave? Son by a Native wife? The Frenchman didn't elaborate and Daniel didn't ask. He'd spent a good many of his fourteen years of army service at remote frontier posts. He'd learned early to respect the privacy of those who chose, for reasons of their own, to leave the towns and cities to roam these untamed forests.

Waving the boy back to work, the trapper offered his unexpected visitor coffee. The brew was thick as mud and bitter as day-old sin, but more welcome to Daniel than a bucket of home brew.

"Sit by the fire," Chartier invited, "and tell me what you do here."

"I'm with a company of soldiers. We're charting the course and navigability of the Arkansaw."

"You are the first, I think. The very first soldiers from your country to come so deep into Osage Country."

As far as Daniel knew, he was right. Aside from the expedition headed by Captains Meriwether Lewis and William Clark, only one other military probe had attempted to penetrate the Louisiana Territory. Headed by Captain Richard Sparks, it had set out from Natchez earlier that spring, but had been turned back by a heavily armed company of Spanish dragoons at the disputed border between the United States and Spanish Texas.

At that point, Major General Wilkinson, military governor of the Louisiana Territory and as slippery an eel as ever swam through murky waters, had chartered the band led by Lieutenant Pike.

Sipping the hot, bitter coffee, Daniel thought back to the day General Wilkinson had called him in and announced he'd personally chosen Rifle Sergeant Morgan as part of the Pike expedition. Daniel's instinctive surge of excitement had quickly been tempered by the burden of his responsibilities at home, but duty had won out.

Only after the troop had departed St. Louis did Daniel learn the real reason behind his selection. Because of Sergeant Morgan's years of experience at frontier posts, the general had specified he was to accompany Pike's second in command when he broke away from the main party to follow the Arkansaw.

Unfortunately, the second in command was none other than General Wilkinson's second son, Lieutenant James Biddle Wilkinson, as nervous and dithering a young officer as ever wore a uniform. Pike's private instructions to Daniel, just before the small detachment started south two months ago, were to keep the lieutenant from getting hopelessly lost or shooting off his own foot, if at all possible.

Daniel had managed to avoid those disasters. Barely. Now if he could just get the lieutenant and the rest of his troop down the last hundred or so miles of the Arkansaw...

"How long have you been voyaging down the river?" the trapper asked, breaking into his thoughts.

"We picked it up in Pawnee Country, about two hundred miles north."

"You've come far, my friend."

"Very far."

Daniel's gaze lifted to the snow-covered ridges topped by a sky so blue it hurt his eyes to look at it. After the flat, rolling plains of Pawnee Country, these rugged mountains seem to stretch clear to heaven.

"This is a vast land," he murmured, "and a savage one."

"And rich," the trapper added. Shaking his head, he spit into the fire. "Me, I cannot believe it when I hear the upstart Napoleon takes these lands back from the Spanish, only to turn around and sell them to your president Jefferson."

"France and England are at war," Daniel said with a shrug. "Wars devour a treasury."

"But to sell eight millions of acres for mere pennies an acre! Pah!" He spit again. "Such stupidity is to be expected of a Corsican bourgeois, one supposes."

The haughty pronouncement sounded incongruous coming from a gray-beard with rheumy eyes and a mouth missing most of its teeth.

"Your president Jefferson knows," the old man grumbled, "if Napoleon does not, the plentiful bounty to be found in these mountains and valleys. So plentiful even the Norsemen once tried to claim them."

"Norsemen?" Wondering what the devil he was talking about, Daniel took another swig.

"Danesmen." The trapper cut circles in the air with his hands in the extravagant way of the French. "Vikings."

The coffee stuck in Daniel's throat. Choking, he coughed it down. "Vikings here, thousands of miles from the open sea?"

"Oui."

Chartier had been in the wilds too long, Daniel decided. He'd started spinning tall tales in his mind to entertain himself.

"It's true," the old man insisted. "I swear to you on the blessed Virgin. The Wichita and Osage tell tales of red-bearded warriors. Me, I have seen the marks they carved there, on that very bluff."

Dubiously, Daniel eyed the ridge he pointed to.

"You do not believe me?"

"Well—"

"It is only a short climb. Come, I will show you."

Before Daniel could protest, the trapper rolled to his feet and rattled off a flurry of French to the crouched figure down at the creek.

Daniel rose more slowly. He should use what remained of the daylight to hunt. He had seven hungry men awaiting his return with fresh meat. On the other hand, one of their expedition's main tasks was to record the location of Indian camps and the natural landmarks of the territory they explored. If Vikings had indeed visited these parts long ago and carved marks in stone, the lieutenant would want to make note of it in his journal.

Incredulous but willing to be convinced, Daniel followed Chartier.

A half hour later, the two men crested the high ridge. Their breath frosting on the frigid air, they paused to survey the vista spread out below.

It was a scene of stunning, primeval beauty that seemed to go on forever. Forests of pine and spruce spilled down the steep ridges, dark and verdant against the snow blanketing the earth. Above, eagles floated on the endless blue sky. Far below, the Arkansaw formed a winding ribbon of silver.

Chartier cradled his musket in the crook of his arm as his rheumy eyes roamed from bluff to bluff. "She is beautiful, this place."

"Yes," Daniel agreed, breathing in the sharp tang of resin. Despite the hardships he and his troop had endured since entering Osage Country, these steep crags and wide valleys stirred something deep inside him. "She is beautiful."

He could live in this great, untamed land, he thought. Too many settlers were pushing west of the Alleghenies for his liking, moving into Kentucky and Ohio and Tennessee territories. Over the often violent protests of the eastern tribes, farmers cut down trees, plowed up meadows, chased away game.

These forests would swallow the sound of an ax. These rivers would provide fish and furs for any who wanted to paddle them. For a moment, he felt a fierce stab of envy for the freedom to roam enjoyed by the grizzled trapper beside him.

"I have trapped these mountains for forty years," Chartier murmured, as if reading his mind. "Always I find peace here, where the rivers run and the eagles fly. Just this morning I tell my little Louis, it is here, on this ridge, where I wish to be buried."

Unless his little Louis sprouted a considerable set of muscles in the next few years, Daniel thought wryly, the boy would have a time of it hauling Chartier's carcass up to this high bluff.

"How much farther to these Viking marks?" he asked, feeling the pinch of his responsibilities to his men.

"Not far," Chartier replied. "We climb past those rocks and—"

The Frenchman broke off, freezing in place as a high-pitched scream split the air. It was a sound like no other, a frenzied cry that stopped Daniel's heart. Whipping around, he brought his musket barrel up and thumbed back the hammer. The trapper did the same, his watery eyes searching the slope behind them.

A small shower of snow from the branches of a massive pine was their only indication that the danger came not from below, but from above. By then, it was too late.

With another high-pitched scream, the mountain cat leaped from an overhanging bough. Fangs bared, claws outstretched, it was a blur of tawny fur and fury.

"Mon Dieu!"

Chartier barely had time to fling up an arm before the snarling, slavering cougar landed on him. Daniel fired off a shot that spouted a blossom of red in the beast's side, but the wound only goaded it to greater fury. Locked together in a tangle of thrashing legs and slashing claws, Chartier and the cat rolled over and over, the cries of one as terrible as the cries of the other. Daniel tossed his musket aside, pulled his hunting knife from its leather scabbard and leaped into the fray.

When the beast finally gave a last, tormented cry and went limp, Daniel scrabbled to his knees. His chest heaving, he used both hands to pry apart the animal's locked jaws and free the Frenchman.

Chartier fell back against the reddened snow. What was once his face was now raw, unrecognizable pulp. Air whistled from his throat, torn open to expose glistening white tendons. Blood pumped from the gaping wound. Panting, Daniel dropped back on his heels. He'd seen enough battle wounds to know the next breath or two would be Chartier's last.

Through his haze of agonizing pain the Frenchman recognized the same awful truth. His one remaining eye fixed on Daniel. With an effort that brought blood spewing from his lips, he whispered a few tortured words.

"Take care...of my Louis."

"I will."

"Swear...it!"

"I swear."

A red bubble formed on Chartier's lips. Before it burst, the Frenchman was dead.

Daniel stayed hunkered down beside the body. Warm blood drenched his hands. Cold air stabbed into his lungs like a bayonet. After the cougar's high-pitched screams and the fury of the attack, the sudden silence thundered in his ears.

He dragged in another shuddering breath and swiveled on his heels to view the dead animal. The cougar's ribs stuck out like barrel staves under its tawny hide. If there was a pound of flesh anywhere on the beast, Daniel couldn't see it. What looked like a bent and broken foreleg gave some clue to its near starvation. The creature couldn't run, couldn't chase its normal prey. But it could pounce.

Slowly, Daniel pushed to his feet. A soldier's life was precarious at best. Between bouts of boring garrison duty, he stood a good chance of being blown apart by a British cannonball, taking a Spanish bayonet to the gut or losing his scalp to a warrior from one of the fierce tribes that roamed the forests and plains. Even here, in this land of majestic beauty, violent death was just a heartbeat away. Daniel's glance swept the snow-capped crags, dropped to the ribbons of silver glistening far below.

Chartier would get his wish. He'd be buried here, where the river ran and the eagles flew.

Grunting with the effort, Daniel hauled loose rocks to mound over the Frenchman's body. He was sweating beneath his buckskins and buffalo coat by the time he cut and stripped two small branches. Tying them with a bit of rawhide cut from the fringe of his hunting buckskins, he planted the crude cross on the mound of rocks.

He thought about gutting the cougar and hauling the carcass back to camp, but there wasn't enough meat on the creature's bones to feed a flock of crows, let alone eight hungry men. He left it for the scavengers.

Except the claws. Those he decided to take to Chartier's boy. The lad might want to make a necklace of them, take medicine from the fierce spirit of the cat that killed the trapper.

Dropping the claws into his leather cartridge case, Daniel gathered Chartier's musket and hunting knife and started back down the ridge. He no longer had either the time or the desire to view the supposed Viking marks that had lured him up the bluff.

What he did have, he thought grimly, was an unexpected charge. What the devil was he going to do with the boy? He was still pondering the best way to honor his vow when he approached the Frenchman's camp for the second time.

The lad was still down at the stream. He appeared hard at work, but the faint crunch of boots on snow brought his head whipping around. He crouched there, the bloody skinning knife clutched in his fist. His eyes narrowed to slits as they took in the two muskets Daniel carried.

"Où est Henri?"

Approaching slowly, Daniel searched his mind for

the few French phrases he'd picked up over the years. "Henri is *mort. Fini.*"

Under the bulk of his wolfskin cap and buffalo robe, the lad went still. The fingers clutching the knife turned white at the knuckles.

"A mountain cat got him."

Still the boy didn't move. Propping the two muskets against the bale of furs, Daniel curled his fingers into talons.

"Puma. Panther."

He raised an arm to rake a hand across his throat in a grotesque pantomime of the trapper's death. Before he could complete the gesture, the boy's lips curled back.

"Muerte!"

Spitting the word like a curse, he launched himself through the air much as the cougar had up on the ridge. His buffalo robe tumbled away from his shoulders. His wolfskin cap flew off. His eyes blazed with fury.

In the space of mere seconds, Daniel made two startling discoveries. The boy's eyes were blue, a deep, sapphire blue. And *he* looked very much like a *she.*

Daniel formed a fleeting impression of glossy, waist-length black hair. Of high cheekbones and a pointed chin. Of small, proud breasts molded by a doeskin tunic.

Then he, like Chartier, went down under the weight of a snarling, spitting she-cat.

2

Daniel landed flat on his back, felled by a hundred pounds of feral fury. Only his hard-learned combat skills kept him from receiving or inflicting real pain. Not an easy task while dodging sharp knees to the groin, elbows to the windpipe and a well-honed skinning knife. It took some doing, but he managed to catch his assailant's wrists in a tight grip.

"Enough!"

She—yes, it was definitely a she—ignored the sharp command and butted her head forward.

Daniel took a solid whack to the nose. Swearing, he transferred both of her wrists to one hand and grabbed a thick hank of hair. A vicious tug brought her head back and her chin pointed at the sky.

Still she fought. Her lips curled away from her teeth. Her body contorted atop his. She got a knee loose and damned near unmanned him.

Grunting, Daniel blocked the vicious thrust with his thigh, dug a heel into the ground and rolled them both over. His weight squeezed the breath right out of her. Squashed into the snow, she squirmed and gasped and jerked.

"Enough, I said!"

He didn't know whether it was his angry bellow that finally stilled her struggles or his dead weight crushing her into the snow. Whatever the reason, she went limp. Unmoving except for the quick, tortured rise and fall of her chest, she glared up at him.

She was a good bit older than the stripling he'd first thought, he saw. Closer to a woman than a girl. Despite her slender build, the breasts mashed against his chest felt full and round, her flanks long and firm. And she had the damnedest eyes. As deep and blue as a high mountain lake.

Chartier must have passed them to her. The trapper's eyes had been blue, too, but not the same mesmerizing shade of his daughter's. Fringed by thick, ink-black lashes, they drew a man in and left him to drown.

For a moment, Daniel forgot he was deep in uncharted territory, forgot the troop of hungry soldiers waiting for him. For the oddest space of time, he saw only a backdrop of white snow. A spill of hair as black as obsidian. Full, red lips set in a defiant line. A blaze of blue fire. She was as wild and dangerous and beautiful as the land that had bred her. Shaking his head, he broke the spell.

"*Parlez* English?"

She didn't respond except to set her jaw. Daniel gave her hair another yank.

"Do you talk English?"

"Yes!" she hissed. "I have the *anglais*. Also a little of the *español*."

"Good."

Very good, since Daniel had pretty much used up his entire repertoire of foreign phrases.

"I didn't kill Chartier," he said, spacing each word slowly and distinctly. "It was a mountain cat. Puma. Cougar."

Jaw tight, she eyed him for a long moment. "Is that the cry I hear?"

A panther's scream could carry for miles on this thin, cold air. He should have realized the girl would hear it and wonder whether it had been made by man or beast.

"Yes, that was the cry you heard."

"You say... You say this cat kills Henri?"

"I brought the claws to prove to you I speak the truth."

"Show me."

He knew better than to react too quickly to that imperious demand. The fight wasn't gone out of her yet. Or the suspicion. The moment he rolled away from her, she'd have her razor-edged blade to his throat.

"I'll show you," he countered, "when you let loose of your knife."

Her black brows slashed together. Her body tensed under his. They lay in the snow, chest to chest, hip to hip, while she mulled over her choices in the matter. Finally she realized she had only one. Her fingers loosed their grip on the skinning knife.

Releasing her hair, Daniel took possession of the weapon. The handle was wrapped in bits of rawhide woven with red yarn and fit awkwardly in his hand, but he kept a sure grip on it as he levered himself up. Freed of his weight, the woman drew in a long, shuddering breath and struggled upright. Regret lanced into Daniel when he saw the angry marks banding her wrists. He hadn't intended to bruise her like that.

He reached down a hand to help her up. Spurning his aid, she scrambled to her feet, dusted the snow from her backside and snatched up her buffalo robe. With the heavy hide draped over her shoulders to block the cold, she reissued her imperious demand.

"Show me."

He dug the claws out of his cartridge case. They lay in his palm, curving, sharp-tipped bits of black still streaked with the blood of the cat and the man it had savaged.

She reached out and closed a hand over the gory trophies. Clenching her fist, she brought it to her breast. Her extraordinary eyes showed no trace of emotion, but the skin stretched taut over her high cheekbones and moved Daniel to pity.

"I buried Chartier up there," he said gruffly, "on the bluff."

Her glance went to the snow-covered ridge. "It is where he wished to lie."

"Your father asked me to take care of you."

Her gaze slewed back. "What do you say?"

"Your father. With his last breath, he asked me to take care of you."

"You think Henri is my father?"

"Isn't he?"

"*Imbécile!* He is my husband. For five winters now."

"The hell you say!"

The old buzzard must have taken her into his bed before she'd laid aside her corncob dolls. Disgusted, Daniel shook his head.

Her chin came up. Mistaking his disgust for disbelief, she gave him a look that would have frozen the Arkansaw if it didn't already wear a coat of ice.

"Our marriage is done by a priest," she announced haughtily. "The same priest who baptizes me and gives me my name."

"Louis?"

"Lou-*ise*. Louise Therese. Before I am Wah-shi-tu, but Henri, he and the priest say now I am Louise. I am Henri's wife," she repeated, more fiercely this time. "The beaver we take from the streams are mine."

"Don't get your dander up. I don't want your furs."

Her inky black brows slashed together. "What is this dander?"

"It's... Well—"

Come to think on it, Daniel didn't rightly know what the devil it was.

"All I'm saying is that I'm not trying to lay claim to the beaver you and your, uh, husband trapped."

He stumbled over the word, still struggling with the idea of the near-toothless Frenchman mounting this supple young beauty. Struggling, as well, with the dilemma of what to do with her.

"I don't know if you caught my name when I gave it before," he said. "It's Daniel. Daniel Morgan, Rifle Sergeant with the Second United States Regiment of Infantry."

She made no response, as if she didn't give two hoots who he was.

"What about you?" Daniel prodded. "Who are your people?"

"My father was of the French, like Henri. Or so I have been told."

Well, that explained her eyes.

"Your mother?"

She chewed on her lower lip, as if debating how much to tell him. She was a suspicious thing, but Daniel didn't blame her. He'd come out of nowhere, climbed a ridge with her husband and returned with a set of bloody claws.

"My mother was of the Osage," she said at last. "From the Quapaw Tribe."

Relief seeped into Daniel. Quapaw was the Indian name for "those who went downstream," denoting a clan of Osage that had broken away from their main tribe some years back and moved south along the Arkansaw. Called the Arkansaw Osage at first, the tribe had become known by the shortened name, Quapaw. Establishing contact with this prosperous clan was a secondary goal of the expedition. Since their winter camp lay only a few days' march to the south, Daniel could get Chartier's widow to her people.

"I made a promise to your husband to see you safe. I'll take you to the Quapaw winter camp…"

"No!"

"…and leave you there."

"No, I say!"

"They're your tribe. Why the devil don't you want to go to them?"

Her chin came up. "My uncle is chief of the Quapaw. When my mother dies, my uncle takes me into his lodge, but—"

"But what?"

She took her lip between her teeth again, worrying it. She started to say something, changed her mind and finished with a toss of her head. "My uncle sells me to Henri to be rid of me. I will not go where I am not wanted."

"You have to go somewhere. I damn sure can't leave you here."

The stubborn set to her jaw told Daniel that's exactly what she wanted him to do.

"Just think for a moment. Your man's dead. Winter's hard on us and there's more snow coming. If you don't freeze to death, you could well starve."

"I know these mountains. I will not freeze *or* starve."

He was tempted, sorely tempted, to wash his hands of her. Damned if she wasn't a mulish bit of fur and feathers. But a promise was a promise, and Daniel

Morgan had never yet gone back on his given word. Closing his mind to the protests he knew his lieutenant would rain down on his head, he suggested another course.

"How about this? You travel with my detachment until we reach a settlement or trading post where you can sell your furs for enough supplies to get you through the winter. Then you can go where you will."

She cocked her head, studying him through still suspicious eyes. "Why do you do this?"

"I told you. I made a promise to Chartier."

"You'll take me *and* the furs?"

"Didn't I just say so?"

She tapped the toe of her bulky bearskin boot. Eyes narrowed behind those thick black lashes, she looked him up and down. Daniel felt himself being weighed and measured. He was half expecting her to order him to bare his teeth for inspection when she gave a reluctant nod.

"I come with you."

He couldn't decide if he was more relieved or sorry. Thinking that he'd just saddled himself with a whole peck of trouble, he handed her back her knife and kept a wary eye on her movements while she stooped down to clean the blade in the snow. Rising, she slid the rib-sticker into a beaded sheath at her waist.

"Bundle what you can carry into that haversack," he instructed. "I'll pack up the meat from the beaver you just skinned."

Beaver steak took a good bit more chewing than deer, but it was too late to follow those tracks in the snow. He was thankful that the beaver meat was cut into neat strips ready for frying or smoking. The girl—woman—had done her job well.

Hell, he couldn't decide just how to think of her. She moved with the grace of a young deer. Her skin was fresh and smooth and clear, with none of the lines carved by wind and sun. Yet five years of sharing a blanket with a grizzled old trapper certainly took her out of the category of girl and gave her the status of a woman.

Shutting out the image of her slender legs wrapped around Chartier's waist, Daniel stuffed the strips into the canvas pouch he carried with him on hunting expeditions and topped them with the livers, hearts and other edible organs. There was enough to feed his men one solid meal, anyway. Tomorrow, he'd have to bring down more game.

With the pouch thudding heavy against his hip, he crossed the clearing to the bale of furs. The woman was on her knees, retying the rawhide strips to include the fresh-scraped pelts. She left wide loops and had just bent to slip an arm through one when Daniel stopped her.

"I'll carry that. You take the haversack."

As big and full muscled as he was, Daniel had to strain to lift the bale. Good Christ above! Chartier had let his wife tote this load? Evidently the Frenchman had got himself a packhorse as well as a bedmate when he'd bought her from the Osage.

Leaning forward, he hefted the weight higher on his shoulders. "You ready?"

She coiled her hair under the wolfskin cap, slung the haversack over one shoulder and wrapped a fur-mittened fist around Chartier's musket. Her gaze swept the camp a final time before lifting to the ridge where her husband was buried.

When her blue eyes turned back to Daniel, they were flat and expressionless. "I am ready."

Daniel fully expected the high-strung Lieutenant Wilkinson to fly into a nervous fit when his sergeant returned to camp with a very young and very recent widow in tow. What he didn't expect was to find the officer down with a raging fever.

Wilkinson thrashed about on a bed of pine boughs. Sweat ran down his temples and drenched the tattered remains of the uniform jacket he wore under his buffalo robe.

"When did the fever come on him?" Daniel asked Private Huddleston.

"'Bout an hour after you left."

Sullen-faced and demoralized by the tribulations of the past few months, the private shifted his glance from his sergeant to the fur-clad figure standing behind him.

The rest of the small troop was just as curious. John Boley and Sam Bradley, almost as disgruntled as Huddleston these days. John Wilson, a skilled hunter and outdoorsman who still sprang to orders with some degree of respect. The two Osage guides,

Nan-wa-sa, or Wind That Cries, and Pa-tu-she-ga, called One Eye by the men because of the drooping lid that all but covered his right eyeball.

Surveying his small detachment, Daniel had to admit they made a sorry sight. The soldiers' few remaining uniform items were little more than rags. Their boots had long since rotted away and been replaced by hides tied in bulky bundles over their frostbitten feet. Red rimmed their eyes. Scraggly beards covered their cheeks. Even the lieutenant now bore more resemblance to a rough-planed woodsman than the overly fastidious officer who'd left St. Louis six months ago. Worried by the young officer's condition, Daniel deposited the bale of furs in the snow and went down on one knee beside him.

"Lieutenant? Can you hear me?"

Wilkinson turned to the sound of his voice. Mumbling incoherently, he lifted a clenched fist and let it drop.

"It's Sergeant Morgan. I've brought fresh meat."

He dragged the heavy pouch over his shoulder and passed it to an eager Private Boley.

"Put some on to boil for the lieutenant before you fry up the rest. A hearty broth may help break his fever. The rest of you, roll out your blankets and prepare a bivouac area. We'll spend the night here. Huddleston, you and Wilson have first watch. Bradley and I will take second."

Huddleston hooked a thumb toward the newcomer. "What about this one?"

"This is—" Daniel couldn't remember her Osage

name. Not that it mattered. The priest who'd baptized her had given her another. "This is Madame Chartier. Louise Therese Chartier."

"Madame?" Huddleston squinted, trying for a closer look at the face and figure almost hidden by the bulky robes. "She's a woman growed and bedded?"

Avid eagerness leaped into Huddleston's face. Of all the men in the small detachment, he'd been the most vocal in his complaints. And in his eagerness to accept offers made by several of the tribal chiefs they'd encountered to send women to warm their beds.

Lieutenant Wilkinson had refused the offers. Much to Huddleston's disgust, Rifle Sergeant Morgan had backed him up. With everything else he had to worry about on this expedition, the last thing Daniel needed was the kind of problems that inevitably arose when men on the march ignored their duties and took their pleasures where they found them.

"I met up with Madame Chartier and her husband earlier this afternoon," he informed the others, "right before a cougar ripped out the man's throat."

"The devil you say!"

"How'd that happen?"

"I'll tell you about it after you set up camp and we spoon some broth into the lieutenant." He leveled a hard look at the short, thickset Solomon Huddleston. "For now, all you need to know is that I made a promise to Chartier to see his wife safe to the nearest settlement."

The man's mouth twisted with the resentment that was never far beneath his skin these days. "Well, I hope you ain't thinking I'm going to tote that heavy bale of furs she brung with her."

"I'm thinking you'll do whatever I tell you to, Private." The swift retort cracked like a whip in the frosty air.

Huddleston looked as though he had more to say, but wisely bit down on it. Daniel would have to do something about that one, he decided. And soon.

"You've got your orders, men. Jump to them."

While the company scattered to attend to their tasks, Daniel addressed the female standing stiff and silent. "I don't know how much of that you understood—"

"I understand enough."

"You don't have to worry about Private Huddleston. Or any of the others, for that matter. They answer to me."

She stared at him with those clear blue eyes. "Yes, I see that they do."

With a nod, he turned his attention back to the lieutenant.

Louise watched him work. He spoke the truth. These men feared and respected him. He carried strong medicine, this wide-shouldered man with the shaggy brown beard and eyes the color of smoke.

Her stomach had clenched when he first stepped out of the woods. Henri's movements had grown so slow of late, his sight so blurred and dim. He'd welcomed the stranger too quickly, blind to the danger he brought with him.

Louise had sensed it, though. One glimpse of this man made her whole body go tight with the wariness of a doe scenting wolf. It wasn't fear. She'd roamed the wilderness with Henri for too many years to feel fear at this one's sudden appearance. Rather, it was the uneasy sense of something to come, a fierce storm or raging river that would sweep her up in its wake.

Her instincts had proved true. So disastrously true! Within the space of mere hours, she'd lost Henri's comfortable companionship and had put herself under the protection of this—this American.

Suddenly, the day that had begun with the rise of the sun weighed down on her. Grief for Henri tugged at her heart. Uncertainty over what was to come burdened her mind. Weary beyond her years, Louise shrugged out of the heavy haversack and glanced around the makeshift camp.

"Where do I spread my blanket?"

Busy tending to the sick one, the man named Daniel jerked his chin toward a pack lying beneath a low-hanging branch.

"Over there, with mine. We'll bundle together for warmth."

She drew in a swift breath. So that's the way it was to be. He wouldn't even give her time to mourn her husband before he claimed her.

Not that Henri had wanted her to mourn. He'd spoken often of the many winters he'd seen, of how he'd leave her soon to find a younger, more vigorous husband. He'd made her promise not to paint her face with ashes and grieve overlong. Their years together had been good, he'd asserted. More good for him, he'd added with a rueful grin, than for her.

When Chartier had paid Louise's bride price and bought her from her uncle, the Frenchman had been long past the point of being able to raise his spear unassisted. Under his patient tutelage, she'd learned to coax it to hardness for him. In the process, she'd also learned how to take satisfaction from his so-clever hands and mouth.

Her husband had offered her the chance to lie with other men, of course. Trappers often shared their women, sometimes in exchange for furs, sometimes merely to relieve the loneliness of their lives. Louise had been tempted. More than once. Henri had awakened her to a woman's passion, and in doing so, he'd stirred needs that often made her wonder what it would be like to take a young, strong warrior between her thighs. But loyalty to her husband had outweighed desire, and she'd chosen to share only Henri's blanket.

Now the choice looked to have been taken from her hands. The American had promised to protect her. In exchange, he expected her to warm his bed.

Her heart thumping, Louise tried to sort through her whirling thoughts. Should she wait until night fell and slip away into the darkness? Use her skinning knife to slash the sergeant's throat when he tried to use her?

If she did the first, she would lose her supplies and her furs, and the cold would soon claim her. Or a cougar, such as had claimed Henri, would fell her. If she succeeded in the second, these men would exact vengeance for their slain leader.

There was a third path, she decided after much thought. She could submit to him. She would not dishonor her husband's memory if she permitted him to take what Henri allowed her to give to others.

Nor would she have to coax his spear to hardness, she thought with a sudden quiver deep in her belly. He'd carried her bale of furs through the snow for hours without so much as a pause to take his breath. More to the point, she'd felt him hard against her when they struggled in the snow. He was as strong and sound-limbed as Henri had been thin-shanked and brittle-boned.

Her throat closing at the thought of the night to come, Louise spread her blanket under the pine.

3

As taut as one of Henri's traps before its jaws clanged shut, Louise made her bed. Hacking boughs from low hanging pines with her knife, she laid her blanket over them. All the while, she fretted over what she should do when the sergeant tried to claim her.

Her task done but her thoughts still turbulent, she sat stiff and silent on a fallen log while the last of the day swiftly gave way to darkness. Her lip curled as she watched the small band of men set up their camp. They went about the business with dragging feet and backs bent from weariness. While one built a large, crackling fire and melted snow for washing and cooking, another put the livers and other organs of the beaver on to fry. He used no salt or herbs of any kind, Louise saw, and wondered how he expected anyone to eat such tough, tasteless meat.

She debated for long moments before delving into her haversack. She packed only enough supplies for herself and Henri and had hoarded them carefully to make them last the winter. It worried her to part with so much as a pinch of salt or a handful of coffee beans. She had to eat, however, and chose not to chew on unsalted meat. Her fur boots crunching on the snow, she crossed to the fire.

"Here."

The cook looked up at her with red-rimmed eyes.

"Salt to flavor the meat," she told him. "And beans for coffee."

"Real coffee?"

"Yes."

"Damn!"

With a grunt, he snatched both offerings out of her hands.

Louise returned to her perch and debated even longer before digging among her pouches for her medicines. She wasn't a shaman or a healer, by any means, but she could see that the lieutenant was in need of relief from the fever that flushed his face and drenched his body in sweat. A folded deerskin packet in hand, she approached the one called Daniel.

"I have dried leaves of the moonflower. If you soak them in melted snow and make a band to put around the head of your lieutenant, it will draw his fever."

"Moonflower?" The thickset one with the small eyes and flat nose jerked around. "Isn't that Indian for 'stinkweed'?"

"I know not this stinkweed, only moonflower."

"Is it a tall plant with big white blossoms?"

"Yes."

"Hell! That *is* stinkweed she's giving you, Sergeant. It's pure poison. It'll kill the lieutenant for sure."

"It kills only if eaten. But if you do not wish to use the leaves, I will—"

The broad-shouldered one settled the matter with a gruff command. "Give them to me. I'll see that they don't go down his gullet."

Louise handed him the folded deerskin and retreated once again to her log.

Daniel didn't spare her a glance as he soaked the leaves in melted snow before folding them into a scrap of linen torn from what was left of his shirt. He couldn't tell whether it was the moonflower or the rich broth he spooned into the lieutenant that stilled the young officer's restless movements, but Wilkinson soon dropped into an exhausted sleep.

Almost as exhausted, Daniel joined the men at the campfire and claimed his share of the coffee and fried meat. The talk was all of his chance meeting with the Frenchman and Chartier's sudden, savage death. More than one glance strayed to the trapper's widow, sitting off by herself.

The Osage guides, in particular, seemed to find her presence disturbing. They made only one attempt to speak to her in her own tongue. Whatever she replied had them keeping their distance and muttering to each other. His meal finished, Daniel took his mug over to join her.

"Do you know them?" he asked, indicating the two guides with a nod.

"No. They are of the Little Osage."

"I heard the Little Osage and Quapaw often hunt together."

"Before, perhaps. Not now. Not since Pierre Choteau and his brother open their trading post."

Daniel knew the enterprising Frenchmen who'd established the first permanent trading post south of the Missouri River only by reputation. General Wilkinson had invited the prosperous Choteau brothers to St. Louis when he assumed governorship of Louisiana Territory. Reportedly it was to gain information about the territory he was now responsible for, but everyone in St. Louis figured the wily general's real purpose was to find ways to cut into the brothers' lucrative fur trade.

Such private enterprise wasn't illegal or even discouraged for men in uniform. More than one soldier earned extra dollars by hunting fresh meat for his garrison or bringing in furs. General Wilkinson, however, was rumored to have his fingers in more pies than a baker. Daniel wasn't surprised his son had spent more time talking furs with the chiefs they'd visited during this expedition than talking peace. Cradling his hands around his mug, he angled for information.

"What do you know about Pierre Choteau?"

"Henri trades with him. So do the Quapaw. Or they did. Henri says Pierre worries the Quapaw might now sell only to the agent of the Spanish."

The casual remark brought his head snapping up. "The Spanish are trading in these parts?"

"They come," she answered with a shrug, "they go."

So much for respecting the boundaries of the United States, he thought wryly. The Spanish had yet to completely concede the territory they'd ruled until the French took it from them a few years ago.

Before Daniel and the rest of the group had broken away from the main body of the expedition and turned south, they'd found ample evidence of Spanish military presence. One campsite wasn't more than a few days old. At a Pawnee village, Lieutenant Pike had had to talk long and hard to convince the chief to lower the Spanish flag and hoist the Stars and Bars. This was the first Daniel had heard, though, that the Spanish were operating so deep in Osage Country.

"Who is this agent you speak of?" he asked the woman beside him.

"I know not his name. Only that he plans to send boats up the Great River and lay claim to these lands."

The hair on the back of Daniel's neck rose. Were the Spanish out to recover the vast territory Napoleon had wrested from them by treaty, then sold to the Americans? General Wilkinson would want to hear about this.

"How do you know about these plans?"

Her shoulders lifted in another shrug. "The trappers, they talk."

They sat for a few moments, each lost in thought. Daniel's mind was still spinning with the possibility of a Spanish agent stirring up trouble in these parts, when Louise slanted him a sideways look.

"The trappers also say your Great Father speaks of moving the Choctaw and Cherokee to this land."

Not just the Choctaw and Cherokee.

Citing the inexorable westward movement of white settlers, President Jefferson's second inaugural address had endorsed a plan to move all tribes living east of the Mississippi to the newly acquired Louisiana Territory. The move would guarantee the tribes rich hunting and farming lands "forever and in perpetuity," and create an immense Indian Country to serve as a buffer between the United States and the Spanish holdings to the west and south. Coincidentally, it would also free up vast tracts of Indian land in the east for white settlement.

The plan had been enthusiastically endorsed by land-hungry citizens and heartily condemned by those who believed the government should stand by the treaties it had negotiated over the years with the sovereign Indian tribes. Emotions on both sides of the issue ran hot and looked as though they would soon heat to a boil. Daniel wasn't surprised rumors about the scheme had penetrated even these remote reaches. It was stirring up enough controversy everywhere else.

"Is this true, what the trappers say?" Louise asked. "Your Great Father has such a plan?"

"It's true."

"Pah!" Her blue eyes flashed with scorn. "It is

foolish beyond words. The Osage war now with the Choctaw and Cherokee. If the Great Father sends them here, the rivers will run red with blood.''

Daniel suspected she was right. He also suspected it would fall to the army to keep traditional enemies from killing each other off—along with anyone else who got in the way—if Congress passed the Indian Removal Plan.

And, he acknowledged with a sudden tightening of his gut, the proposed plan would provide a crafty Spanish agent with just the fuel he needed to fan the flames of rebellion among the tribes already living in Louisiana Territory. A rebellion that would allow Spain to move in and take back the territory they'd lost.

Had the chiefs they'd met with so far during the expedition expressed their concerns to the lieutenant? Or made mention of this Spanish agent? If so, young Wilkinson hadn't commented on it.

He'd ask the lieutenant if he'd picked up these disquieting rumors. In the morning. When the young officer had shaken off his fever and regained his senses. Downing the last of his coffee, Daniel left Louise and went to secure the camp for the night.

After checking the placement of the sentries, he instructed Private Wilson to lay his blanket next to the lieutenant's and notify Daniel immediately if the officer should take a turn for the worse.

Weariness pulled at him like anchor chains when he approached his own bed of pine boughs covered with his tattered blanket. He wanted nothing more than to drop down, drag his buffalo robe over his head and snatch a few hours' sleep. The shadowy mound a few feet from his blanket reminded him of his newest responsibility.

"Are you warm enough?"

The mound didn't stir.

"Madame Chartier. Louise."

Slowly, a corner of the buffalo hide peeled back. The flickering campfire illuminated the pale oval of her face.

"Are you warm enough?" he asked again.

"Yes."

The curt reply stirred a stab of pity in Daniel. In the space of a few hours, the woman had lost a husband and been forced to throw in her lot with a band of scruffy, half-starved soldiers. Small wonder she'd retreated after sharing her precious supply of stores with his men, and now huddled beneath that pile of hide.

"Sleep well, then," he said gruffly.

Dropping a knee onto his blanket, he claimed his bed. The pine boughs rustled under him as he worked into a comfortable position and dragged his robe up around his ears. With the scent of resin sharp in his nostrils and an endless expanse of star-studded sky above, he noted the sounds of his men settling down for the night. The muted remarks. The muttered complaints. A hiss as John Wilson spit his wad into the fire. Sam Bradley's hacking cough.

The sounds were as familiar to him now as the

sensation of lying next to a female was strange and unsettling. Despite the exhaustion weighting his limbs, Daniel couldn't seem to empty his mind of her. Or of the thought of Henri Chartier taking his ease on her young, lithe body.

To his profound disgust, images of Chartier's wife lost to passion leaped into Daniel's head again. His belly clenched as he pictured her on her back, her coal-black hair fanned against a blanket and her extraordinary eyes heavy with desire.

Guilt stabbed into him, sharper and far more intense than the pity that had gripped him just moments ago. He had no business thinking such thoughts about this woman. He'd sworn to protect her, to see her safe to the nearest settlement. He'd rid himself of the burden she represented as soon as he was able, get his small, tattered troop to the mouth of the Arkansaw and go home.

Deliberately, he wiped all thought of Chartier's widow from his mind and filled it instead with a face framed by hair as pale as a winter moon.

Louise lay still and rigid beside him. With each thunderous beat of her heart, she expected him to roll over, raise her buffalo robe and reach under her tunic to probe for the slit in her leggings.

Her pulse fluttered like that of a startled quail when the pine branches rustled under him. She sucked in a quick breath, held it. Long, tense moments passed. When he made no further move, she unclenched her fists and released the air trapped in her lungs.

More moments slid by. With the heavy robe pulled up around her ears, her world was narrowed to a thick, impenetrable darkness scented with the familiar scent of tanned hide. She could sense him, though, feel him on every prickly inch of her skin.

The grim anticipation that had gripped her since he'd instructed her to lay her blanket next to his held her in its maw. She'd been so sure of his meaning, so convinced of his intent, that it was some time before she interpreted the low, snuffling cadence her straining ears picked up.

He was asleep.

Fast asleep.

Relief lanced through her, followed almost immediately by the oddest sensation. It wasn't disappointment. It couldn't be disappointment. She needed time to mourn Henri properly, time to accord him the respect he deserved. Yet the realization that the American evidently didn't intend to claim her this night left her feeling strangely unsettled.

It was the events of the day, she decided. So much had happened in so short a space of time. Seemingly in the blink of an eye, the entire course of her life had changed, and she now walked an unfamiliar path. That was what caused this—this disquiet.

Squeezing her eyes shut, she said silent prayers to Wa-kon-dah and the other spirits who gave balance to all things on earth and in the heavens. If the spirits were kind and so inclined, they would welcome Henri Chartier into their midst.

She woke the next morning to the stench of burnt meat and the taste of snow in the air. Pushing aside her heavy robe, she blinked the sleep from her eyes and surveyed the various occupants of the camp. They looked no better in the harsh light of morning than they had in the waning light of the previous day.

They must have endured much hardship for their skin to stretch so tight over gaunt cheeks and their garments to hang in such tatters. They moved listlessly, she noted, as though their morning tasks gave them no pleasure or anticipation for the coming day. One poked at the meat sizzling in a fry pan with a stick. Another squatted on his haunches, waiting for snow to melt and boil in a battered tin coffeepot.

She felt not the slightest urge to join the two at the fire and help prepare their meal. She'd perform tasks necessary to her own survival, like gathering wood and carrying her haversack. She'd share what she could of her supplies. But she certainly didn't intend to act as a slave to any of these men. With that resolve firm in her mind, she rose and slipped into the woods to attend to her personal needs.

That was where the heavyset soldier found her some moments later. She'd finished relieving herself and was on her knees, scrubbing her face with snow, when he stepped out from behind a tree.

"Well, well. When you come out from under all

that fur and hide, you're a pretty enough little piece, aren't you?''

She didn't like this one. He looked at her with the eyes of a hungry wolf and spoke with a jeering tone. Turning her back on him, she wiped her cheeks with a corner of her robe, slung the garment over her shoulders and started back for the camp.

He sidestepped, deliberately blocking her way. ''I'm talkin' to you, squaw.''

''But me, I have no wish to talk with you.''

Her contemptuous glance raked a path from the burrs caught in his beard to the dirty buckskin shirt showing beneath his buffalo cloak. When her gaze lifted to his again, his mouth had tightened in anger.

''What do you think you're about, turning your nose up at me like that?''

''If I turn up my nose, it is because you carry the stink of a dead skunk.''

The blunt response made the veins in his forehead bulge. ''I'm thinking your man should have learned you a little respect.''

Louise stood her ground as he started for her, but her hand moved beneath her robe to the beaded sheath at her waist. ''Henri, he teaches me to respect those who deserve it. You, I think, do not.''

His arm came up. ''Why you little—''

''What goes on here?'' The sergeant stomped through the woods.

Slowly, Louise loosed her grip on the handle of her skinning knife. How strange, she thought. Yesterday at this hour their paths had not yet crossed.

When they did, she believed him responsible for Henri's death and viewed him through a blaze of hate and fear. Last night, she considered taking her knife to his throat if he lifted her skirts. Now she greeted his arrival with a shiver of relief.

So quickly do things change!

"What's amiss here, Huddleston?"

The soldier hooked a thumb toward Louise. "She slipped out of camp. I followed to see what she was up to and she served me a field ration of sass."

"That's no reason to raise your arm to her. Don't do it again."

"Jesus! You'd jump me and the boys quick enough if we was to backtalk you or the lieutenant."

"You have the right of it. I would. The difference is, you're under military orders and Madame Chartier is not. Nor does she answer to you. I'll tell you once more, Huddleston. Just once. She's my responsibility. I'll see to her."

"Well, maybe you should keep a closer eye on her, then. Wind That Cries says she's bad medicine. Real bad medicine."

"What are you talking about?"

"I heard him and One Eye muttering and asked them what they was jawin' on about." He shot a glance at Louise. "They said there's a legend. Some folderol 'bout a blue-eyed maiden bringing disaster to her tribe. They seem to think you showin' up with this particular female in harness will bring disaster down on us, too."

Daniel had a sick lieutenant to see to, a troop to

ready for the march and fresh meat to hunt. "If we believed in bad medicine we would have turned around the first time our canoes went under," he snapped. "We've come too far to worry about such matters now. Go on back to camp and get your gear together."

His mouth thin and tight, the soldier speared another glance at Louise. Daniel waited, keeping his own temper on a tight rein, until the man had shouldered past and was out of earshot.

"Don't go wandering off again," he instructed the woman curtly.

"Am I to squat right in front of your men, then?"

"Of course not. Just let me know before you go into the woods."

He started for the camp, took all of two or three paces before he realized she wasn't following. Swinging back, he saw that she was still standing right where he'd left her.

Well, hell! That's all he needed. A female with sore feelings.

"I'm sorry I spoke so harsh," he said, striving for patience. "I've got a load on my mind."

"And I add to your burdens."

There was no denying that. "You do, but you're a burden of my own choosing." Hoping he'd soothed her ruffled feathers, he swept an arm as if to usher her back to camp. Still she didn't move.

"He speaks the truth."

"Who does?"

"Wind That Cries. I am bad medicine."

"How do you figure that?"

"There *is* a legend about a long-ago maiden with eyes the color of mine. She brought disaster to her people. As I did to mine."

"What disaster? Our reports show that the Quapaw are a rich nation, with many fields of corn and squash, and rivers filled with fish."

She took her lip between her teeth again in a gesture Daniel was coming to recognize. Stifling his impatience to return to camp, he waited.

"When my mother dies," she said slowly, reluctantly, "I am taken to my uncle's lodge. That year the hunt was bad and we ate little meat. Then, after his wife delivers a babe with no arms, people begin to speak of the curse. That's why he sells me to Henri. Why—" She swallowed and forced out the words. "Why, perhaps, Henri dies as he does."

Daniel had a healthy respect for the Almighty in all His shapes and guises, including the spirits worshiped by the various tribes. But his years in uniform had bred in him a gut-deep belief that death came more by chance than by divine intervention. How else could he explain the musket ball that had ricocheted off his powder horn and gone through the eye of the man next to him? Or a murderous fusillade that had dropped his captain's horse but left the officer without a scratch?

He was no barracks-room philosopher, however, and all he could offer Chartier's widow was the brutal truth. "Your husband died because a mountain cat ripped out his throat."

"And if your lieutenant dies? Who will bear the blame for that? Your men will say it is the one who gives you the leaves of the moonflower."

"If he dies, it will be because the cold went to his lungs. But his fever broke during the night. He's better this morning."

Her breath escaped on a sigh of relief. "That is good."

"Very good."

With a roll of his shoulders, Daniel pushed this business of bad medicine to the back of his mind. As he'd pointed out to Huddleston, they'd come too damned far to turn back now.

"The sun's coming up over the trees. Let's get back to camp."

4

The lieutenant was sitting up when they returned to camp. Although his fever had indeed broken, he was still weak and fitful. So much so that it took some time for him to grasp the explanation Daniel offered for the addition to their small band.

"A Frenchman's widow, you say?" Blinking owlishly, he gaped at Louise. "And you want to take her with us to the Quapaw winter camp?"

"Not just to the Quapaw camp. I told her she could travel with us as far as a settlement where she can trade her furs."

"We're weeks away from the nearest settlement. She can't trek along with us all that way. This is a military expedition, not a walk through a country garden."

As if Daniel needed reminding of that fact! Schooling himself to patience, he passed the lieutenant a tin mug of coffee.

"I promised her husband I would see her safe."

Wilkinson thinned his mouth, obviously displeased and not entirely sure what he could do about it. Like his father, he was small of stature, but he possessed none of the general's blustery charm or immense self-confidence. Daniel supposed most women would consider the son more handsome than the father, though. He tied his fine, if now matted, brown hair back in a queue and looked out at the world with pale blue eyes. He wore his uniform well—when it wasn't in rags—and could exude an air of sophistication at times.

This wasn't one of those times.

Swallowing a sigh at the officer's querulous expression, Daniel guided the coffee mug to his lips. "The woman won't be any bother," he promised, ignoring the fact that she'd already created a stir among the men.

"You know better than that. A woman in a military camp always spells trouble."

"I've given my promise," he said again, shrugging.

Young Wilkinson looked as though he wanted to argue the matter further, but gave way before his sergeant's calm implacability. Daniel ended the matter by steering the conversation to the question that had been nagging at the back of his mind since last night.

"When we camped with the Little Osage a few weeks back, did the chief let drop anything about a Spanish agent operating in these parts?"

Wilkinson lifted a startled gaze. "A Spanish agent?"

"The woman, Louise, says the trappers have heard rumors the Spanish might send boats up the Arkansaw and try to reclaim this territory."

The lieutenant buried his face in his coffee mug and took another swallow. When he lowered the battered tin cup, sweat dewed his forehead.

"If the Spanish are thinking to reclaim this territory, that's all the more reason for us to finish charting the river. My father's most anxious to know if it's navigable by anything larger than a canoe."

Terminating the discussion, the lieutenant set his empty mug aside and dropped back on his blanket. "I'm still feeling poorly. I don't think I have the strength to walk today."

"You'd better go by dugout."

Pasty faced, he nodded weakly.

After a breakfast of fried beaver liver and coffee, Daniel loaded the girl's bale of furs in their one remaining boat.

They'd started down the Arkansaw with a skin-covered canoe and a pirogue hollowed out of a log, both of which their small band had constructed. A submerged limb had ripped through the canoe and sunk it. The damned pirogue wallowed like a drunken sow, but at least it would carry the heavy bale of furs.

Daniel hauled the pelts to the boat and made a nest for the lieutenant. Hooking a shoulder under Wilkinson's arm, he half walked, half carried the officer to the dugout and settled him beside their remaining store of powder and shot.

"Boley, you take first shift at the prow. Bradley, you've got the rear."

The two privates took their places and pushed away from shore. Boley had to use an ax to chop through the ice crusting the banks. Cursing and soon soaked to the waist, he and Bradley finally managed to get the dugout into the narrow, free-flowing channel at the river's center.

The rest of the troop trudged along the banks. The snow was hard and caked enough to keep them from sinking up to their knees, but the march took a toll on their waning strength. To make matters worse, the air carried a dank bite and the sky turned an ominous gray. They'd have fresh snow to struggle through, and soon.

As if a sick lieutenant, surly troops and the weather weren't worry enough, Daniel now had the added responsibility of the trapper's widow. She kept up with the men easily enough, but where their eyes were red-rimmed from frost and their shoulders were hunched against the biting wind, she moved with the sleek, surefooted grace of an antelope. The cold gave her cheeks a pink glow. The wind tugged silken strands of black from under her cap.

Her youth and resilience showed more with every passing mile, and Daniel caught the glances his men directed her way. He didn't like the idea of leaving her alone with them when he broke off to hunt. He'd kept John Wilson ashore for just that reason. The

lanky Kentuckian was the only one of the four privates he trusted to follow orders without question
these days.

"Wilson!"

"Yes, Sergeant."

"I'm going out to hunt. I'm detailing you to keep
an eye on Madame Chartier."

"Yes, Sergeant."

"See she comes to no harm."

"And causes none," he added under his breath.
With a last glance at the woman, he struck off on his
own.

He ranged as far as he dared from the river in
search of game, but bagged only one wild turkey.
Dusk was falling by the time he caught up with his
men and directed them to make camp for the night.

While Boley cleaned and spitted the turkey, Daniel
saw to the lieutenant. Wilkinson hadn't yet shaken
his sickness. He took the brew Daniel brought him
with trembling hands, but his gratitude toward the
woman who'd supplied his troop with the beans for
his coffee soon turned to peevishness.

"You should have traded with her for the beans,"
he muttered, his glance going to the figure sitting
alone across the campfire. "Not brought her with
you."

"Traded what? All we've got left are a few of the
medals your father had struck to give to the chiefs
of the tribes we encountered. A bit of metal wouldn't
have kept her alive through the winter."

"Keeping her alive through the winter isn't our responsibility."

Since they'd already ridden over this ground once, Daniel saw no need to cover it again. Deliberately, he turned the subject.

"We passed a saline about noon and stocked up on salt."

"Did you mark the location on the map?"

"Yes."

Given the importance of salt to survival, the expedition had orders to take note of every natural deposit. They'd already charted the Great Saline, just west of the main branch of the Arkansaw, and the Grand Saline at the mouth of the Negracka. After watching the local residents use turkey feathers to scrape up the precious salt and deposit it in wooden trenchers, Lieutenant Wilkinson had made copious notes in his journal. The man lacked both maturity and leadership skills, but he had a keen eye for detail and a fine hand with a map. Daniel would give him that.

Tonight, however, the young officer couldn't work up any enthusiasm for his duties.

"You'll have to take the circumferentor and fix our location," Wilkinson told Daniel listlessly. "I'm too weak to handle the task."

"Yes, sir."

Pushing his own fatigue aside, Daniel reached for the lieutenant's leather pouch. Inside was a wooden box bundled in oilskin to keep its contents dry. A sort of portable desk with a sloping lid that could be used to write on, the box contained Wilkinson's journal, a spare compass and the expedition's brass surveying instrument.

"Be sure to check the settings against the book."

"Yes, sir," Daniel drawled again.

As many times as he'd performed this duty in the past six months, he not only knew the circumferentor's settings, but could recite Robert Gibson's whole damned *Treatise of Practical Surveying* by rote.

He took the leather pouch to the edge of the river. The tattered treatise stayed at the bottom of the box while he fitted the rotating compass onto a fixed ring, then attached the four sight vanes into their dovetail slots. The two sets of graduated sights allowed him to measure angles independent of the compass's magnetic needle and thus calculate heights as well as bearings. Daniel shot line of the river, the bluffs on the opposite side, the high ridges in the distance. Each measurement he recorded in the lieutenant's journal with a blunt-tipped pencil.

When he lowered the instrument, his breath puffed on frigid air. Cold nipped at his ears and nose, but the vista held him motionless. The sky hung low and threatening. The broad Arkansaw moved sluggishly under the ice, showing only a narrow open channel in its center. Wind rustled through the bare branches of oak and maple and sighed through the pines. Despite the desolation, the beauty of the land pulled at his heart much as it had yesterday, when he'd stood beside Henri Chartier on that high ridge.

The woman was right, he thought. The Osage

would fight fiercely to keep intruders out of this wilderness, as would the other tribes who hunted here. President Jefferson would have a time of it convincing their chiefs to accept his proposed Indian Removal Plan. And if the president did push the plan through Congress, the troops assigned to remote outposts in Louisiana Territory would have an even tougher time keeping the peace between traditional enemies like the Osage and Choctaw.

Daniel might well have volunteered to be one of those troops if not for the woman waiting for him back in St. Louis. His chest squeezing at the memory of their farewell, he disassembled the circumferentor, boxed it and bundled the instrument in the oilskin. As he walked back to camp, the first white flakes began to drift out of the sky.

The snow fell all that night and for most of the next two days. Soft, fluffy flakes at first, the kind that looked powdery enough but soon soaked a man clear through to his skin and made lifting each foot and planting it down in front of the other a tiresome chore.

The snow by itself would have been bearable if the temperature hadn't dropped clear to hell. Icy cold knifed in the lungs with every breath. Fingers, toes and noses soon went numb. Following fast-disappearing deer tracks through a copse of bare-branched oak, Daniel thought his eyeballs would freeze in their sockets.

Finally, he came upon an antlered buck pawing in

the snow for roots and acorns. Hoping his powder had kept dry, Daniel shouldered his musket and thumbed back the hammer. He shook so badly from the cold that he couldn't get the animal in his sights. Swearing, he gritted his teeth, steadied his back against a tree trunk and fired. The recoil slammed the rifle butt into his shoulder and his back against the tree, but he brought the buck down.

It took almost all his remaining strength to drag the carcass up and hook its horns in a low hanging branch. Slicing open the belly, Daniel plunged his hands into the body cavity to thaw them in the steamy warmth. When feeling came back into his fingers in stinging spurts, he gutted the animal, hauled the carcass over his shoulders and started for the river.

The men had already made camp by the time he caught up with them. The snow was coming so thick and fast by then that he might not have found them at all if not for the sharp scent of their fire. Following his nose, Daniel stumbled into camp. Eager hands reached out to relieve him of his burden.

"Damn, Sergeant! We thought you was lost for sure."

"You got us a prime one."

"Enough meat to last a few days, anyway." That came from Private Boley, the designated cook. He wasn't any better at it than the other men, but liked being first at the fry pan.

The others huddled close to the fire, cursing the cold, the snow and the madness that had made them agree to take part in this ill-fated expedition. Only the woman sat apart, as she always did. And as he'd come to do, Daniel cradled his coffee mug in both hands for warmth and went to join her.

Louise watched his approach with eyes that stung from the cold. It struck her again how quickly her life had changed. Three days ago, she'd had no thoughts in her head but cleaning the take from Henri's traps and making sure he wore enough furs to still the cough that rattled in his chest. Now, she greeted the approach of this broad-shouldered American with a curious sense of anticipation. And relief.

It was his manner, she decided, as much as his wide shoulders and lean, muscled flanks. He brought his ragged band into order with just a word or a glance. She'd learned by now that the sick one, the lieutenant, was the chief. But this one, this rifle sergeant, was their leader.

He stayed with her throughout the meal. He even accompanied her into the woods when she went to relieve herself. And, as he had on each of the previous nights, he made his bed where she did. This time, though, he spread his blanket atop hers.

"It's going to get colder than a grave tonight. I've told the men to huddle up. We'd best do the same."

Her fingers tightened on the robe draped around her shoulders. She said nothing, could say nothing.

"It's just for warmth," he said gruffly.

Louise might have believed him if not for the way he held himself as stiff as a lodge pole when she crawled into the cocoon made by their blankets. He didn't bend, didn't curve his body so much as an inch to fit hers. They lay with her back to his front, neither moving, until the cold seeped into her bones and she began to shiver.

"Here." His breath was a wash of warmth in her ear. "Snuggle closer."

Hooking an arm around her waist, he drew her into the cradle of his thighs. She wiggled her bottom to escape the prod of a broken branch and heard him pull in a sharp breath.

He jerked away, but not before she felt another prod at her rear cheek. Her womb clenched, a swift, mindless response that sent heat spearing through her belly. They lay stiff, their lower bodies angled away, neither speaking but each, Louise suspected, thinking the same thoughts.

The litany of Henri's oft-repeated teachings drummed through her head. There was no shame in the pleasures of the body. No shame in the desire that joined a man and a woman. The only shame lay in denying those desires.

Louise had often suspected he repeated that chant as much for himself as for her, but she didn't dispute the truth of it. She'd taken pleasure from his hands and mouth, and given as much as she could in return.

But this—

This joining wouldn't compare to Henri's fumbling attempt to pierce her maiden's shield. Nor to the infrequent times he'd entered her body after that. With everything that was female within her, Louise sensed this man, this soldier, would pleasure her in ways Henri could not.

A liquid heat formed between her legs. She no longer tried to tell herself she didn't want him, that she would dishonor Henri if she allowed this man to mount her.

Except he made no move to do so.

His arm lay heavy on her waist. His breath was hot in her ear. But he didn't slip his hand under her tunic. Didn't try to find the slit in her leggings. Didn't rub his fingers against flesh that had grown hot and slick.

Deciding she would not spend another night lying awake and tight with anticipation, she rolled over until they lay knee to knee.

"Why do you not lift my skirts?"

"What?"

"Why do you not join with me, as a man does with a woman? I felt your spear grow stiff."

"I didn't mean for that to happen."

The gruff reply confused her until she remembered Spotted Dog, a skilled hunter who'd brought down many buffalo and took his pleasure only with other warriors to avoid draining his powerful medicine.

"Ahh. Are you one who chooses not to lie with women?"

"Yes. I mean, no." His breath puffed out on a chuckle. "It's just that— Well…"

When he hesitated, Louise began to wonder if perhaps he was like Henri, after all. So often the Frenchman had waited for her to set the spark to his fire.

Stealthy as a coyote on the scent of prey, curiosity crept through her veins. Curiosity, and the stirrings of need. She'd never curled up under the blankets with any man but Henri. Had never felt the desire to taste any man but her husband.

This one roused strange urges she'd never felt before. He was so near she could feel his breath on her cheek. So warm, his heat drew her like the low, flickering flames in a drafty lodge. Without stopping to think, without weighing the consequences, she leaned forward, put her mouth on his and used her tongue in the way Henri had taught her.

"Jesus!"

Daniel jerked his head back, stunned by the fire that slashed into his belly. Even more stunned by the savage urge that ripped into him. He came within a blink of rolling the woman onto her back and returning the thrust of her hot tongue.

He sucked in a sharp breath, welcoming the blade-edged cold of it, and forced himself to speak calmly. "You've got me wrong all the way around, Louise. I don't choose to lie with other women because I have a wife who waits for me in St. Louis."

She curled an arm under her head, tried to see the pale blur of his face.

"Many men, I think, have wives in one village and lie with women of another. Henri, he has a wife in France. He tells the priest who marries us she is dead, but me, I think he doesn't speak the truth."

"Well, I speak the truth. My wife is very much alive."

Alive, but living in shadows.

The pain that always lay just under Daniel's breastbone squeezed at his chest. He closed his eyes, struggling to remember Elizabeth's face before she'd lost her merry smile and retreated into herself.

A knock of a knee against his yanked his thoughts from the fair-haired bride he'd married ten years ago to the ripe young widow now sharing his blanket.

With a somewhat less than gentle shove, he rolled her over until they were back-to-front again. Pain, frustration and—damn him!—lust laced his voice as he issued a terse order.

"Go to sleep."

5

Fresh snow lay hip-deep by dawn.

Coiled tight by the hunger that had kept him lying stiff and awake most of the night, Daniel dug out of their cocoon and almost savored the lash of the cold.

Louise crawled out after him. Shivering, she dragged her buffalo robe over her shoulders. He didn't know how she could look so young and innocent, yet use her mouth and tongue in ways that would put a Spanish whore to the blush. She'd learned those tricks from Chartier, Daniel guessed. The lecherous, lucky bastard.

"I'll take you into the woods," he said shortly. "Then we'd best get on the move."

She nodded, apparently unfazed by the fact that she'd all but set a torch to him last night. With some effort, he banished the memory of her body molded to his and escorted her into the trees. By the time they returned, the men were up and moving.

Lieutenant Wilkinson was still in the grip of his illness. Too weak to walk, he climbed into the boat.

The soldiers manning the paddles were forced to chop and hack at the ice obstructing the channel as the river carried them along. The rest shuffled along the bank in snowshoes fashioned from bent hickory frames interwoven with strips of rawhide.

Daniel took point and ranged ahead with One Eye. The going was slow and arduous. They'd traveled far fewer miles than either liked when they reached a wide bend in the river. Squinting through the snow, Daniel tried to see what lay beyond the turn.

"How far to the winter camp of the Quapaw?"

One Eye held up two fingers, thought for a moment and uncurled a third.

Hell! Two days' march yet. Maybe three if the storm didn't let up. At this rate Christmas would be come and gone before they reached the camp.

All reports indicated it was a good-size gathering. Lieutenant Wilkinson was especially anxious to meet with Cash-she-se-gra, chief of the Quapaw. The general had given his son specific orders to establish friendly relations with the chief, known by the English name of Big Track. Daniel had an idea the general was more interested in the lucrative fur trade centered around the Three Rivers area than in formal treaties between the Osage and the United States, but at this point, he didn't much care. All he wanted was to get his ragtag band out of the cold and snow.

He shuffled forward and had covered another quarter mile or so when he heard shouts. His stomach tightening, he whirled and plunged back through the tracks he and One Eye had just made. When he reached the others, he saw at a glance what had happened.

The damned dugout had snagged on a submerged tree and tipped over again, dumping its occupants and cargo into the river. The current had already carried Private Wilson some ways downstream. Huddleston and Boley had gone after him. Lieutenant Wilkinson clung to the overturned boat with one arm, his other wrapped around the leather pouch containing the box with his journal and the circumferentor. Private Bradley had gone into the river, too, but he'd floundered onto the ice and was scuttling toward the bank on hands and knees. The ice splintered under him, each snaking *crack* sounding as sharp and ominous as a pistol shot in the cold air.

Wind That Cries stood on the bank, unwilling to add his weight to the ice for fear it would shatter and take both him and Bradley in. It was the girl who threw off her heavy buffalo robe and stretched out onto the ice.

"Take my hand!"

Bradley lifted his head at her shout, lurched forward and made a grab for her arm. Their fingers touched just as the ice came apart. For a second Daniel thought Louise might have him, but their hold was too loose or his weight too much for her. With a curse that carried clearly on the frigid air, Bradley sank into the dark water.

"Help them!" Daniel shouted to One Eye. "I'll go for the lieutenant."

Dropping his rifle, he kicked off his snowshoes,

tossed aside his buffalo robe and plunged down the riverbank. The hides wrapped around his boots slithered on the snow-covered ice, but he moved fast enough to make the channel mid-river before the slick crust broke under him. Gritting his teeth, he sank into the icy water.

The cold was like a blade plunged straight to the heart. It drove the air from his lungs, stunned him into immobility. He went down, eyes open, arms dangling like dead weights at his sides. With his mind shut down and his whole body frozen in shock, he stayed under for what seemed like two lifetimes, until finally—finally!—he forced his limbs to move.

He broke to the surface mere feet from the overturned craft. Shoving its prow toward the bank, he swam the hollowed-out log and the officer clinging to it to shore. By the time they reached the bank, Bradley was out. Wet and shivering, he helped One Eye and Louise pull Daniel and the lieutenant on to dry land. Daniel left them to get a fire started and went to aid Huddleston and Boley.

When at last he'd gathered his troops all again, he couldn't remember ever seeing a more wretched lot. The wet ones stripped down and huddled under blankets and borrowed buffalo robes. Squeezing the water out of their clothes, they stretched their garments on branches and waved them over the fire to dry. The ones who hadn't gone into the river chopped more wood for the blaze, melted snow for coffee and generally commiserated with their comrades. Only one remained apart. She stood alone at the riverbank, the drifting snow almost obscuring her bundled figure.

"Look at her," Huddleston muttered. "Cryin' over her lost furs, I don't doubt."

"You'd cry, too," Bradley retorted, feeling more kindly toward the woman after her attempt to aid him, "if everything you owned just went to the bottom of the river."

"She ain't lost everything." Huddleston's eyes shifted away to the haversack lying across the fire. "She's still got that. No tellin' what's in it besides the few beans she doles out one by one like a miser does his pennies."

John Wilson shook his head. "You're a fine bucket of brine, Solomon. You guzzle down her coffee fast enough and misspeak her while you do."

"All I'm sayin' is that I'm comin' to believe she's bad luck, just like One Eye and Wind That Cries here said. Look how our boat tipped over today."

"Hell," Wilson protested, "we done tipped over a half dozen times before today!"

"Not in this kind of cold 'n' snow. We'll be lucky if we don't be froze by morning. And what about the way she let Bradley here go into the river?"

"She didn't let me go," the shivering private put in, although with less force than he had a moment ago. "I was too heavy for her."

"Maybe, 'n' maybe not."

"That's enough, Huddleston." Disgusted, Daniel tossed the dregs of his coffee into the fire. "If you put as much muscle into your assigned duties as you do into stirring up trouble, we'd all be home by now.''

The disgruntled private subsided, but shot his sergeant a sour look as Daniel pulled on his almost dry long-johns, britches and socks. The socks had more holes than yarn left to them, but they gave his toes some measure of warmth, as did the strips of hide he wrapped around his feet as an outer covering while his boots dried. Dragging his buffalo robe over his shoulders, he went to join Louise.

She acknowledged him with a sideways glance, but didn't speak. Tucking her chin down in her robe, she returned her glance to the river. In the waning afternoon light, Daniel couldn't help but notice how the snowflakes clung to her dark lashes, sugar-tipping them. His glance roamed over her proud cheeks, caught on the silky strands straggling out from under her cap.

It was a marvel to him now that he'd ever mistaken her for a boy. He'd grown so familiar with her features over the past few days. And with the curve of her slender body. Sternly, Daniel shut out the searing memory of her rounded bottom pressed against his groin.

''I'm sorry your furs went to the river bottom.''

''The fault is not yours.''

No, but the responsibility was.

''I'll collect six months' wilderness pay when I get back to St. Louis. I'll use it to see you're taken care of.''

''St. Louis? Is that where your wife waits?''

"Yes."

"Me, I have no wish to live in the lodge of another woman."

The reply took Daniel aback. He hadn't been thinking of taking the girl all the way to St. Louis with him, much less into his home. Elizabeth's hold on her senses was frail enough without thrusting the responsibility for a trapper's widow on her. Hastily, he scrambled for another solution.

"You don't have to live in my lodge. I'll make arrangements for you when we reach Arkansaw Post. You can remain there until I send you funds, then do as you wish. Unless you change your mind when we reach the winter camp of your people," he added hopefully. "You might decide to stay with them."

"No!"

"Just until I send you funds to cover the loss of your furs."

"No!" She drew in a deep breath. "I have told you of the legend. Always I have lived in its shadow, but it does not change my life until my uncle's wife delivers her child without arms." Her voice went flat. "The shaman smokes the pipe and talks with the spirits and says I am bad medicine. The next week, my uncle sells me to Henri. I cannot stay with the Quapaw. I am not welcome in their camp."

Well, that settled the matter, Daniel thought as he escorted the woman back to the fire. Not that it made much difference at this point. If this snow didn't let up, they'd all likely freeze to death before they made it to the Quapaw village.

* * *

Louise spent the night huddled against Daniel's back and the morning avoiding hostile glances from the two Osage guides. They blamed her, she knew, for the stinging sleet that gradually replaced the soft snowflakes. Blamed her, too, for the winds that now howled through the trees like the spirits of the unmourned dead.

It was a curse. Her curse. She'd escaped it only during the years she'd roamed the wilderness with Henri. He, like Daniel, shrugged aside the ancient tale.

Now Henri was dead, and Daniel wanted Louise to remain with her mother's people. She couldn't. She wouldn't. Once there, she knew with a mounting dread, the whispers would begin again. The sideways looks. The prayers designed to pacify the angry spirits.

So great was her reluctance to hear the ancient legend once again, she almost—*almost!*—welcomed the storm that howled all through the day and into the next. Only the certainty that she would freeze along with Daniel and his men if they didn't take shelter gave her the courage to stumble into the Quapaw winter camp late the following afternoon.

The sprawling camp was located not far from where three great rivers came together—the Arkansaw, the Grand and the Verdigris. The waterways provided easy means for the Quapaw to travel, as well as plentiful fish and game to see them through the winter months.

The camp itself looked little different from when Louise had last seen it more than five years ago. Set well back from the bank of the Arkansaw, the village was a jumble of more than a hundred longhouses constructed of bent poles covered with cypress bark. Each lodge housed several families joined by blood or by marriage, with the headman and his wife occupying the choice, fur-covered platform farthest from the smoke of the cook fires. A great council house, where games and ceremonies took place, sat at the center of the village. Pens for the horses were squeezed in among the lodges, to protect the animals from raiding bands and to provide them some shelter from the winds.

Louise's stomach twisted as dogs barked and men and women bundled in fur robes braved the pelting hail to stare at the band straggling wearily into camp. The moon-faced officer wheezed with each step, but managed a brave smile for the chief who came out of his lodge to meet them.

The wind and sun had carved deep lines into Cash-she-se-gra's face, but he still stood straight and tall as an oak. When his gaze swept over the bedraggled group, Louise ducked her face into the folds of her buffalo robe. Like a coward, she dreaded the moment he'd recognize her.

"I am Cash-she-se-gra," he announced, "called Big Track by your people. I am chief of the Osage who live here, where the rivers run together."

One Eye put her uncle's words into English for the lieutenant, who replied solemnly.

"I am Lieutenant Wilkinson. Son of Major General James Wilkinson, military governor of the Louisiana Territory. I bring you greetings from him and from our Great Father in Washington."

"This one is like an untried girl," One Eye informed Big Track, making no effort to give a faithful account of the lieutenant's spoken words, "but his father is a great chief among the whites. He has come to smoke with you and speak on behalf of the general."

"I will smoke with him."

"He also brings a woman of your clan. She is called Wah-shi-tu."

Startled, her uncle whipped his head around. Louise's stomach rolled as she lifted her chin and met his piercing stare.

"Why are you with these men?"

"I travel with them," she answered in her own tongue, adding quietly, "I stay only as long as they do."

Frowning, her uncle searched the group again. "Where is your man?"

"He is dead."

His mouth settled into tight lines. "We will speak more of this inside."

Lifting the bark-covered door, Big Track gestured his visitors inside. Gratefully, they ducked through the square opening. A good number of the curious bystanders crowded in after them. Louise hesitated, dragged in a deep breath and followed.

Dark, smothering warmth flowed around her as she

drank in the sights and smells of her childhood. Big
Track's wealth was evident in the rich furs draped
over his sleeping platform and the many pouches
hanging from the lodge poles. The pouches were
crammed with the summer harvest of pumpkin,
squash and corn, Louise knew, carefully hoarded to
see his family through the winter. Despite her prickly
nervousness at being back among the Quapaw, her
mouth watered at the remembered taste of pumpkin
cakes fried in bear grease.

She'd spent so little time with her mother's people,
only those few years after her mother's death. Her
memories of the Quapaw seemed to be centered on
such small things. The way the married women wore
their hair loose, while maidens wove two braids and
secured them in loops at each ear. The sway of a
baby swinging in its board-backed cradle. The earthy
warmth of many people living together.

Perhaps she didn't want to remember anything
else. Perhaps she thought of herself as French instead
of Quapaw because her mother's people had shunned
her. Fighting an all-too-familiar sense of loneliness,
she edged to a far corner of the lodge.

Louise might not be welcome, but the Quapaw
were known for their hospitality to strangers. She
wasn't surprised when Big Track ordered the women
of his lodge to begin preparations for a feast and sent
criers to invite the more senior warriors to join him.
Louise kept to her dark corner, guessing her uncle's
wife would not want her assistance. She'd guessed
right. Running Deer sent her one cold look and spoke

not a word to the female who'd once shared her lodge.

"We will smoke while we wait," her uncle told his visitors, inviting them to the fur-covered platform.

It was a time-honored ritual, sometimes spiritual, sometimes social. The long-stemmed pipe decorated with beads and feathers was passed from man to man. Smoke drifted through the lodge, light and fragrant, another memory from Louise's years with her mother's people. Breathing in the familiar scent, she sat with her legs crossed under her and her hands folded loosely in her lap, while the lieutenant dug into his haversack.

"I bring you a gift from my father. A bronze medal to show he wants only peace and friendship with the Osage."

One Eye's lip curled as the young officer held out a disk dangling from a blue ribbon. "He gives this same gift to all chiefs," the Osage guide advised the Big Track. "Even those who lead few warriors."

Her uncle grunted, but hung the bit of bronze around his neck. "Tell him I have heard many tales of his father. I accept his gift and will consider what to give in exchange."

"My father wants only peace with the Osage," the lieutenant replied after the words were relayed to him. "As military governor of this territory, it is his sole desire to protect you and the lands where you hunt."

Protect them? Louise knew better. The whey-faced

one spoke a great lie. If he were truthful, he would tell Big Track of this absurd plan to move the Cherokee and Choctaw into Osage Country.

"My father is also very interested in expanding trade with you and your people," the officer continued. "This area is rich in furs."

"Very rich." The chief's gaze was thoughtful as it rested on his visitor. "I, too, wish to see trade increase between your people and mine. I will give you a place between the rivers for a trading post."

Surprised, Wilkinson blinked his owl's eyes. "I, uh, thank you, but we don't have any immediate plans to—"

"Lieutenant." Daniel leaned forward, his words quiet and urgent. "Accept the offer. What better spot for a fort than where three major rivers converge?"

"My father gave me no instructions regarding a fort."

"Think, man! We might well need a contingent of troops in the area if we want to keep the Spanish out and control the trade on these rivers."

And control the Osage, Louise thought, if their Great Father proceeded with his plan.

The urge to warn her uncle that he had invited a pack of hungry wolves into his lodge battled with her bone-deep reluctance to call attention to herself. If she spoke up, if she predicted another disaster for her people, she would be blamed for it as she'd been blamed for the scarcity of game and the boy-child born with no arms.

Biting her lip until she tasted blood, Louise sat

alone in her dark corner all through the feast that followed. Her pride kept her head high, but she wanted nothing so much as to see the end of this night and the resumption of her journey with Daniel.

Her glance lingered on his broad back and wide shoulders. He didn't want her as a man wants a woman. He'd made that clear enough. Yet he continued to honor his vow to Henri by throwing the shield of his authority over her. He would pay for that, Louise knew with a sick feeling in her stomach, as soon as the feast was finished and her uncle turned his attention to his niece.

She knew the moment had arrived when Big Track hooked a finger and beckoned her forward. Throat dry, Louise rose and wove her way through the cross-legged warriors.

"You say Chartier is dead."

"Yes, Uncle."

"Who among these men claims you?"

"None of them claims me."

"What? None of them has offered you his protection?"

"Yes, the tall one, with the hair the color of tobacco. He made a promise to Henri."

Frowning, the chief eyed Daniel's ragged buckskins and boots held together with strips of rawhide.

"Tell him he has taken a woman of my house. He must pay a bride price."

"He doesn't want me for a wife, Uncle."

"Does he share your blanket?"

"Yes, but—"

"Then he must pay. Tell him," he ordered sternly.

Helplessly, Louise turned to Daniel. "He asks if we share a blanket. I tell him yes, but that you do not take me to wife. It makes no difference. He says you will pay a bride price."

"The hell I will."

She was too proud to beg, but she couldn't keep a hint of desperation from seeping into her voice. "If I am to go with you to Arkansaw Post, this must be done."

"Louise, I couldn't buy you if I wanted to. I don't have two lead pennies to rub together. I won't until I return to St. Louis and draw my pay."

The one called Huddleston leaned forward, his eyes gleaming. "I've got a silver dollar tucked in my haversack. Tell the chief I'll buy her."

"No!"

This was what she had feared, what she had dreaded. Her uncle would give her to one who stunk like a dead fish to be rid of her, just as he'd given her to Henri. Trying to keep the desperation from her face, she turned to the sergeant.

"Daniel—"

He blew out a long breath and reached for his rucksack. His face set into grim lines as he pulled out a small package wrapped in oilskin. Carefully, he peeled back the folds. Inside lay a gold pocket watch.

"My wife gave me this the day we were wed."

By now Louise had come to know the rise and fall of his voice. It grieved him to part with the watch.

She heard the reluctance in his words, saw the fleeting pain in his eyes. He must hold this wife in St. Louis in great regard, she thought with something close to envy.

"The case is gold. It's worth many beaver and muskrat pelts."

Carefully, Daniel wound the stem and held it to Big Track's ear. After a moment, the chief nodded and folded his fingers around the watch.

"Tell him it is good," he instructed Louise. "But not enough."

"Uncle! You sold me to Chartier for a sack of dried corn and two beaver pelts."

"You were young then and had no more meat on your bones than a stewed rabbit. Now you are a woman, worth more. It is not enough."

As angry now as she was desperate, Louise bitterly regretted the loss of her furs. She had nothing to contribute to the trade.

Except, she remembered suddenly, the cougar's claws.

"I will add to the bride price myself."

Rushing back to the corner where she'd left her things, she searched through her depleted stores for the claws Daniel had brought her.

"Here." Her heart hammering, she spilled the shiny black talons into her uncle's hand. "These were taken from the cat that killed my husband. They have powerful medicine. They and the timepiece are enough, Uncle. More than enough."

Big Track debated the matter for long, agonizing moments before nodding in agreement.

"They are enough. I give you to this man."

When Louise spread her blanket beside Daniel's later that night, he grunted and rolled over so that his back was to her. It piqued her pride a bit that he did not want her even now, when her uncle had joined them in the ways of the Quapaw. But she was so relieved at the outcome of the negotiations, she merely drew her buffalo robe up to her ears and let the snuffles and snores of the lodge's occupants lull her to sleep.

6

By the next morning, the storm had passed and the sun smiled down from a cold, clear sky.

Louise stumbled out of her uncle's lodge, anxious to be away. After extracting such an exorbitant price for his niece, Big Track showed a more generous mood. He gifted the expedition with a good supply of meat and dried corn. He provided as well two sturdy canoes.

Louise climbed into the second. Wind That Cries took the prow, Daniel the back. Torn between relief and the shame of being so unwelcome in her uncle's lodge, she stared straight ahead as Daniel pushed away from the bank.

The expedition's three boats caught the current and moved swiftly on the river swollen by the recent snows. Ice still narrowed the channel, and the paddlers had to work to avoid another dunking, but the banks flowed by rapidly.

The days passed just as rapidly. They stopped at several small Osage villages, and hailed two hunting parties. Gradually, the river channel widened and the high, pine-studded mountains of Osage Country gave way to the rolling hills of the Wichita.

Louise had never journeyed this far south. She'd visited St. Louis once with her father, and had traveled to a fur traders' rendezvous on the Missouri with Henri. But those places lay north of Osage Country. This land was new to her. Not as cold, not as rugged. She saw only open skies, stunted trees that would not make good lodge poles and villages less than half the size of the Quapaw camp.

With the flattening of the land came the rapids. Not violent washes of stone and water, such as Louise had seen on other rivers, but fast, rippling currents that carried the boats swiftly and required constant vigilance. So much vigilance that when the exhausted men dragged the boats ashore each night, they ate their meals in sullen silence and dropped onto their blankets.

With the lessening of the brutal cold, there was no need for them to huddle together at night. Or for Daniel to curl Louise into his body to share his warmth. She told herself it mattered not, that she would soon part from him, but with each new dawn the feeling grew within her that she was leaving behind all she knew and entering a strange and unfamiliar world. For now, for the few remaining days of their journey, Daniel formed the one link between her past and an uncertain future.

So it was with a mix of joy and relief that she recognized the red-bearded Englishman who approached them as they made camp late one afternoon, led by a scout from an Osage war party.

"Robert!"

The trapper's face folded into lines of lively astonishment. "Louise Therese!"

Hobbling to her on the stumps that remained of his feet after a savage mutilation by the Pawnee some years ago, he bussed her heartily on both cheeks. "What the devil are you doing here?"

"I travel to Arkansaw Post."

"Do you? I've just come from there." He threw a glance around the camp. "Where's Henri?"

"He dies in the place where the river runs and the stones carry strange marks."

"Damnation! I'm sorry to hear that."

The flame-bearded Robert McFarlane dropped a sympathetic hand on her shoulder. He and Henri had often shared a campfire, swapping news of the fur trade and the endless wars that pitted their distant countries against each other. Like Henri, McFarlane held nothing but bemused contempt for Napoleon for selling the rich wilderness of Louisiana Territory to the United States for mere pennies an acre. And, like Henri, he'd heard the rumors whispering through the oaks and pines. Rumors he put directly to the lieutenant when that worthy introduced himself.

"So you're General Wilkinson's boy, are you?"

"I am."

"What's this I'm hearing about a scheme to set up a separate kingdom west of the Mississippi?"

The lieutenant's already pale face went gray. "Are you—? Are you speaking of the proposal to move the eastern tribes off their lands and into this part of the country?"

"No. I'm speaking of the brouhaha about your father's old friend, Colonel Burr."

"What—? What brouhaha?"

"You haven't heard?"

When the lieutenant couldn't seem to choke out a reply, Daniel stepped forward and answered for him. "We departed St. Louis in July and separated from Lieutenant Pike's expeditionary force in October. We've had no news at all since then."

McFarlane's shrewd brown eyes sized him up. "And who might you be, sir?"

"Rifle Sergeant Daniel Morgan."

"Well, Sergeant Morgan, if you'll let an old man warm what's left of his feet by your fire, I'll tell you what I know. It makes for a lively tale, I promise you."

It made, Louise soon decided, for an astonishing tale. She struggled to make sense of the names and places McFarlane tossed out, but Daniel and his men had no such difficulty. Seated on fallen logs, they listened avidly as the Englishman told of a web of treachery and deceit spun by one called Aaron Burr, once a great chief of the whites.

From what Louise could grasp, this Burr was a soldier, a warrior. He rose to hold a powerful rank in his tribe, second only to the Great Father, Jefferson. As great as this Colonel Burr's stature was, however, it did not satisfy him. He laid plans to seize lands from both the Spanish and the Great Father, and found a separate nation where he would be chief. He had gathered warriors to his cause, bought arms, and was moving to implement his scheme, when he was betrayed.

"It was your father who put Jefferson wise," McFarlane informed the lieutenant.

The young officer looked as though he'd been hit with a war ax. "My...? My father?" he stuttered.

"The general sent President Jefferson a letter he had received from Burr. The letter was in cipher, it seems, and gave details of the boats and troops Burr was amassing in New Orleans and at Blennerhassett Island on the Ohio."

The lieutenant opened his mouth as if to speak, but no sound emerged.

"The Ohio militia seized the Blennerhassett boats," McFarlane related, "but the troops escaped. Jefferson has issued an order for his navy to seize and destroy any boats under Burr's command in New Orleans. Your father has been relieved of his duties as governor of Louisiana Territory and sent to New Orleans to provide the governor of Orleans Territory military support."

"What of the Spanish?" Daniel asked. "How are they involved in this scheme?"

He was thinking of the Spanish agent Henri had heard rumors of, Louise guessed, the one she'd told him of.

''The Spanish have no involvement that I've heard,'' the trapper answered with a shrug, ''though I've no doubt they were glad to have the plot uncovered. One rumor has it Burr hoped to incite the citizens of Spanish Texas to revolt and join his empire.''

''How did General Wilkinson uncover evidence of the plot?''

The Englishman glanced at the lieutenant. ''Some are saying he was in on the scheme from the start.''

Wilkinson jumped up, his cheeks as flushed now as they had been white just moments ago. ''How dare you, sir!''

''But only to lure Burr into betraying himself,'' McFarlane finished. ''Why else would he provide Jefferson with the coded letter?''

''Why else indeed?'' Daniel murmured.

Louise studied his face, as familiar to her now as her own. Beneath his beard, his jaw was set. His gray eyes stared into the campfire, but she guessed he saw something other than the dancing flames.

The talk went on and on. McFarlane spoke of captains called Lewis and Clark, who'd made a journey of many, many moons and recently returned to St. Louis. He spoke as well of the war between France and Britain, and how the chief of the French, the very Napoleon whose name had so often caused Henri to spit into the fire, had made his brother chief of some kingdom called Naples.

Bored with names and places she knew nothing about, Louise yawned. After a moment, she drifted away from the circle of men to go into the woods and relieve herself. McFarlane met her as she returned. His beard flamed with the same fire as the rapidly setting sun and his eyes were kind as they skimmed her face.

"Do you mean to stay at Arkansaw Post?"

"For a while."

"You're welcome to hitch along with me. Henri taught you well how to work the traps and clean pelts. I could use a companion with those skills."

She arched a brow. "Only those skills?"

A quick grin split his bushy beard and displayed rows of blackened stumps. Stepping forward, he chucked her under her chin.

"All right, I'm not ashamed to admit it. I wouldn't mind if you warmed my old bones the way you did Henri's."

Louise tipped her head, considering his offer. He was of her world, had traveled its rivers and forests. Henri had judged him to be a brave hunter and skilled trapper. McFarlane would be kind to her, as Henri had been kind in his own way. Part of her wanted to snatch at the world she knew. But she had only to glance over McFarlane's shoulder to know how she would answer him.

Daniel stood a few yards away. His face wore a fierce scowl as he took in the way McFarlane cupped her chin. A scowl, and something more. Something that made her heart rush and skip like the rapids they'd traveled over earlier.

It was gone in a flash, and when the trapper

glanced behind him to see what had caught her gaze, Daniel showed only an expression of polite interest.

"Do I interrupt?"

"Yes," McFarlane replied testily.

"No," Louise countered, smiling as she pulled her chin from his grasp. "Robert and I, we speak of Henri."

And the possibility of Louise warming McFarlane's bones. Daniel had heard the words. Damned if they weren't ricocheting around inside his skull like spent musket balls. With some effort he kept his hands from fisting at his sides. The idea that she might snuggle up with McFarlane put a tight, painful twist in his gut.

"Robert asks me to go with him," she said. "But me, I do not wish to share his blanket."

He didn't stop to question her decision. Or the relief that knifed through him.

"Then you'd better go back to camp and get packed up. The lieutenant wants to push on."

"By night?"

"There's a full moon rising and the river's flowing fast. He thinks we can make another five miles or more."

McFarlane tugged at his beard. "That news about Burr got his feathers up, did it?"

"Something did."

"Well, I'd best go and make my farewells, then."

The trapper tucked Louise's arm in his and hobbled back to the fire. The men had already begun to gather their possessions and break camp, muttering among themselves as they did so. Private Huddleston's complaints were the loudest and earned him a sharp reproof from Daniel.

"It was good sharing a fire with you," McFarlane told the lieutenant. "See that your sergeant there takes good care of Louise Therese here. She's got ties to royalty, you know. Henri always claimed he' could trace his line back to the Sun King."

"Did he?" Still distracted by the news that the man had imparted earlier, Wilkinson merely nodded. "I'm sure that will be of interest to my father."

McFarlane grinned and turned away. For the life of him, Daniel couldn't tell whether the Englishman was jerking on the lieutenant's powder horn or trying to provide a mantle of respectability to the penniless, half-breed widow of an old friend.

After the meeting with McFarlane, the lieutenant pushed his men as hard as he dared. He made only sketchy notes in his journal, jotting down just the names of the major tributaries feeding into the Arkansaw and the rough location of various Indian villages.

On the last day of 1806, they passed the mouth of the Poteau, named for the Frenchman who'd first skimmed its bounty. From there, the land flattened even more and the shores were lined with cane, indicating rich bottomland.

Several days beyond the Poteau, they stopped at the plantation of a Monsieur Labomme, who treated the bedraggled party with far less civility than the

Osage had. Finally, on the ninth of January, the detachment rounded a bend of the river and spied the rambling settlement of Arkansaw Post.

As the boats angled across the rippling water, Louise's heart thumped against her ribs. This outpost marked the boundary between her two worlds.

Behind her lay the land of the Pawneee and Osage and Wichita, an endless sea of high bluffs, sparkling rivers and rolling prairies where thousands upon thousands of buffalo grazed.

Ahead…

Ahead lay the land of the whites, who wore strange, uncomfortable clothes, rode in wagons and carriages, and built great villages of brick and stone.

She was part of both worlds, yet belonged to neither. Gripping the sides of the boat with tight fingers, she took a last look over her shoulder before turning her face to the bustling outpost.

Called Poste de Arkansea by the Frenchman who'd claimed this bend of the river some twenty miles above the point where it emptied into the Mississippi, the village had grown into a thriving trade center. A hundred or more lodges lay scattered along a riverbank crowded with dugouts and canoes. Dogs yapped, children chased feather-covered balls and women bundled in furs chattered as the latest arrivals pushed their boats up on the bank and wearily climbed out.

A wooden palisade of tall, sharp-pointed logs housed the buildings of the chief factor, a Frenchman of considerable girth and loose loyalty to the government that now claimed jurisdiction over his post.

"So many flags have flown here," Pierre Duval said as he tipped generous portions of brandy into pewter mugs for the tired travelers. "These days I know not whether I'm to pay taxes to the French, the Spanish, the English or the Americans. Perhaps soon," he added with a shake of his head, "I will run another flag up the pole. One belonging to Colonel Burr, the man who would be king."

His eyes watering from the fiery brandy, Daniel lowered his mug. "So the rumors about Burr are true?"

"But, yes! News comes up the river daily. The latest is that Burr gathers some thousands of men in Natchez." Duval nodded to the lieutenant. "Your father has declared martial law in New Orleans. He thinks to keep the citizens there from joining forces with Burr."

Face flushed, Wilkinson downed his drink in a single gulp. Daniel's heart sank. It wasn't just the brandy putting that high color in the man's cheeks. He looked to be coming down with another bout of fever.

"That changes our plans," the lieutenant declared. "If martial law has been declared, things must be at a serious impasse. My father will want my report as soon as possible. We, too, will go to New Orleans."

Huddleston voiced an immediate protest. "The hell you say! We left our kits and our families in St. Louis. We figured on returning there."

"And so you will, after New Orleans."

"Now, look. I didn't sign on for—"

"You signed on for the duration of the expedition," Daniel reminded him sharply.

"Didn't you hear Duval, man? The general's declared martial law. You know what that means. Foot patrols and barricade duty all day, every day, with not a penny of extra pay to show for our efforts." Huddleston's red-rimmed gaze darted from face to face. "I say we head back to St. Louis, where we set out from, and forget New Orleans."

"My orders are to deliver the report of our expedition directly to my father," the lieutenant said with an attempt at authority. "We leave first thing in the morning for New Orleans."

Lifting an arm to swipe the sweat from his brow, Wilkinson missed the sneer that twisted Huddleston's mouth. Daniel saw it, however, and barely refrained from planting a fist in the man's face.

Gritting his teeth, Daniel reminded himself that the private was bone-tired and ready to be done with this damnable expedition. They all were. God knew Daniel would be happy to see the last of this ragtag band.

Or so he thought, until he glanced at Louise and saw the quiet desperation in her blue eyes.

Reluctance seeped into him, replacing the weariness. They'd come so far together these past weeks. He'd grown used to taking her into the woods each morning, to seeing her face across a campfire. Her low, musical voice and lilting accent were a part of his day now. And, he suspected, memories of how her lithe young body had curved against his would fill his nights for a long, long time.

Understanding her worry at being left in a strange outpost, Daniel turned to Duval. "Do you know of a good family who would take Madame Chartier in for a few weeks? I'll reimburse them for her keep when I draw my pay."

"She can stay here, in my storeroom. It has a bed. My woman is from the Caddo Tribe," he added. "She'll be glad to have the company of another female."

"Good. It's settled then."

"Come with me," Duval said with a smile for Louise. "I'll show you where to put your things."

She gathered the straps of the haversack that contained all she now owned. With a nod that included the lieutenant and the others in the troop, she stopped before Daniel. Her extraordinary eyes lifted to his.

"I thank you for your care. You have kept your promise to Henri."

"Not quite. I'll send you funds as soon as I collect my pay."

"Perhaps our paths will cross again someday."

"Perhaps they will."

His gut tightened. Like a sharpened blade, need knifed into him. He ached to lift his hand. To draw a knuckle down the smooth curve of her cheek. To keep her with him for the rest of their journey, wherever it took them.

Deliberately, he stepped back. He had a wife waiting for him in St. Louis. A wife who clung to the shadows more than she clung to him. But the vow he'd made to her was more compelling than the one he'd made to Chartier, more urgent than the hunger that now fired his blood.

Louise left him with a smile and a soft wish. "May you walk with the sun and ride with the wind."

Daniel spread his blanket on the hard-packed dirt floor of the trading post later that night and drifted into sleep thinking of her smile.

He jerked awake some hours later to the shrill of her screams.

7

Primed pistol in hand, Daniel burst through the door to Duval's storeroom a half step ahead of the trader himself. A single glance at the two figures facing each other across a sack of dried beans told the story.

Huddleston was drunk. So drunk he spewed brandy fumes into the musty air with each enraged bellow.

"Bitch!" Hand clamped to his bloody face, he roared with pain and fury. "You damned near cut off my nose!"

Louise waved her red-stained skinning knife, her screeches every bit as loud and infuriated as the thick-necked private's.

"Snake! Son of a snake! Touch me again and I will cut off more than your nose!"

Daniel was sorely tempted to stand back and let her make good on her threat. He'd had a bellyful of Solomon Huddleston. With Pierre Duval, a sickly faced lieutenant and the rest of his men shoving at his back, however, he had no choice but to stride across the storeroom, grab the bull-like private by the nape of his neck and fling him toward the door.

"Get him out of here," he told the gaping men. "I'll deal with him in the morning."

"It's her," Huddleston bellowed as Wilson and Boley hauled him out. "Her and her damned eyes. She's put a curse on me, just like in the legend. On all of us!"

Louise started after him. Just in time, Daniel threw out an arm and hooked her around the waist. She fought his hold but couldn't break it. Incensed, she screeched at the man being dragged away, his heels digging ruts in the dirt floor.

"I did not curse you before, but now I will pray to the spirits to shrivel your sack! I will sing songs to the sun and the wind and the fire to dry your seed so you cannot spawn any more like you! I will—"

"That's enough."

"Pig! Son of a pig. I will—"

"Enough, I said!"

Daniel had recalled shouting the same command into this hissing, spitting she-cat's ear the first time they'd met. Then, as now, he was forced to use brute strength to subdue her. Tightening his arm, he cut her off in mid-screech. She responded with a kick that damned near shattered his shinbone.

"If you don't shut your mouth and still your thrashing," he ground out through a jaw clenched so tight he thought it might crack, "I swear to God I'll do what your husband was no doubt forced to do many a time!"

"Hah!" Her eyes flashing, she twisted in his hold until they were face-to-face. "You want to do what Henri did to me? Here? With all watching? You would not do it when we lay belly to belly, but if that's your wish—"

The taunt leaped between them like live sparks from a blazing fire, torching the air. She knew, damn her! She knew how viciously he wanted her. Knew how he ached to slam the door on the gaping crowd, throw her down on her blanket and drag up her tunic.

Disgusted with himself, with her, with the wide-eyed spectators, he loosed his hold and thrust her away. "I'll deal with you in the morning, too."

The small crowd fell back as he stalked toward them. With a crash that rocked the storeroom's rickety wooden door on its leather hinges, Daniel shut the girl from their view and, he vowed savagely, from his own lascivious, licentious thoughts.

He woke the next morning feeling as friendly as a bear with a broken tooth. It didn't help his temper any to find the lieutenant lying once again in a pool of feverish sweat and Private Huddleston gone.

"Not just him," Private Wilson reported glumly. "John Boley and Sam Bradley lit out during the night, too. They took the dugout with what was left of our supplies and one of the canoes."

"Damned fools! They'll take a hundred lashes each for desertion."

"If they're lucky."

The Rules and Articles of War laid out by the

Continental Congress in 1776 still governed crimes committed by men in uniform. Although the maximum punishment for just about every misdeed, from falling asleep on sentry duty to stealing whiskey to desertion, was death by firing squad or hanging, court martials could impose lesser penalties. Often they ordered branding, running the gauntlet, head shavings, wearing a uniform coat inside for extended periods or being drummed out of the corps. The standard punishment, however, was flogging with a wire-rope whip.

Hardier souls boasted of their ability to withstand the beatings. One of the men in Daniel's regiment was a member of the "Damnation Club," an informal group consisting of those who carried five hundred or more scars on their backs. Huddleston and his two cohorts would undoubtedly face the whip when they returned to the ranks.

"Unless the lieutenant orders them shot," Wilson muttered.

Young Wilkinson wouldn't issue any such order. Not if Daniel had any say in the matter. Huddleston and the others might have taken French leave, but they'd gone through more hardships in the past three months than any soldiers should be asked to endure.

And, he reminded himself, they'd done what no other American soldiers had. They'd followed the Arkansaw to within twenty miles of its mouth. In the process, they'd help chart a river and a region that would figure large in the westward expansion of a young, hungry nation.

But when he caught up with them, he swore silently, he'd tear a yard-long strip off each of their hides.

"One Eye and Wind That Cries leave us here in Arkansaw Port," he reminded Wilson. "Looks like it will just be you and me ferrying the lieutenant to New Orleans."

"And me."

He spun around, swallowing a growl when he saw Louise standing at the open door to the storeroom. He wasn't ready to deal with her. Nor was he in any way prepared for the feeling that assaulted him when she calmly announced that she had decided not to remain at Arkansaw Post.

"Henri, he speaks often of a friend in New Orleans. A trader who buys his furs. Me, I have never met this man, but I think perhaps he will let me stay in his lodge out of friendship for my husband."

"Why the devil didn't you tell me about him before now?"

"I did not know you go to New Orleans," she said with a shrug. "But now that you go, I have decided I will go, too."

Daniel wasn't happy about the prospect of spending more weeks in her company. Hadn't he just passed a whole damned night trying to force her out of his head?

"You've decided," he echoed, sour-tempered. "Just like that?"

"*Oui.* Just like that."

"And I'm supposed to jump to your command, princess?"

Her brow furrowed. "What is this 'princess'?"

"Didn't McFarlane say your husband could trace his blood back to a king? That makes you a princess. The wife of a great chief," he explained sardonically.

"Of this I know nothing. I know only that I will go with you and help you care for your lieutenant." Her gaze dropped to the young officer lying in a twist of sweat-drenched blankets. "He is very sick. You will have need of my moonflower leaves, I think."

Daniel thought so, too, which was the reason he agreed to take her with him to New Orleans.

The only reason.

Within hours of departing Arkansaw Post, young Wilkinson's face grew so flushed and his fever rose so high that Daniel wasn't sure he'd survive the twenty miles to the Mississippi, much less the journey downriver to New Orleans.

The lieutenant lay in the center of the one canoe left to the expedition, too weak to even twitch. Louise took his head in her lap and wiped his face with a strip torn from what remained of his uniform.

"Rest easy," she murmured. "I will soak the moonflowers and put them on your brow."

Her compress of jimsonweed leaves seemed to give him some relief. He opened his eyes and stared up at her blankly for some moments, then essayed a weak smile.

"I...I thank you for your care of me."

She smiled down at him. "It is I who must thank you for allowing me to journey with your expedition."

Blinking the sweat out of his eyes, he looked at her as if he was seeing her for the first time.

"You really...are quite...beautiful."

Her smile softened. She murmured some idle nonsense until he sank back into sleep with his head in her lap. Louise brushed a strand of lank brown hair from his brow and wondered how this man and Daniel could be so much alike and yet so very different.

They both had hair the color of tobacco, but Daniel's was rich and dark while the lieutenant's was like the leaf when it first turns from green to dun. They both were warriors, soldiers in the army of their country. The officer carried the rank, but the sergeant carried the authority. They both had been kind to her, in their own way.

The lieutenant could have ordered her left behind at the Quapaw camp or at Arkansaw Post. Daniel could have refused Big Track's demand for payment of a bride price. Yet here she was, on her way to a city she had heard of many times but had never thought to see. Crooning softly, she stroked the lieutenant's cheek to keep him calm.

Neither the crooning nor the compress worked for long. The officer's fever peaked, and by the time Daniel spotted a settler's cabin built close to the bank and begged a place under the sturdy shingle roof for the night, Wilkinson had sweated out so much they all thought him gone for sure.

Daniel, Louise, Private Wilson and the settler's wife took turns spooning weak tea and venison broth into him that night and all the next day. The fever finally broke the morning of the second day, leaving the officer so weak and drained he couldn't lift his head.

"You'd best leave him here," the apple-cheeked goodwife suggested. "He'll need careful nursing and plenty of stout food to regain his strength."

The lieutenant agreed with her. "You go on," he urged Daniel. "Take my journal and the report I wrote out at Arkansaw Post. My father is waiting for it."

Daniel was caught squarely between two poles. He'd been charged to keep an eye to the general's son. But he was aware that their assessment of the navigability of the Arkansaw could well factor into the movement of army troops in the event of a war with Spain—or a rebellion fomented by Aaron Burr, former vice president of the United States.

"You have your orders," Wilkinson said in a thin, reedy whisper. "You'll leave immediately. Take Madame Chartier with you, but leave Private Wilson to accompany me when I'm able to travel."

Take Louise. On a journey of some weeks. Alone. Feeling as though he was about to forfeit his soul, Daniel slowly nodded.

"Yes, sir."

8

February 25, 1807
New Orleans
Capital of Orleans Territory

Daniel and Louise arrived in New Orleans by flatboat on a rainy February afternoon. She greeted the
city with wide-eyed wonder, he with profound relief.

The weeks since they'd left Lieutenant Wilkinson
and Private Wilson had been the worst kind of hell.
He'd held to his marriage vows. That much of his
honor at least he'd salvaged. But the days and nights
spent alone with the young widow had brought him
to a state of near desperation.

She was so much like the woman his wife had
once been. Brimming with energy. Curious about
everyone and everything they encountered on the trip
down the Mississippi. And brave. So very brave.
She looked out on the world with clear, fearless
blue eyes.

Her courage alone would have won Daniel's heart. Glimpses of her lithe young body, revealed more and more as they left the cold behind and packed up their buffalo robes, kept him surly by day and aching at night.

He wanted nothing more than to settle the woman with this friend of her husband's, make his report to General Wilkinson and head back to St. Louis before he gave in to the craving that clawed deeper at his gut with every hour he spent in Louise's company. Slinging his haversack over one shoulder, he helped her onto the stone quay.

She stood transfixed, a small figure in a buckskin tunic and leggings, almost lost amid the barrels and bales stacked high on the quay. The heavy mist dewed on her hair and gave it a glossy shine. Her eyes wide, she looked around in wonder.

"It is so big, this village."

"Yes," he replied, hefting his musket. "It is that."

"With such great lodges!"

His gaze followed hers and swept the plaza facing the busy riverfront. The Cathedral of St. Louis dominated the square. The first time Daniel had seen the structure, he'd gawked very much as Louise now did. Constructed by the French when this city first served as their capital in the New World, it had been destroyed once by hurricane and once by fire. Rebuilt in the Spanish style, it now thrust twin, rounded turrets up to the pewter sky.

"The governmental offices are there," he said,

nodding to the building to the left of the church, "in the old Spanish *cabildo*."

In that rambling, two-story building the treaty transferring Louisiana Territory to the United States had been signed. There, Daniel knew, W.C.C. Claiborne conducted his civil duties as governor of Orleans Territory. And there, he'd learned, Major General Wilkinson now exercised military authority over the city he'd put under martial law.

As Daniel escorted Louise down the length of the stone quay, he saw ready evidence of that war-ready state. Barricades had been thrown up across the major streets. Long lines of people and carriages waited impatiently for armed guards to pass them through. Two-man squads patrolled the square, the riverfront and the narrow alleys intersecting the city. Notices posted on tree trunks and fence posts warned citizens to adhere to a dusk-to-dawn curfew or risk being taken into custody or shot.

Yet despite these measures, Daniel didn't get a sense of a city on the brink of invasion by a hostile army. Vendors thronged the streets, hawking everything from painted fans to skewers of spiced shrimp. Merchants in frock coats tipped their hats to one another. Women in high-waisted gowns, plumed bonnets and mutton-sleeved coats shopped the market stalls crowding the square.

The bonnets especially caught Louise's attention.

"But look! Big Track himself does not wear so many feathers in his war bonnet. And that woman's robe. It is of such colors!"

The scarlet and yellow demi-dress she referred to cloaked a particularly well-endowed whore. She leaned over a second-story wrought-iron railing, advertising her abundant wares to the men in the plaza. Her face was caked with white lead paint and her hennaed hair hung in lank curls over one plump shoulder. Louise stared at her, fascinated, before announcing that she, too, must have such a robe.

"If I'm to live for a while among my father's people, I will dress as they do."

Daniel's mouth opened, then shut again with a snap. She wouldn't be his responsibility much longer. She could dress herself up in scarlet and yellow silk if she wished. He only hoped this friend of Chartier's possessed a wife with a strong enough sense of fashion to guide the trapper's widow in her choice of gowns.

As Elizabeth might have guided her. Clenching his jaw, Daniel tried to summon the image of his wife when he'd first courted her. Her merry smile was only a dim, distant memory, but he remembered the sunlight gilding her hair to fine-spun gold and the cherry-pink bows on the muslin dress she'd worn the first time he took her walking.

"Daniel?"

Blinking away the memory of a cobbled street shaded by chestnut trees and the tinsmith's daughter who'd stolen his heart, he frowned down at a face framed by hair the color of darkest night.

"Does something disturb you?"

"No."

"Then why do you hold me so?"

With a start, he realized his fingers had dug into her upper arm. Muttering an apology, he loosened his grip.

"The customs office is in the *cabildo*," he said, shepherding her toward an entrance at one end of the building's elaborate facade. "We'll inquire there about this friend of Henri's, then I must make my report to the general. He should be—"

He stopped, his eyes narrowing on the guard posted at the entrance. The soldier wore a coat of army blue with red facings over his white trousers and smalls. Daniel didn't need to read the insignia on the pewter plate attached to his black leather shako to identify him as Second United States Regiment of Infantry.

"Iverson?"

The guard snapped his head around. He stared at the figure in travel-stained buckskins for a moment or two before recognizing the face behind the beard.

"Rifle Sergeant Morgan! By damn, we about gave up on you and the others! When did you reach New Orleans?"

"Just this morning. Is the whole regiment here?"

"Most of it. The old man left Major Thomas and one company in St. Louis. The rest of us shipped down here when that bastard Burr escaped custody in Natchez. Now that he's been recaptured, though, we're thinking the martial law will be lifted soon and the regiment will move out again."

"Is the general here at the *cabildo*?"

"No. Didn't you hear?"

"Hear what?"

"His wife died two days ago. He's keeping to his quarters."

"Where are his quarters located? I have news of his son he'll want to hear."

"Don't know where the old man's bedding down. Some big plantation on the river, I think." Iverson jerked his thumb toward the entrance to the *cabildo*. "Colonel Matthews is inside. He'll tell you."

Pushing his way through the crowd thronging the outer offices of military department headquarters, Daniel collared a clerk and requested an audience with Colonel Matthews, General Wilkinson's harried chief of staff. The colonel sent word that he would see Sergeant Morgan immediately. Leaving Louise with the clerk, Daniel straightened his stained buckskins as best he could and reported to the senior staff officer.

Matthews welcomed him distractedly. He was a tall, rail-thin officer who wore a perpetually pinched look. Daniel supposed his own face would take on the same sour lines if he served as chief of staff to a wily old bastard like Wilkinson. Keeping up with the general would tax any man's wits.

Matthews accepted the oilskin-covered package containing Lieutenant Wilkinson's journal and written report. "I'll see these are delivered to the general right away. I've no doubt he'll want to speak with you personally. Report to your company, draw what pay and uniform items you need and hold yourself ready.''

''Yes, sir. And when that's done, I'd like a few weeks leave to go back to St. Louis and see to my wife.''

''I'm afraid that's not possible. We're in a state of martial law here. We need every soldier under arms, particularly a sergeant with your rank and experience.''

''I understand, sir, but I'm hearing martial law might soon be lifted now that Colonel Burr's back in custody.''

''He may be in custody, but this city—this whole territory—is in a precarious state.''

Setting aside the journals, the colonel rose and clasped his hands behind his back. ''I think you should know we received word only yesterday that the Spanish have taken Lieutenant Pike and the rest of his detachment into custody. They're holding them prisoner in Santa Fe.''

''The devil you say!''

''The Spanish seem to think your expedition was part and parcel of the Burr conspiracy. That Lieutenant Pike and his men were sent west to incite those citizens living in New Mexico territories to rebel against their Spanish rulers and become citizens of a new, grandiose empire.''

''Why would they think that? General Wilkinson himself chartered our expedition. From what we heard, he was the one who uncovered the Burr conspiracy and denounced it to the president.''

"Yes, well..."

The colonel glanced away. When he brought his gaze back to Daniel, his face wore a grim cast. "I suppose you'll hear this soon enough. It's only barracks talk, mind you. Gossip rising from the scurrilous rumors put about by these damned Creoles who resent the restrictions we've imposed on them. But, well, there are those who claim General Wilkinson was part of the conspiracy. That he plotted the scheme with Burr, then turned on him when word about it began to leak."

Robert McFarlane had hinted at the same possibility. Hearing the rumor repeated by the general's chief of staff made the skin on the back of Daniel's neck itch.

Matthews hesitated, looking as though he wanted to say more, and Daniel's gut tightened. He had a guess what was coming.

"You spent six months and more with the general's son," the colonel said slowly.

"Yes, sir."

He stopped short of asking whether the son had by word or deed, in any way implicated his father. Instead, he issued an oblique warning.

"If Colonel Burr goes to trial, as it appears he will, the barristers will be looking for anyone who might have information about his scheme to carve a private empire out of Louisiana Territory."

Daniel looked him square in the eyes. "I have no such information."

"Good."

"But—"

"But what, Sergeant?"

It was Daniel's turn to hesitate. His sense of duty warred with a bone-deep reluctance to plunge Louise in the dark, swirling waters of a traitor's schemes. Every instinct warned him to keep his mouth shut, to let the lawyers delve into the matter of Aaron Burr's coconspirators. Fourteen years of service to his country forced him to speak.

"There's a woman," he said slowly. "The wife of a French trapper. We came upon her near the end of the expedition. She mentioned a Spanish agent. Someone with an interest in stirring up the Osage, as well as the French and Spanish in the area. She said the trappers spoke of this man coming up the river with boats and men."

"Did she give a name?" Matthews asked sharply.

"No, sir."

"Where did you leave this woman?"

"Her husband died and, well…" He let out a breath. "I brought her here."

"To New Orleans?"

"Yes, sir."

"The general will want to know about her."

Daniel could only nod. With a feeling that he'd stepped into waters far too dark and deep for a mere rifle sergeant, he took his leave.

The adjutant seated in the outer office supplied him with authorization to draw funds from the paymaster, a requisition for a new uniform from the quartermaster and the location of his company, quartered only a few blocks from the *cabildo*. Daniel's thoughts whirled so fast that he walked right past the small figure seated on a bench beside the door. Jumping up, she hurried after him.

"Daniel! What has happened? Why do you wear the face of a dog with a thorn in his paw?"

He couldn't begin to explain the momentous events that seemed to be occurring by the day, if not the hour. He hadn't yet fully grasped them himself.

"I've given the lieutenant's report to the colonel," he told her. "I've told him about you. He thinks General Wilkinson may wish to speak with you."

"Bien," she said, not particularly concerned by the prospect. "But before I meet with him, I must buy a scarlet and yellow robe such as the woman with the so-white face wears."

That alone was enough to wrench Daniel's thoughts from his interview with Colonel Matthews. He fixed them squarely on the need to get Louise settled, preferably with someone who possessed a sense of fashion.

"Let's find this friend of Henri's," he said, taking her elbow to steer her through the crowd. "Then you can think about a dress."

A tax collector at the customs office searched the ledgers for information about one Bernard Thibodeaux, merchant. Twenty minutes and a dozen twisting turns later, Daniel located Thibodeaux's establishment.

The narrow, three-story building was situated on

Doumaine Street, close to the river. The ground floor served as a shop and warehouse. The upper balconies provided a sweeping view of the flatboats plowing through the wide, gray waters. Wrought iron painted a bright turquoise lavishly adorned the building's facade.

When Daniel followed Louise through the door into the ground-floor shop, the scents of a lively and profitable trade enveloped him. His nose twitched with the dark flavor of coffee beans, the rich aroma of exotic spices and the stink of tightly baled pelts. Louise found the rack of muslins and silks more to her interest. With an exclamation of delight, she fingered a bolt of shimmering ruby silk.

A clerk in brown gaiters and a loose-cuffed linen shirt stepped forward. "Be careful, if you please! That silk is very costly."

His tone was no more to Louise's liking than to Daniel's. He started to put the bespectacled little toad in his place, but she took matters into her own hands.

Her chin came up. Her brows lifted. In a haughty manner that would have done justice to a duchess, she flicked a hand over the bolt of silk.

"It is good that this is costly. Me, I have a wish to buy it."

The clerk's glance darted from her to the man at her side and back again. "You have the wish, but do you have the funds?"

"*Mais oui!* Daniel, he shall pay you from what he gives me for my furs."

"Ahh. You've brought furs to trade."

"But, no. Daniel, explain to this one how I shall have this silk."

"Best we explain to Monsieur Thibodeaux. Tell him Rifle Sergeant Morgan would like to speak with him," he instructed the clerk. "And Madame Louise Therese Chartier, wife to—" He caught himself. "Widow to Henri Chartier."

The clerk's eyes widened. He shot another look at Louise before scurrying off.

He was back within minutes with his master at his heels. Thibodeaux was a portly man clad in a blue broadcloth frock coat and embroidered waistcoat. His welcome more than made up for his underling's lack of warmth.

"Madame Chartier! At last we meet. Henri mentioned you often in the letters he sent each spring with his cache of furs." Taking her hand in his, he bowed over it. "My wife and I are most distressed to hear you are now a widow. Come upstairs and take a dish of tea with us while you tell us what happened to Henri. And you, Sergeant Morgan. Please, join us."

Daniel followed them up the stairs to a well-appointed set of apartments furnished with great luxury. Thick carpets softened the tongue-and-groove oak floors. Brass sconces held beeswax candles. Velvets and brocades covered the furniture, crafted in the French style with flourishes and gilt-edged scrolls.

Thibodeaux's wife and two daughters fit well into their surroundings. As befitting the womenfolk of a wealthy merchant, they were dressed in the height of fashion. Louise eyed their lace caps and high-waisted gowns with interest while they in turn listened open-mouthed to the series of misadventures that had brought her to New Orleans.

"But of course Madame Chartier must stay with us," the merchant's wife exclaimed when the tale was done. A dimpled matron, she possessed an ample bosom, a generous smile and a warm heart.

"And she need not worry about the matter of funds," her husband put in. "Henri asked me to bank half his profits each year we did business."

"You and Henri did business for many years, I think," Louise said.

"Yes," the merchant confirmed with a smile. "For almost four decades. If you can establish your legal claim to his account, you'll inherit something close to fifteen thousand gold louis."

Daniel's jaw dropped. He'd worried for months about this woman, had fretted over how to keep his promise to her dying husband to see she was cared for, had pledged her every penny of his wilderness pay. Now, it appeared, she didn't need him or his paltry pay. She'd inherited a damned fortune!

He should take great satisfaction from knowing she'd be well set up. Instead, he felt the most ridiculous sense of loss, as though someone had just relieved him of a burden he very much wanted to be rid of but wasn't quite ready to give up.

Louise seemed less concerned about the amount

of her inheritance than how to make it hers. Frowning, she leaned forward in the brocaded chair.

"What is this, 'legal claim'?"

"You must prove you were indeed married to Henri."

"I have the marriage lines the priest writes." She gestured to the haversack resting beside her chair. "The paper is there, with the gold cross Henri gives me when I am baptized."

"That's good. Very good. But, ah, you see…"

He looked to his wife. Madame Thibodeaux reached for Louise's hand and gave it a small pat.

"When Henri married you, he— Well, there's a possibility he may have already had a wife back in France."

"Henri says she is dead," Louise responded with a shrug. "Me, I think he lies, but by then we have already shared a blanket for two winters and it matters not."

"Yes, well, we'll sort it out," the older woman said hastily to preclude any more such indelicate disclosures in front of her daughters.

"In the meantime, I'll advance you any monies you need," the merchant assured her. "No doubt you'll want to buy yourself some dresses and bonnets and such."

"Yes!" Louise exclaimed. "That is exactly what I want."

Her delighted laugh should have eased the turmoil in Daniel's mind. She'd be happy with these people, he told himself. Thibodeaux would look after her and no doubt earn a hefty commission on the settlement of Henri Chartier's estate. Still, he wasn't prepared for her casual air of acceptance when he stood to make his farewell.

"I'll leave you now. I must report to my company."

"Here in New Orleans, yes?"

"Yes."

"Then I shall see you again. You will come to visit me."

"If my duties permit."

"You must make them permit. You will come to visit me," she repeated with a merry smile, "and I shall be wearing a robe of silk."

"That will surely be a sight worth seeing."

Yes, Louise vowed, her smile fading as his broad back disappeared down the stairs. It surely will.

Her feelings for this man confused her. He confused her. During the weeks of their journey, she'd given him her trust and gifted him with her friendship. She'd also come to respect him for holding to his vows to the wife so far away.

Yet the woman in her, the woman who'd come to crave his smile and his touch and the sound of his voice, wanted nothing more than to open his eyes to all else she offered him.

She would do that, Louise vowed, in a robe of red silk.

9

Warmly gracious, Madame Thibodeaux and her daughters escorted Louise to a guest chamber on the third floor.

"It's a bit small," Helene apologized, "but bright when the sun shines. I think you'll be comfortable here."

"We're right next door," the youngest daughter, Bertrice, informed her. A berry-eyed maiden with blond hair cut and crimped into curls, she plopped down on an alcove bed. An iron ring was suspended above the bed. Folds of sheer white cloth hung from the ring.

"To keep the mosquitoes from you while you sleep," the helpful Bertrice said in answer to Louise's query. "You pull the netting around you like so." With two quick tugs, she drew the fine cloth around the bed.

"And you have your own water closet," the elder daughter said shyly.

"What is this, 'water closet'?"

As tall and slender as her sister was short and plump, the doe-eyed Marie smiled and opened a door built into the wall.

"A private place for you to bathe and use the chamber pot."

Louise poked her head into the closet. The rose-patterned china pitcher and washbowl delighted her almost as much as the covered pot. She wouldn't have to trudge down three flights of stairs and go outside to relieve herself!

"You can hang your things here in the clothes-press," Madame Thibodeaux informed her, indicating a high cupboard decorated with hand-painted ceramic ovals containing pictures of flowers. Dubiously, the matron eyed the haversack that contained all Louise owned. "Do you wish me to send one of the servants to help you unpack?"

"I pack and unpack for many weeks now. I need no help with it."

"Very well. We'll leave you to rest."

"Rest?"

"You must be tired after your arduous journey."

"But, no! Me, I wish to buy a dress."

She soon discovered one dress, in Helene's words, *simply would not do*. As the plump matron earnestly explained, a lady—particularly a wealthy widow such as Louise looked to be—required several changes of clothing a day.

Calling to her manservant to ready the carriage, Helene pulled on kid gloves and a caped pelisse and hustled Louise and her girls down the stairs. Her husband's clerk loaded the carriage with the bolt of shimmering ruby silk that had caught Louise's eye, along with a half dozen other bolts selected by Helene and the girls.

A short drive took them to the shop of Madame Celeste du Clare. The seamstress greeted Helene with a smile. Her eyes widened at her first glimpse of Louise, but she gasped with delight when she was informed that Madame Chartier required fitting from the skin out.

"Georgina! Eloise!" Clapping her hands, she summoned her assistants. "Bring the striped muslin morning gown we just sewed for Madame Tolbert. And the underlinens I stitched for Justine Alberville's trousseau."

Bustling Louise into a backroom, she drew a curtain and stripped her to the skin with cheerful ruthlessness. The stained buckskin tunic and leggings were tossed into a corner.

"Shall I discard them?"

"But, no! I tan the skins and sew them myself."

"Very well. I'll have my girls clean them. Here, step into these."

She held up a pair of drawers double the width of Louise's buckskin leggings.

"They are too big! They will fall off."

"No, they draw in at the waist."

Tugging on the string, she cinched the soft fabric, then dropped a chemise trimmed with lace over Louise's head. The straps settled on her shoulders, but the neckline of the garment dipped almost to her nipples.

"You hardly need this corset," Madame du Clare observed as she laced the boned garment around Louise's waist. "You are small of stature, but well formed. Very well formed. Slender of hip, narrow of waist and full at the bust. You shall do justice to my gowns. And those eyes—"

Louise stiffened.

"So blue," she murmured. "So beautiful. I have a sapphire silk that matches them perfectly."

While Helene and the girls sipped some orange-colored drink, the seamstress and her assistants trotted out a bewildering array of morning gowns of kerseymere, walking gowns of striped muslin, afternoon robes, dinner dresses and frilled, laced nightgowns.

She also displayed a rainbow of fringed shawls, pelisses, evening capes and silk stockings embroidered with clocks.

"To draw the eye to your ankle when you walk," Marie explained with her shy smile.

One of Madame du Clare's assistants was sent running to the boot-maker next door, who hurried in a few moments later with an assortment of high-heeled shoes in leather and silk. A hatter was also called in. He produced straw chip hats, poke bonnets trimmed with dyed ostrich plumes and something he called a turban.

"There," Madame Thibodeaux announced after insisting her new houseguest choose an astounding number of garments and their accompanying fripperies. "That should do you until Madame du Clare has time to make up the rest of the gowns you'll need."

With an airy wave of her hand, she told the seamstress to send the bills to Doumaine Street and shepherded her charges out of the shop.

Dressed in a lilac afternoon dress with a matching pelisse trimmed in green braid, Louise wobbled out of the shop. Her high-heeled red shoes pinched her toes and she was sure her lacy drawers would drop around her clock-trimmed ankles at any moment.

Daniel spent his afternoon being re-outfitted as well.

Glad to be shed of his buckskins, he drew a new fatigue uniform from the quartermaster. The white woolen britches felt scratchy after his supple buckskins, and the dark blue cutaway coat stretched tight across his shoulders, but the supply clerk found a pair of boots that fit. The clerk also provided him with a new black leather cross belt, a short-sword and scabbard, and the white worsted epaulets denoting his rank. Daniel rubbed his sleeve over the plate on his tall black shako until the U.S. Army insignia gleamed.

Feeling like a proper soldier again, he joined his captain and the men of his company at mess that night. Over tankards of ale, he regaled them with the details of his journey down the Arkansaw. They in turn supplied him with the latest barracks gossip and a detailed update of the conspiracy that now gripped the attention of the entire nation.

After amassing men, arms and a small flotilla of boats on the Ohio, Burr had left with a small contingent for New Orleans, where he was to gather more men and boats. He had learned he'd been betrayed when he reached Natchez and read a newspaper transcript of his coded letter to General Wilkinson. The governor of Mississippi Territory had then demanded his surrender. He'd complied, had been brought before a grand jury and, amazingly, had won his release. Disguising himself as a boatman, he'd then melted into the wilderness.

As additional information about his plot became known, a new warrant was issued for Burr's arrest. He'd been taken into custody once again in mid-February and hustled to Fort Stoddart, where he was now being held under close guard. Rumor was, he'd be sent to Richmond to stand trial for treason and other high misdemeanors.

"They're saying he intended to rouse the whole of Louisiana, Texas and New Mexico territories to arms," one of Daniel's company commented. "Word is, he intended to march clear to Mexico City, drive out the Spanish and set himself up as king of a new country."

"They're also saying our general was up to his ears in the plot," another put in. Puffing on his pipe, he blew a cloud of fragrant Virginia tobacco into the air. "We all know how the old man fawned over Burr when he came to St. Louis last spring. Damned if he didn't turn us all out in the pouring rain for a formal review."

"Parading the troops is one thing," the captain said sharply. "Conspiring to commit treason is another. Smoke your pipe, Jackson, and shut your hole."

His mind whirling, Daniel left the group clustered around the mess table and went to his room. The last hour before he doused the lanterns he spent writing a letter to Elizabeth. He couldn't tell her whether his company would return to St. Louis or when he'd see her again. All he could do was provide her written authorization to draw upon his wilderness pay—and hope she'd remember who he was.

He sent the letter off with a courier leaving for St. Louis the next morning. He had no sooner returned from that task than his captain plunged him back into the duties and responsibilities he'd left behind when he trekked into the wilderness seven months ago.

By noon, Daniel had reviewed the company rosters, revised the schedule of work details and walked patrol with his men to get a better feel for the mood of the city. He'd also ordered the appropriate punishments for the inevitable infractions of military discipline that occurred when troops were housed in close proximity to strong spirits and accommodating women. He was at the stables, inspecting the horses and wagons used to transport the company's extra supplies and ammunition, when the order came to report at once to General Wilkinson.

Clean-shaven and a good stone lighter than when he'd last met with the general, Daniel reported to the *cabildo*. His new shako tucked under his arm, he waited while Wilkinson's aide de camp announced his presence. The aide came out, held the door, and Daniel strode inside.

"Rifle Sergeant Morgan reporting as ordered, sir."

Wilkinson returned his salute and strutted forward, his hand outstretched. It was an egalitarian gesture inconsistent with his rank, but not unexpected considering how he'd handpicked Daniel for a particularly hazardous expedition.

"I was overjoyed to hear you'd returned safely."

"Thank you, sir."

"Sit down, sit down!"

Daniel hooked his sword out of the way and took a chair carved in dark wood in the Spanish style. Wilkinson rounded his desk to claim the chair opposite. He was a short man, with dark, busy eyes, a deep cleft in his chin and a protruding belly, but he wore his uniform with an impressive air. Gold braid dripped from his blue jacket and his epaulets glittered with the embroidered stars of a general officer. The loss of his wife and, Daniel guessed, the intrigues swirling around him had carved deep brackets on either side of his mouth that hadn't been there when they last met.

Not that Wilkinson was any stranger to intrigue. This was the man who'd taken part in a plot to remove General Washington as commander of the Continental Army. Who'd been relieved as clothier-general of the army for alleged discrepancies in his accounts. Who'd faced a court-martial following allegations by a subordinate that he'd deliberately held back badly needed reinforcements at the Battle of Fallen Timbers in order to embarrass his rival, General Anthony Wayne.

This was also the same officer who'd conducted a brilliant campaign against the Iroquois, Daniel reminded himself. The general who had risen in rank to become commander in chief of the Army of the United States. The man who now coadministered with Governor W.C.C. Claiborne an area larger than the country that had purchased it.

It wasn't the officer he faced now, however, but the anxious father.

"How did you leave my son?"

"Weak with fever, sir. Very weak. He's in good hands, though. Private Wilson is with him, and the goodwife of the house where he rests seems to know what she's about."

"I pray to God she does."

His distress was real. Daniel could do little more to relieve it and offered his sympathies on the death of his wife. The general accepted them with a sigh.

"Her lungs troubled her for some time, and the climate here in New Orleans did not agree with her. I shall miss her greatly."

With an almost visible effort, he wrenched his thoughts from his family to his official duties.

"My son's report is most thorough until the last weeks of your expedition."

"The fever struck him in mid-December. He made only brief entries in his journal after that."

"From what he's written, the Arkansaw appears to be navigable only in certain stretches."

"Yes, sir."

Daniel moved to the elaborately inscribed parchment map of Louisiana Territory nailed to the wall. The sheer size of the wilderness he'd just journeyed through almost stole his breath. Slowly, he traced the course of the Arkansaw.

"Here to the north, where the river crosses the plains, it's shallow and sandy bottomed. Further south, it widens, deepens and flows with dangerous currents. Particularly after a snow melt."

Inked lines on a parchment couldn't begin to encompass the endless sky, the rolling hills, the forested slopes. A dozen images flashed through Daniel's mind. Of the warlike Pawnee with black-painted faces. The Osage who roamed the hills and bluffs. The French and English who trapped the rivers and lived their lives in splendid isolation.

"And the Native tribes?" the general asked. "My son writes they received you well, for the most part."

"For the most part."

"Where is this parcel of land Chief Big Track wants to gift us with?"

Daniel thumped his forefinger on the map. "Here, where the Arkansaw, the Grand and the Verdigris flow together."

"Those rivers are rich with beaver and otter," Wilkinson murmured. "Their confluence constitutes an ideal location for a trading post."

"Or a military fort."

"What? Oh, yes. Of course. It may come to that, particularly if Congress approves the Indian Removal Plan. We'll require a military presence in the area to keep the Osage and Choctaw from warring with each other."

They'd require more than a presence, Daniel thought. They'd require a whole damned regiment.

He spent the next twenty minutes answering detailed questions about the topography of the terrain and the character of the tribes his small detachment had encountered. Finally, Wilkinson brought up the subject of Louise.

"What of this widow? My son makes no note of her in his official report, but his private letter includes a rather interesting reference to the woman."

"What sort of reference?" Daniel asked carefully.

Now that he'd had a day and a night to grasp the scope of Burr's treachery, he very much regretted mentioning Louise to Colonel Matthews. She'd heard only vague rumors about someone coming up the river with men and boats, nothing that would in any way substantiate the charges and countercharges sure to come in what looked to be a wildly sensational trial.

"My son says her husband could trace his roots back to Louis the Fourteenth of France."

Imperceptibly, Daniel relaxed his tense muscles. The general didn't appear to be interested in what Louise might know, but in who she was.

"Is it true?" Wilkinson asked curiously.

"I don't know. We met up with an English trapper

who knew Chartier. Robert McFarlane. He's the one who spun out that tale. And…''

''And?''

Daniel shrugged. ''Chartier spoke of 'that upstart Napoleon' with contempt, as though the man who'd crowned himself emperor was far beneath him.''

''Hmm.''

Rubbing a finger along the side of his nose, the general thought for a moment. ''My son also writes that she cared for him most tenderly in his illness. I would like to meet with her and express my thanks.''

''She's lodging with a business associate of her husband, Bernard Thibodeaux.''

''I know Thibodeaux. I shall invite him and his wife for dinner tomorrow night, along with his guest.''

The idea of Louise sitting down to dinner with this schemer raised a damp sweat on Daniel's palms.

''No, it can't be tomorrow night,'' the general said with a frown. ''I'm dining with Governor Claiborne and the bishop of Orleans parish. It will have to be next week. I'd intended to give a ball to celebrate Fat Tuesday. Such a ridiculous name for a festival, is it not? But one must humor these Catholics.''

Since the comment obviously required no response, Daniel sat silent.

''Due to my wife's death, I've curtailed the Fat Tuesday festivities to just dinner. I'll instruct my aide to send an invitation to Madame Chartier and the Thibodeaux family. He has two daughters, I believe.

Quite pretty girls, as I remember. At one time, I thought about one of them for my son. But now—''

He caught himself. It wasn't appropriate for a major general to discuss intimate family matters with a mere rifle sergeant, Daniel knew.

''You must come to dinner as well, Morgan. My staff and guests will be most interested in hearing a firsthand account of your adventures.''

Daniel was trying to find some way to decline for both himself and Louise when the general stood and signaled the interview was at an end.

''Next week, then. Dress uniform.''

Hell! The quartermaster didn't issue dress uniforms and Daniel's was in the clothespress back in St. Louis. He'd have to borrow one from another sergeant. He'd also have to give Louise some understanding of the quagmire they'd both have to pick their way through.

The mere thought of seeing her again quickened his pulse. Saluting, he performed a sharp about-face and left the general's office.

He was only going to warn her, he told himself as he closed the door behind him. To advise her to tread carefully when dealing with the general. But despite the stern admonition, he couldn't keep his blood from racing.

When the door thudded shut behind Morgan, Wilkinson walked slowly back to his desk.

He was a man of unlimited talents and supreme confidence, who'd survived many setbacks in his career. Hadn't he disproved accusations of the scurrilous subordinate who'd all but charged him with treason during the Ohio Valley campaign? Hadn't he weathered the enmity of Secretary of War Knox, who'd labeled his promotion to major general a disgrace to the military reputation of the country?

He would survive this business with Burr, too.

Oh, he'd heard the rumors that blew through the city with every breeze off the river. How could he not? The citizens of New Orleans, who'd welcomed him as their savior a few short weeks ago, now chafed openly against the restrictions he'd imposed on them. They retaliated by gossiping over their disgustingly bitter coffee and sugar-dusted beignets. They also speculated openly about the military governor's various business ventures with Daniel Clark, rumored to be in league with Burr.

So openly that Wilkinson had been forced to write Clark's partner, Daniel Coxe. In it he assured the man that he'd betrayed Burr to President Jefferson only because Burr had already betrayed himself. The former vice president's railings against the Federalist government in Washington had roused suspicion enough. His blatant attempts to enlist others in the capital to their cause had opened the floodgates. The trickle of rumors had become a torrent that looked to drag Burr and all who consorted with him under. Wilkinson had seen no choice but to cover his part in the scheme by turning on his friend and coconspirator.

True, he'd used somewhat incautious language in

his letter to Coxe, branding Jefferson a fool and Governor Claiborne a contemptible fabricator. Unfortunately, he'd also made reference to some very private business dealings with the Spanish and the French. He'd never imagined Coxe would pass the letter to Vice President Madison, who professed himself astonished by General Wilkinson's duplicity. Now Jefferson was breathing fire and threatening to call his senior general to Richmond to stand trial alongside Burr.

Jefferson could threaten and bluster all he wished. He held no evidence against anyone but Burr, and that evidence had been supplied by Wilkinson himself.

Yes, he'd survive this swiftly unraveling conspiracy. And perhaps, just perhaps, concoct a new scheme in the process, one centered around the wife of a French trapper who'd fallen into his lap, like a ripe apple from a tree. The niece of a great chief, his son had written. An Osage princess of sorts. Widow of a man who could trace his line back to the Sun King of France.

His mind still imbued with the grandiose dreams he'd shared with Burr until just a few months ago, the general dipped a sharpened quill in the inkstand and began to scratch out an urgent letter to the Spanish governor in Florida.

My friend,
The press of my responsibilities and the loss of one so dear to me must be my apology for this

short missive.

I must stress again that the suspicion of Jefferson has been awakened. He does not know I kept you apprised of Colonel Burr's plan to incite the citizens of Spanish Texas to rebel, or that you agreed to pay me handsomely for such information, but he now questions my role in the conspiracy.

I don't think matters will come to such a point that I shall have to defend myself in public court. If they do, I shall require immediate payment of the $10,000 promised to me.

In the meantime, I continue to work toward our mutual goal of removing the yoke of the United States from Louisiana Territory. I have another plan in mind, one which I believe will meet with your most enthusiastic approval and support. I shall think more on it and elaborate the details in another letter after I've received the aforementioned payment.

I do not sign my name to this, nor must you ever again mention it in any correspondence. Instead I close with the appellation your government bestowed on me some years ago....

Secret Agent No. 13

10

"Rifle Sergeant Morgan! How good to see you again." Helene Thibodeaux welcomed her unexpected visitor with a gracious smile and twinkling black eyes. "You look very changed in your uniform."

And very, very handsome!

Helene had married Bernard Thibodeaux right out of the convent school and dutifully produced two daughters in three years. She'd grown to love her husband dearly, but even a plump-cheeked matron wed for close to two decades could feel a flutter around her heart at the sight of a tall, broad-shouldered sergeant with smoky gray eyes and skin tanned to the hue of old oak.

"I'm surprised you allowed me in your house when I brought Louise—Madame Chartier—to you," he answered with a grin. "We both looked like savages."

"Neither of you much look like a savage now,"

Helene returned complacently. "I suspect you'll be quite surprised when you see Louise."

"I suspect I will. Is she at home?"

"No, she's out visiting the shops with my daughters."

"When will she return? I need to speak with her on a matter of some urgency."

"I'm sure they'll return shortly. You're welcome to wait and take a dish of tea with me. Or coffee, perhaps?"

"Coffee would go down well, thank you."

She led the way to the sitting room and tugged on the bellpull. A stately manservant came up the stairs.

"Oui, madame?"

Rattling off an order in French, she sent the man back down the stairs. Daniel hooked his sword to one side and lowered himself into a chair covered in rose damask.

"I'd like to thank you for your kindness to Madame Chartier," he said. "She had a rough time of it, losing her husband the way she did."

Helene nodded. She'd met Henri Chartier only once, many years ago, when he'd come to New Orleans to work arrangements with Bernard to sell his furs. She'd thought him a rude sort of man, and the artless confidences Louise had let drop in the short time since she'd arrived hadn't changed Helene's opinion one whit. Fifteen thousand gold louis were all very well and good, but every time she tried to imagine one of her daughters lying under Henri Chartier she could barely repress a shudder.

What a shame Sergeant Morgan already had a wife. It hadn't taken Helene long to discover the place this man held in Louise's heart. Although the young widow claimed Morgan had merely served as her escort, Helene was too old and too wise to miss the signs of a young girl in love. After all, she had two daughters.

Feeling a maternal responsibility for her house-guest, Helene decided it behooved her to drop a gen-tle warning in the sergeant's ear. "Louise will be quite sought after when word leaks out about her inheritance."

Morgan's eyes lost a little of their warmth. "Yes, I imagine she will."

"With her fortune, her youth and her beauty, I don't doubt she'll have every bachelor in New Or-leans at her feet."

He took the hint. His eyes met Helene's and he acknowledged the truth of her statement with a brief nod.

Oh, dear! Pity settled in Helene's chest. Morgan ached for Chartier's widow as much as she ached for him. Pray God her daughters never longed for a man they could not have!

A cheerful babble of voices on the stairs spared her from further comment. Sinking back in her chair, she watched as Rifle Sergeant Morgan caught his first glimpse of Madame du Clare's creation.

His jaw didn't drop as it had when Bernard an-nounced the amount of Louise's inheritance, but his glance certainly did. In one stunned sweep, he took in the lustrous black curls, the poke bonnet lined with straw-colored silk, the moss-green caped pelisse and red-heeled shoes.

"Daniel!"

Joy suffused Louise's face as she crossed the room, hands outstretched. "I am so glad you have come. I have such things to tell you. Such things to *show* you. But look at these stockings! Are they not beyond all things foolish?"

Lifting her skirts, she wagged her foot to show him the embroidered clocks decorating her ankle.

"They are to catch a gentleman's eye, Bertrice says. But they remind me of the watch you give my uncle as a bride price. I ask Bertrice and Marie to go with me to the shops so I may buy you a new watch."

Digging into the tasseled reticule dangling from her wrist, she pulled out a small velvet pouch. "It is gold, like the one your wife gives you."

Louise was too busy pressing the pouch into his hand to catch the gray, wintery look in his eyes, but Helene didn't miss it. The artless reminder of his wife had struck a raw nerve with the sergeant.

Biting back a sigh, she pushed out of her chair. "Come, girls, let's go to your room so you can remove your coats. Rifle Sergeant Morgan has come to speak with Louise on matters that don't concern you."

"Open it," Louise begged as the girls departed. Untying the ribbons of her bonnet, she tossed the hat on the chair Helene had just vacated and knelt at

Daniel's knee. Impatience and eagerness filled her face.

Slowly, he parted the strings. The timepiece slid into his palm. It was finer than the watch Elizabeth had given him. Far finer. The familiar ache started just below his ribs.

"It cost fifty louis," Louise told him, laughter in her eyes. "My uncle would be greatly surprised to know I am worth that."

He closed his fingers around the watch. "You shouldn't have spent so much."

"The feathers on that so-silly hat cost almost as much. Oh, Daniel, never would I have imagined such a city as this."

"Tell me."

"It is a place of constant noise! Wagons clatter over the cobbles before the sun rises. There are dog-carts filled with the leavings from chamber pots. Flat-sided drays. Carriages with high perches and every sort of vehicle."

Shaking her head, she sank back on her heels. "And the people. There are so many! Bernard says more than eight thousand people live in the French Quarter and the back city. They crowd these raised walkways Madame Thibodeaux calls banquettes. Men in coats with long tails like swallows. Girls draped in fringed shawls. Street sellers singing every kind of ware. Voodoo women chanting charms. Some women carry this—this so strange object. A parasol, Helene says it is. To shield the sun from one's face."

Her merry laughter rippled through the room. "Me, I think it very odd that the women of this city must shield their faces from the sun, yet wear thin robes that all but bare their breasts. But look at this gown!"

Fumbling with the buttons of the pelisse, she peeled it back. Head cocked, she surveyed the swell of creamy flesh she'd just exposed.

"Henri, I think, would like these fashions."

"I don't have a doubt about it," Daniel said, more brusquely than he'd intended. Those mounds of ripe flesh had hit him like the kick of a mule.

She looked up at him, startled. He damned himself for a fool and begged her to take a seat.

"I spoke with Lieutenant Wilkinson's father this morning. He wishes to meet you."

"Me? Why?"

"Because of the service you rendered his son."

"I do little, but if the general wishes to meet with me, I will gladly do so."

"Have a care what you say to him, Louise."

"Why?" she asked again.

He hesitated. "Has anyone spoken to you about the Burr conspiracy since we arrived in New Orleans?"

"Pah! It is all I hear. Even Bertrice and Marie, they speak of nothing else."

In truth, Louise had heard the name of Aaron Burr on the lips of everyone from slaves to shopkeepers. Some branded him a traitor. Others hailed him as a savior, particularly those who chafed at the restrictions the Americans had imposed on their city. They spoke with real regret of his impending trial, and speculated wildly about why General Wilkinson had supplied the evidence against him.

It was this general, the father of the lieutenant Louise had traveled so many miles with, who now wanted to meet with her. She might find the ways of the people of New Orleans strange and confusing, but she was no fool. She would not walk into a wolf's lair unarmed. Neither would she meet with the general unprepared.

"Tell me why I must have a care what I say to him."

His brow creasing, Daniel tried to explain the tangled web surrounding General Wilkinson and the man he'd betrayed.

Nine days later, the Thibodeaux carriage rolled down the long tunnel of gnarled oak trees that led to the plantation where General Wilkinson had taken up residence. February had given way to a cool, blustery March. A breeze rustled through the still-bare tree branches and caused the carriage lamps mounted beside the driver to flicker and sputter.

Louise sat between Bertrice and Marie, taking care not to crush their skirts or the shimmering crimson folds of her own. Bernard and Helene squeezed their comfortable girths together on the forward-facing seat.

"This curfew has put such a damper on the traditional celebrations before Lent," Bertrice grumbled to Louise. "Usually we have such parties! You can't imagine."

"The Quapaw, too, have ceremonies where they feast and sing and dance."

"Not like they do on Fat Tuesday, I'd wager!"

"What is this, 'Fat Tuesday'?"

While the merchant and his wife tried to explain this confusing feast tied to another called Easter, their younger daughter craned around to peer through the carriage's rear opening.

"There must be at least five or six carriages ahead of ours," she reported.

"Obviously the general doesn't hold to his own curfew," her sister said with a touch of dryness.

"Belle Terre is lit up with dozens of flambeaux. And the soldiers! They're wearing such splendid uniforms. Wait until you see them."

"We'll see them soon enough," her mother scolded. "Do turn around, Bertrice. You're treading on Louise's slippers."

Louise hardly felt the pain. The long, pointed tip to her shoes had already pinched her toes so much that they were numb.

If her feet were dead to all feeling, the rest of her was not. Anticipation shivered through her veins. She would see Daniel tonight.

He'd called at Doumaine Street twice since coming to warn her to have a care how she spoke to the general, but each time she'd been out. The invitation to Belle Terre had led to a flurry of visits to Madame du Clare's shop. In preparation for the fete, Bertrice had insisted on roasting Louise's hair on hot tongs. A gold ribbon caught it atop her head in a cluster of curls. A length of the same ribbon circled her neck above the bodice of her gown.

And such a gown it was! The ruby silk shimmered as she walked. So thin, Louise wore petticoats to keep the dress from molding to her legs. So low at the neck, she dared not draw a full breath for fear her breasts would spill out. Tightly tied garters held up stockings spun as fine as a spiderweb. Gloves of the softest leather covered her hands, and a fringed shawl protected her from the evening's chill.

She could not wait for Daniel to see her in such fine feathers.

When they entered the great lodge where the general had taken up quarters, his aide took their names and announced them to the assembled crowd. Several heads turned, including that of an officer in blue and buff. Threading his way through the crowd, he bowed before her.

"Madame Chartier?" His round, owlish eyes looked her up and down in admiration. "By George, I wouldn't have recognized you!"

Louise hardly recognized him, either. The last time she'd seen him, he was gray-faced and shaking and lying in a pool of his own sweat. His skin still wore a sickly cast, but she had to admit he looked almost handsome in a uniform coat with a stiff-necked gold collar.

"My father told me he'd invited you here tonight.

You and Sergeant Morgan. But I couldn't imagine— That is, I didn't think—'' He broke off, his cheeks flushing.

She took pity on his obvious astonishment and gave him a merry smile. ''Me, I could not imagine this, either. When do you arrive in New Orleans?''

''Two days ago.''

''I am glad to see you well. Do you know my friends, Monsieur and Madame Thibodeaux and their daughters?''

''Yes, of course.''

While the lieutenant exchanged greetings with the Thibodeaux family, Louise searched the room. It was a great hall, as large as any Osage council house, and filled to overflowing with officers in brilliant uniforms and women in silks of every color. A few of the male guests wore high-collared frock coats in shades of black and gray and brown. Louise guessed they were men of business, like Bernard Thibodeaux.

Her nose twitching at the unfamiliar scents of fine wax candles, heavy French perfumes and the heat of many bodies pressed close together, she skimmed her gaze over the milling crowd. Nowhere did she see the broad shoulders of the man she sought. Frowning, she tapped a slippered toe and waited until the lieutenant had finished his brief conversation with the Thibodeauxs.

''I do not find Daniel.''

''Sergeant Morgan? He's here somewhere. I spoke with him only a few moments ago.'' He tucked her gloved hand in the crook of his arm. ''If Monsieur

and Madame and their delightful daughters will accompany us, I have orders to bring Madame Chartier
straightaway to my father. The general is most anxious to meet her.''

He led them toward a group standing at the far
end of the hall. Even from a distance Louise could
see the general was a great chief. So much gold lace
and braid spilled from his uniform he could have
blinded a hawk in flight. The circle around him
opened when Louise and the lieutenant approached.
She felt many curious eyes on her as she extended
her gloved hand in the way Madame Thibodeaux had
taught her.

The general grasped her fingers lightly in his,
bowed and dropped a kiss on the back of her glove.
He greeted the merchant and his family with similar
graciousness before returning his attention to Louise.

"It's a pleasure to meet you, Madame Chartier.
My son informs me you provided invaluable assistance to him and his men in the last week of their
expedition.''

"They assist me, as well, after Henri dies.''

"Ah, yes. Your husband. Tell me about him.''

Confused by the command, she tipped him an in-
quiring look. "What am I to tell? He traps the rivers
for many years and dies when the cougar rips out his
throat.''

The blunt reply had several of the general's guests
blinking. He merely smiled.

"I meant I should like to know more about Chartier's background. His birthplace. His parents.''

"Me, I do not know this. But Monsieur Thibodeaux has hired lawyers. They send letters to France."

"Indeed?"

The merchant confirmed her artless revelations. "Henri Chartier left a considerable estate, which his wife stands to inherit. It will take some months before her claim is processed. In the meantime, I thought it wise to verify her, ah, legal status."

"I see." The general exchanged a quick glance with his son before turning a bland look on Louise. "You yourself have both French and Osage blood, I understand."

She nodded. "My father was French. My mother was of the Quapaw."

"And your uncle is Big Track, a great chief. I'm indebted to him for his gift of land where the rivers run together. We think to build a trading post there."

"Me, I think you will build a fort."

"I beg your pardon?"

"You must, if your Great Father in Washington goes forward with his so-foolish plan."

The comment drew several shocked glances from those around her and a frown from Lieutenant Wilkinson. His father merely lifted a brow.

"May I ask which foolish plan you refer to?"

"The one the trappers speak of."

"And that is…?"

"I believe she's referring to the Indian Removal Plan."

The deep voice just over her shoulder spun Louise around.

"Daniel! You wear a different uniform since last I saw you," she commented with an admiring glance for his blue coat with its high, stiff collar of red trimmed with gold. Epaulets added more breadth to his wide shoulders, and a red silk sash circled his waist.

His mouth curved in a crooked grin as he took in the splendor of her red gown. "So do you."

Tucking her arm in his, she turned back to the general. "It is what Daniel says. The Indian Removal plan."

"What do you know of this Plan?" Wilkinson asked curiously.

"I know it is beyond anything foolish. If the Great Father moves the Choctaw and Cherokee to the lands of the Osage and Pawnee, the tribes will war with one another. The rivers will run red with blood and the women will weep many tears."

"We'll weep, too," Thibodeaux added. "War between the Osage and the Cherokee won't be good for the fur trade."

"No," the general murmured. "It won't."

"You must tell the Great Father it cannot happen," Louise stated firmly.

His lips pulled back in a thin smile. "President Jefferson doesn't always listen to my counsel, but I shall certainly pass on your sentiments."

Louise cocked her head, sensing that he made light of her words. And of her. Her chin lifted and a dangerous glint came into her eyes. He might be a great chief among his people, but he would be wise to heed her warning.

Before she could tell him so, Daniel squeezed her arm tight against his side. Belatedly, she remembered his warning and clamped her mouth shut on the hot words that rose to her lips. Head high, she held on to his arm and said no more until others claimed the general's attention.

"You were right to warn me to have a care around that one," she murmured as Daniel led her away. "He has the look of a hungry wolf."

"I'd say that pretty well describes the man."

He looked back and caught a glimpse of the general and his son out of the corner of one eye. They stood surrounded by others, yet both had fixed unblinking gazes on Louise.

A shiver rippled down Daniel's spine. He felt an almost overpowering urge to whisk her out of this house. Out of New Orleans, for that matter. The instincts that had kept him alive during fourteen years of service at frontier posts told him the murky waters swirling around General Wilkinson were already lapping at her toes.

Frowning, Daniel kept her arm pressed closed to his side. She wasn't his responsibility any longer. He shouldn't feel this nagging worry for her deep in his gut, but he did. Damn it, he did.

The guests had all departed. The house slaves had retreated to their quarters. Belle Terre wore the silence with the grace of a grand duchess who had just kissed her lover goodbye.

The general sat with his feet up on an embroidered stool and drew in deeply on the pipe he'd lighted earlier. When he exhaled, the rich, seductive scent of Virginia tobacco laced with opium drifted across the room.

"This widow is more presentable than I had hoped."

"Yes," his son replied. "She quite surprised me when she walked in."

The lieutenant wished he had a pipe of his own to draw on. These late-night sessions always made him nervous. He never quite knew whether he was chambered with his father or his commanding officer.

Unfortunately, he'd had to give up the pipe. His delicate lungs couldn't take the irritation of tobacco, and the Turkish opium favored by his father over that imported from India always left him with a sick head.

"I hear she's worth fifteen thousand gold louis," the general murmured, tapping the tobacco down in the bowl with a silver tong. "Did she bed with Morgan?"

"They shared a blanket, but..." James lifted his shoulders. Morgan hadn't worn the look of a man who'd found release. On the contrary, he'd often rolled out from under the furs of a morning with a tight, frustrated cast to his face.

"I shouldn't like for you to take damaged goods, but she is a widow, after all." His father blew another sickly sweet cloud. "We'll have to do something about Morgan. The chit's in love with him."

James couldn't refute the flat statement. He, too, had seen the joy that leaped into Louise's eyes when she turned to greet the sergeant.

"Send the man back to St. Louis," he suggested.

"Use your brain-box, boy. She'd only follow him. No, I have a better plan, one that need not concern you at the moment. Your only task—and a pleasant one it looks to be—is to pay court to Chartier's widow."

The lieutenant hooked a finger in his stock to loosen it. Truth be told, he found the widow just a little daunting. She'd more than held her own with the men during the expedition and had almost gutted Huddleston during that fracas at Arkansaw Post.

Not that James would mind taking her to bed. He'd thought her pretty before, and had been quite stunned by her tonight. And he suspected she'd bring a fire to the bedchamber lacking in the fat, flaccid whores who usually serviced him.

Lost in his thoughts, he looked up to find his father watching him with his unnerving stare.

"Don't fail me in this, James. I had to throw Burr to the wolves to save my own skin, but I have yet to abandon my ambitions."

"No, sir, I won't."

"This widow is the perfect instrument for our purposes. I expect you to begin pressing your suit immediately. You must do whatever is necessary to win her."

11

The afternoon following the dinner at General Wilkinson's quarters, Colonel Matthews summoned Daniel to his office.

"It's my pleasure to inform you that you've been promoted to the rank of sergeant major. Congratulations, Morgan."

Surprised, Daniel accepted the colonel's handshake.

"Thank you, sir."

"You've also been relieved of your company duties and reassigned to the regimental staff."

That didn't please Daniel anywhere near as much as the promotion. He was a rifleman, not a headquarters clerk. When he said as much to the colonel, Matthews waved aside his objection.

"You've fourteen years of experience in the field. A little time on regimental staff will give you some seasoning."

"What will my duties be, sir?"

"The general wants you to supervise the conduct of marksmanship training for the regiment."

The entire regiment? That task would have Daniel jumping from dawn to dusk, every day of the week. Well, he'd rather keep busy than not, and the lack of training for the Johnny Raw recruits had long been a real concern within the ranks of experienced veterans.

Almost instantly, his mind began racing with the firing drills he'd institute and the increased allocation of powder and lead each company would require. The general might regret assigning him to this duty, he thought wryly, when he saw the cost of Daniel's proposals.

He was so caught up with his swiftly forming plans that he almost missed Colonel Matthews's next announcement.

"I've designated a set of quarters for you. The apartments are small," he warned, "but include a private sitting room and a bedroom. Your wife will no doubt be happy to hear you won't have to share rooms with another family."

"My wife?"

"You're married, are you not? I'm sure I remembered you asking for a furlough to see to your wife."

"Yes, sir, I did. She's in St. Louis."

The colonel's voice took on a dry note. "I know I denied you a leave of absence when you requested one earlier, but General Wilkinson reminded me of the months you spent with his son during the expedition. You may take a furlough to bring your wife to New Orleans. If you leave today, I'm sure you can accomplish the move within a month.''

Daniel had made a dozen or so moves to different posts. He anticipated little difficulty in bundling up the few possessions his wife still seemed to care about, putting them and her on a wagon or a flatboat and getting them to New Orleans within the allotted time.

The question in his mind was whether he should do it.

With each move, Elizabeth seemed to shrink more inside herself. Each departure from familiar surroundings took her a little farther away from the world around her. He'd thought— He'd hoped to keep her in St. Louis. The corporal's wife who helped care for her there was kind and gentle and the only reason Daniel had consented to take part in the Pike expedition. He'd known he was leaving Elizabeth in good hands.

''Sir, my wife's settled in our quarters in St. Louis. I think it's best if she stays there.''

''You don't understand, Morgan. This assignment to the general's staff is a permanent posting. You'll no longer qualify for quarters in St. Louis, only here. I'm afraid there's no choice. You must either move your wife to private lodgings in St. Louis or bring her to New Orleans.''

''Yes, sir.''

As Daniel walked out into the bright March sunshine, the little ache he always carried just under his ribs became a sharp, knifing pain.

I'm sorry, Elizabeth. So sorry.

He took time only to move his gear out of the inn where his company was posted, check out the new quarters and scribble a hasty note to Louise. By evening, he'd found a place on a train of wagons hauling military supplies upriver to Natchez.

Fifteen days later, he reached St. Louis. Daniel knew the journey back down the Mississippi would take far less time, but for once he wasn't driven by the urgency of his military orders. The truth was, he was in no hurry to uproot Elizabeth and move her again.

He'd thought about leaving the army and settling in one place. Many times. He wasn't a farmer, though, knew nothing of working the land. He could easily earn a living hunting or trapping or guiding the ever-increasing stream of settlers pushing west, but those occupations would take him away from home as much or more than his army duties had.

At one point, when things had first begun to look bleak, he'd considered sending Elizabeth back to North Carolina. Unfortunately, her parents were dead and her only sister had a brood of thirteen to care for. Rebecca had made it plain she'd have no time to look after a full-grown woman who chose to sit idle and spin cobwebs in her head all day. No, Elizabeth was Daniel's responsibility. He'd have to see to her.

She was more than his responsibility, he thought

as he disembarked at the bustling waterfront in St. Louis. She was all he had.

He hitched a ride on one of the wagons hauling the supplies to the fort located north of the city. Cantonment Belle Fontaine sat on the low-lying south bank of the Missouri, near its confluence with the Mississippi. The first U.S. military outpost constructed in Louisiana Territory, it served as both a defensive fortification and a trading factory for the Sac, Fox and other local tribes.

It was here General Wilkinson had established his first headquarters, attending to his duties as military governor of Louisiana Territory with the same zeal he put into his personal trading ventures. Here, Lieutenant Pike had launched his expedition last July. Here, Captains Lewis and Clark had completed their two-year exploration and spent their last night with their Corps of Discovery only a few months back.

The fort sat at the bottom of a high bluff—not a particularly strategic location in Daniel's considered opinion, but then no one had asked him. Blistering heat and mosquitoes plagued its residents from spring to fall, ice and snow throughout the winter. A high palisade enclosed buildings constructed of wood and stone. Daniel's senior rank had entitled him to one of the small houses huddled against the pallisade.

He approached the log house, his heart pounding with anticipation and dread. He tried not to picture Elizabeth as she'd once been—a young, laughing bride with hair the color of new wheat. Instead, he forced the memory of how she'd looked when he'd left St. Louis some eight months ago. Silent. Vacant eyed. Empty.

Armored by the wrenching image, he lifted the iron latch and pushed open the wooden door. His glance went immediately to the single window in the front parlor, where he knew he'd find his wife.

She sat in a ladder-back chair, staring through the open shutters. Her hands were clasped loosely in her lap. She wore a gown of blue homespun that hung loosely on her thin frame. Sunlight gilded her hair to a pale, shimmering gold. She didn't so much as blink at his entrance.

A dozen arrows pierced right through the armor Daniel had just wrapped around his heart. His throat tight, he murmured a soft greeting.

"Hello, sweeting."

She turned her head at the sound of his voice. For a moment, only a moment, Daniel thought he saw something stir in the green void of her eyes.

Hope leaped inside him, only to die a swift, agonizing death when the faint glimmer faded and Elizabeth turned her face to the window once again. He was fighting the pain when a ginger-haired woman bustled out of the back room.

"Sergeant Morgan! We didna know you were a'comin home!"

"I didn't know I was, either."

"Ach, it's good to have you back after all these months. Isn't it, dearie?"

Elizabeth made no response. With a little frown, Nora Shaunnessy crossed the room and patted her shoulder to get her attention. "Can you no say hello to yer husband?"

A blank stare was the only response.

The corporal's wife sighed and turned to Daniel. "She's like this all the time now. I try, but the puir thing has naught to say to me anymore. Maybe you can get her to speak."

Daniel dropped his haversack and musket just inside the door. Long, painful experience had taught him to approach slowly so as not to frighten the fragile woman in the chair. Hunkering down on his heels, he carefully gathered one of her hands into his.

"I've just come from New Orleans. Remember, I wrote you to let you know I'd rejoined my company there?"

She gave no answer. The armor back in place, Daniel didn't really expect one. "I thought we'd only stay for a few weeks. A month or two at most. Just until the threat posed by Burr and his supposed army had passed."

Gently he stroked the back of her hand. Her skin felt so thin, the bones so small and delicate. "Looks like I'll be in New Orleans longer than I figured on. General Wilkinson has assigned me to his staff. It's a permanent posting, and a set of quarters comes along with the billet. It'll mean another move for you. I'm sorry, Elizabeth."

If she was cringing inside at the thought of leaving these two rooms, she gave no sign of it. Daniel forced a cheerful smile.

"You'll like New Orleans, sweeting. It's bigger

than St. Louis and far more refined. I'll take you to the shops when we get there and buy you a new dress. What color would you like? Your favorite violet? Or green, to match your eyes?''

Unbidden, the image of a slender, dark-haired woman in ruby silk leaped into Daniel's mind. He could see her face as clearly as the one right before him, her blue eyes filled with the lively curiosity Elizabeth had once possessed.

Clenching his jaw against a rush of regret and grief and guilt, he rose. ''I'm sorry to give you so little notice, Nora, but I'll be taking Elizabeth back to New Orleans with me as soon as I can pack her up.''

''Ach, 'tis no worry at all, Sergeant. Corporal Shaunnessy was tellin' me only the other night, he thinks our company will be movin' out soon, too. Truth be told, I was wonderin' what to do about Elizabeth.''

She threw a glance at the woman by the window. Sympathy and a pity she didn't try to disguise filled her face when she turned back to Daniel.

''Do you want me to help you pack up, then?''

He swept a look around their quarters. The furniture was simple and sturdy. He'd constructed a pine table with legs that detached for transport. The four ladder-back chairs were easily tucked in corners of a wagon. The dish cupboard was heavy, but Daniel had carried it in and out of many a set of quarters on his back. Two clothes chests held their spare garments, and the bed frame came apart easily.

They had few personal items of any value. The

rose-patterned china pitcher and bowl Elizabeth used to love so much. The set of eight finely crafted pewter mugs her father had presented them with on their wedding. The pianoforte Daniel had bought his wife one Christmas. She hadn't touched the yellowing ivory keys in years, but he couldn't let go of the hope that she would.

"I thank you for the offer of help," he told Nora, "but Elizabeth and I have packed up many times in the past. We know just how to do it."

"Good enough." Suddenly teary, the corporal's wife dabbed a corner of her apron at her eyes. "I'll leave you to it. I wish you well. Both of you."

Desperately, Elizabeth tried to shut out the sounds of hammering and crating. The constant noise pierced the walls she'd built around herself, forced her mind from the empty spaces where she willed it to the tall, tanned soldier with hammer in hand. The man she'd once loved with all her being.

Pulling her gaze from the window, she let it linger on his broad shoulders, on the muscles bunching under his linen shirt. She'd once craved the feel of those arms around her, opened her body joyfully to his, hoping to give him the babe they both longed for.

Pain splintered through her heart. She felt again the awful agony of losing first one child, then a second. Once more she tasted the bitter tears she'd shed when her third died in her arms. She could see the small coffin Daniel had built with his own hands, could see the tiny, stillborn babe he'd swaddled in blankets and laid inside.

Unable to bear the grief, she turned her face away from her husband.

The Mississippi's powerful current carried them downriver in half the time it had taken Daniel to travel up.

He kept Elizabeth close to him day and night. Patiently he bathed her face and hands, guided her spoon to her lips, changed her linens when she soiled herself. She was docile as a child and just as helpless.

He lay awake beside her long into the night, trying desperately not to remember how she used to throw her arm across his waist and cuddle her head on his shoulder. Instead, he filled his mind with his new duties, with the need to find someone to help him care for her in New Orleans, with the latest news about Burr, now on his way to trial in Richmond. Often his thoughts turned to the woman who'd shared his blanket during those dark, bitterly cold nights along the Arkansaw.

Louise was on his mind when the flatboat tied up at the same quay they'd both stepped onto only a few short weeks before. She wasn't his responsibility any longer, but worry for her nagged at him. He couldn't quite get over his unease at the way the general and his son had stared at her so fixedly.

If Louise claimed even a portion of the estate Thibodeaux had hinted at, she could count herself a very wealthy widow. That alone would be enough to prick the general's interest. Yet Daniel sensed there was more.

Frowning, he lifted Elizabeth onto the quay and found a spot for her among the stacked bales and barrels. "Wait here. I'll find a cart to carry our baggage to our new quarters."

She stood where he left her, never moving, never so much as turning her head to look at the bustling, busy city crowding the riverfront.

As Colonel Matthews had stated, the apartments occupied by officers and noncommissioned officers assigned to General Wilkinson's staff were small but more than adequate. They were located in a three-story building on Bienville Street, some blocks northwest of the *cabildo*. Like most buildings in this city, the outer facade was graced with elaborate wrought iron.

Daniel guided Elizabeth up the front steps and down a dim hallway reeking with the scents of leather polish, tobacco smoke and spicy stewed fish. The rooms he'd been allocated were at the end of the hall. He was thankful that they looked out on the raised banquette—the parade strolling by outside would give Elizabeth something to watch during the long, empty hours, while Daniel attended to his military duties.

The front room contained a fireplace fronted with hand-painted tiles and a swinging metal hook for boiling water and cooking. The backroom was bare except for a rickety three-legged stool left by the previous occupants. A small walled garden behind the apartments gave access to a well for fresh water and a brick oven for baking.

Daniel carried the stool into the front room. "Sit here by the window, sweeting, while I help the draymen carry in our furniture."

She went where he led her.

Working alongside the cart men, he got the clothes chests up against the wall of the bedroom and assembled the bed frame. The oak plank table and spindle-back chairs went into the sitting room, along with the dish cupboard and Elizabeth's long-unused pianoforte. The boxes and bundles he'd unpack later, after he found someone to help care for his wife.

"I'm going to speak to our neighbors," he told her after paying off the draymen. "Maybe one of them will know someone who can come and keep you company while I'm on duty."

Luckily, the sergeant's wife two apartments down was in dire need of funds to supplement her husband's pay. The small, birdlike woman returned with Daniel to meet Elizabeth and get a grasp of her needs.

"I can't promise to stay with her every minute," Polly Tremayne warned when they stepped back out into the hall. "I've got eleven of my own to care for. I'll look in on her every chance I get and see she's fed a good meal at noon. My youngest can sit with her between times."

That would do. It would have to do. Passing the

woman sufficient funds to cover the first week, Daniel went back to settle his wife into her new home.

The next morning, he reported to the officer who was now his superior. Captain Obadiah Bissell was a good man and a fine officer. Daniel had served with him in the field and held Bissell in every bit as much respect as the captain did his new sergeant major.

"It's good to have you here, Morgan. What with keeping the local militia to arms and our regulars at the ready, I'm up to my ears, I can tell you."

"I've no doubt."

"We've had the devil of a time meeting the requirement for firing drill. You'll have to get with the company sergeants and work out a schedule."

"Yes, sir."

"As soon as possible, Sergeant Major."

The title raised a ghost of a smile. With everything else pressing down on him these past weeks, Daniel hadn't had time to get used to, much less celebrate, his new rank.

"I'll make the rounds of the companies today, sir."

He soon realized that it would take more than a day to get a grasp of what was needed in terms of training. Worry over Burr's private army had compelled President Jefferson to call up the militia from several states. General Wilkinson's imposition of martial law had put a good number of New Orleans's citizens under arms, as well. Adding to their ranks were the companies of regulars the general had brought with him when he moved his headquarters from St. Louis.

Every company carried a wide variety of arms. Regulations required the militiamen to report for duty with "a good rifle, if to be had, or otherwise, with a common smoothbore firelock, bayonet and cartouche box." Daniel found the militia's definition of a "good rifle" varied considerably from company to company and man to man.

The regulars were every bit as diverse in their armament. Most were equipped with horse pistols and Wilson military fusils, a lightweight version of the British army officer's rifle. A lucky few carried the French Charleville or the 1795 Springfield, one of the first American-made muskets produced after the War for Independence.

Each weapon handled differently and required slightly different firing drills. As a consequence, Daniel worked from dawn to well past dusk for the first three days following his return from St. Louis. The hours after he returned to his quarters were spent caring for his wife.

He made his way back to Bienville Street on the evening of the fourth day, determined to change into his dress uniform, bundle Elizabeth up in the silk shawl he'd purchased for her the day after their arrival and take her with him to the Thibodeaux house. The need to see Louise, to make sure she'd fared well during his absence, gnawed at him....

So much so that he stopped dead when he opened the door to his quarters, sure he'd conjured up her image out of smoke and air. But the woman seated on a low stool beside Elizabeth's chair was flesh and blood, and so alive that his wife looked like a pale wraith beside her. His heart squeezed painfully as Louise sprang up, her face alight.

"Daniel!"

In the few seconds it took for her to rush across the room, hands outstretched, he knew he was damned to the fires of his own private hell.

12

Daniel took Louise's extended hands in his and managed to find a smile.

"James tells me you have returned," she scolded. "But you do not come to see me. I wait and wait, and decide I must come to you."

"I meant to call on you sooner, but my new staff duties have kept me hard at it."

"Yes, I hear you have the promotion." She eyed the shiny new epaulets adorning the shoulders of his uniform jacket. "You look most important."

"And you look most fashionable."

"It is this bonnet James buys me," she replied with a laugh. "Me, I think these feathers make me look like the wild turkey, but Bertrice says it is— How do her words go? It is quite the thing."

He surveyed the high-brimmed creation lavishly decorated with green-dyed ostrich plumes. It was as dashing as her figured silk walking dress and lavender kid half-boots. She'd cropped her hair, he saw. The feathery black curls framed her face in a way that stopped the breath in his chest.

"I agree with Bertrice." Somehow he managed to keep both his voice and his smile easy. "It is quite the thing. But who is this James who's buying you bonnets?"

"Your lieutenant."

"My lieutenant?"

"The general's son. James Wilkinson."

She gave a trill of laughter at his astounded expression. "James calls on me almost every day since you leave for St. Louis." Her eyes danced under the feathery ostrich plumes. "It is of all things the most foolish. He has decided he wishes to marry me."

Shock slammed into Daniel. Shock and something else, something he didn't want to think about with his wife sitting a few yards away. He clamped his mouth shut on the hot response that leaped to his lips. He didn't realize he'd clamped his hand as well until he saw Louise wince. Abruptly, he released her.

"I'm sorry. I didn't mean to hurt you."

"You do not," she said, but he knew she lied.

Once he worked his way past a swift, instinctive denial and considered the matter with his head, he supposed young Wilkinson's attentions made sense. The man had displayed no sign of being enamored of Louise during their weeks in the wilds, but now she stood to inherit considerable wealth. No doubt the lieutenant had had his eyes opened to her charms. By his father, Daniel would guess.

"I tell James I have no wish to share his bed, but—"

"But what?"

"He is most insistent," she said with a small sigh.

"Do you want me to talk to him?"

"I thank you for the offer, but it is not necessary. If he begins to annoy me, I shall speak plainer."

Her glance went to the fair-haired woman sitting by the window. "I hope you do not mind that I come to see your wife."

"You know I don't."

She brought her gaze back to Daniel. For the briefest moment, he saw a regret in their blue depths that seared his soul. Then she tipped her chin and gave him a bright smile.

"She is very beautiful, your Elizabeth."

"Yes, she is."

"She has come to New Orleans as I did, alone but for you. I think perhaps she needs another woman to befriend her, as Helene Thibodeaux and her daughters did me. Shall I take her with me when I go to the shops with Bertrice and Marie and Helene?"

He didn't answer, loath to subject his wife to the stares of strangers and shopkeepers. Louise understood his hesitation and laid a hand on his arm.

"You gave me your protection when I was in need of it. Let me give your Elizabeth my friendship. I will see she takes no harm."

Her quiet offer eased a small portion of the guilt and helplessness crushing in on Daniel's chest. The weight didn't go away entirely. He suspected it never would, but it lifted enough for him to answer with a smile.

"Thank you."

Louise gave his arm a quick squeeze before gliding back to the figure sitting silently in her chair.

"I shall come again to visit you. Tomorrow afternoon, yes? We shall put on our finest bonnets and go out to take the air. Perhaps visit Madame du Clare's shop. She has of all things the most beautiful."

Louise kept her promise.

A hazy spring sun warmed the city streets when she walked the few blocks to Daniel's quarters the following afternoon. She'd thought better of including Helene Thibodeaux and her two daughters in the expedition, though. The few moments she'd spent with Elizabeth the previous evening were more than enough to make her aware of the dark spirits holding Daniel's wife in their maw.

Lifting her skirts to avoid catching the dust and refuse on the raised walkway, she wondered again at her impulsive offer to befriend Daniel's wife. Truth be told, her heart had twisted inside her chest when she'd first peered inside the open door to his quarters and spotted the woman with the so-pale hair and green eyes. Her first reaction had been the fury and hurt and all-consuming envy of one who longed fiercely for this woman's man.

So many nights had Louise spent wishing Daniel would join with her. So many times had she wished he would forget his vows to his wife and feed the hunger gnawing at them both. Often she'd reviled him in her mind for holding true to his honor, yet she now suspected she would not crave his smile or his touch nearly as much as she did if he *had* taken what she'd offered him.

After seeing Elizabeth, Louise understood the rope that bound him. It was woven with more than the affection for the woman he'd taken into his bed and his heart. More than the responsibility of a warrior to provide for those in his lodge. This rope had been braided by the spirits who called to Elizabeth.

For the first time in many months, Louise wished heartily for the chance to speak to someone of her world, a shaman who could build a sacred fire to read omens in the smoke. Or to concoct a powerful medicine that would call to the winds to blow away the mists in Elizabeth's mind.

Lacking a priest, she would have to use her own skills, such as they were. She would do this for Daniel, to ease the anguish in his heart that he tried so hard to hide. She owed him this and more, so much more.

She found Elizabeth sitting in the same chair as she had the afternoon before, beside the same window. Her hair was unbound, her shirtwaist haphazardly buttoned over a skirt of blue homespun. An empty wooden bowl and spoon sat on the floor beside her. Across the room a gap-toothed girl sat cross-legged beside the hearth, playing with a rag doll.

Louise rapped on the door that had been left partway open and stepped inside. "Hello."

The girl sprang up. A thumb went to her mouth.

"Who are you?" Louise asked with a smile.

"Tess," she mumbled around the thumb.

"I'm Madame Chartier. I've come to take Madame Morgan to walk with me."

"The sergeant major told mam you was a'coming. She said me 'n' dolly was to stay here till you did. Kin I go now?"

"Well, I—"

"I'm supposed to do my letters. Mam said to come straightaway when you got here."

"Then, of course you must go."

The towheaded girl gathered the bowl and spoon along with her doll and slipped out without a word to the mute Elizabeth. As Louise crossed the room, she caught the faint stench of urine. She chewed on her lower lip for several moments before untying the ribbons of her bonnet and setting it aside.

"I see you are not quite ready for our walk. I will brush your hair and put it up, yes? And perhaps wash your face a bit. There is porridge on your cheek."

Pulling off her gloves, she went into the other room. Someone had left fresh water in a pitcher painted with delicate pink roses. The same someone had left clean, neatly folded underlinens on the quilt-covered bed. Daniel, Louise suspected. Her heart aching for him and the woman he'd taken to wife, she returned to the sitting room and took Elizabeth's hand in hers.

"We will go into the other room," she said, drawing the older woman gently out of her chair. "The bowl and pitcher are there. You will wash and change, and then we shall go out in the sun."

The stroll proved more difficult than Louise had anticipated. She kept her pace slow and Elizabeth's arm tucked firmly in hers, but the other woman shrank away from every passerby and started violently at every sudden, unexpected sound.

And there were many sounds. This so-crowded city buzzed with them. Sang with them. The *clip-clop* of hooves on the cobbles. The cry of merchants hawking their wares. The shouts of children chasing wooden hoops with sticks. After almost a month in this city where people spoke in so many different languages, Louise had come to feel at home amid the noise and clatter. Keeping a steady hold on Elizabeth's arm, she guided her along the banquette.

Perhaps she'd buy her a fan, she thought. One of chicken skin painted with the designs that seemed so favored right now from this faraway country called China. The days were growing longer and the afternoon carried a muggy warmth. A fan would help to stir the air.

When Louise suggested as much, however, Daniel's wife merely gripped her arm and crowded close against her side. Louise kept up a stream of chatter and had begun to think she'd eased the other woman's fears, when Elizabeth jerked to a halt in the middle of the banquette.

Startled, Louise glanced at her. "What is it?"

The blonde said nothing, but a sheen of tears collected in the corners of her eyes. With a small whimper, she stared at some point in the distance.

"Elizabeth! What do you see?"

Worried, Louise swept the scene before her. She spotted merchants in embroidered waistcoats, sailors from the nearby ships, a voodoo woman with dancing dolls on sticks. Nothing to alarm, unless it was the slavers marching a long line of manacled men to the auction house. The captives must have just come off a ship. They looked dull-eyed and half-starved. Louise could have counted their ribs as they passed. Their scant clothes hung in rags. Many wore raw, unhealed scars on their backs.

The Osage took captives and used them as slaves. All tribes did. Yet Louise couldn't remember seeing any that looked as badly treated as these wretched men. Wondering at the foolishness that would cause a slaver to starve and otherwise mistreat his captives, she started to turn Elizabeth away from the sight.

Only then did she notice her companion's gaze wasn't on the slaves but on a couple strolling along the opposite banquette. The woman walked alongside the man, making lively gestures with one hand as she spoke. Her other arm held a swaddled babe at her shoulder.

"Elizabeth? Do you know these people?"

She gave no answer.

"Why do you watch them? What do you look at?"

Louise glanced at the young couple again, trying to see what it was about them that had upset Daniel's wife. They'd strolled past by now, and all she could see was the baby peering over its mother's shoulder, its cheeks fat and its eyes berry bright.

She turned back to Elizabeth, caught a glimpse of shattering grief in her pale green eyes. Understanding came on a swift rush.

"Did you have a babe?" she asked softly. "You and Daniel?"

Elizabeth closed her eyes. When she opened them again the grief was gone, leaving only an empty mask behind.

Louise chewed on her lower lip for a moment, then gently turned the other woman back the way they'd come. "I think perhaps I tire you. We shall walk to Royal Street another time, yes? Today we shall buy fish for your dinner. And fresh bread."

Less than an hour after escorting Elizabeth down the front steps of the house where she and Daniel were quartered, Louise guided her back up again. Relieving the pale, trembling woman of her shawl and bonnet, she led her to the rocking chair by the window.

"Sit now and rest. I will put a kettle on to boil. We shall have coffee and some of this still-warm bread."

When Daniel returned to his quarters just past dusk, the tantalizing aroma of fish stew started a rumble in his stomach halfway down the hall. The rumble grew to a growl when he discovered the spicy scent came from his own hearth.

His glance shot to the woman stirring the bubbling contents of the cast-iron pot hanging from the iron hook of the fireplace.

"I didn't expect to find you here," he said, fighting the pleasure that spread through him like an onrushing tide. "Bending over a cook pot, and in a silk gown yet."

Louise waved a careless hand. "The gown does not matter. Elizabeth and I, we go to the shops this afternoon and buy bread and fish instead of feathers and shawls. We decide to cook you dinner."

"Did you?"

His clutch of worry faded when he sent his wife a quick look and saw she'd come to no harm during her foray into the outside world.

"But I do not find wild onions in the shop," Louise warned with a frown, giving the stew another stir. "Only potatoes and these dried red roots the fish seller says to put in the pot. They burn my tongue when I taste one, so I use only one or two for flavor."

Propping his musket against the wall, Daniel hung his shako on one of the wrought-iron hooks beside the door. As he went to his wife and knelt beside her chair, regret bit into his unexpected pleasure. It had been so long since he'd come home to a hot meal and a warm smile. So long since a woman had made him feel welcome in his own quarters.

"Hello, Elizabeth." Gently, he took her hand in his. "So you went to the markets this afternoon? They're quite something, aren't they? Not like in St. Louis. Did you see the flower stalls? They're like a rainbow."

He stayed at her side for some moments, speaking slowly, hoping for a flicker of a smile, a sideways glance, anything to indicate she heard him.

Across the room, Louise stood beside the bubbling pot and chewed on her bottom lip until she tasted the salty tang of blood. She had not thought it would hurt so much to watch Daniel with his wife, his big frame stooped low, his voice gentle. Feeling as though a fist had plunged into her chest and closed around her heart in a brutal grip, she tugged at the cloth tied around her waist and used a fold to swing the pot away from the fire.

"The stew has cooked enough," she announced briskly. "There is fresh bread on the table. Now I must go."

Daniel rose and crossed the room. "You'll not stay to take dinner with us?"

"I cannot," she lied, scrambling for an excuse. "I tell Helene Thibodeaux I will return early, and it is already late. Me, I do not wish to worry her."

"I could send a message."

"It is best I go."

"I'll walk you back to Doumaine Street."

"There is no need. Truly."

She had to leave before jealousy and want stripped

away her smile. Folding the towel in two, she laid it over the back of a chair.

"I walk here. I will walk to Doumaine Street. There's no need for concern," she added when he looked as though he would insist. "I bring my skinning knife with me always, in this so-handsome pouch James buys for me."

Daniel's face tightened as she slid the drawstrings of the elaborately embroidered and tasseled purse over her wrist.

"I went to see the lieutenant this afternoon," he said stiffly.

"James? But why?"

"To discover if he is sincere in his desire to marry you. I have not forgotten my vow to Henri to have a care to you."

"I see. What did you discover? Is the lieutenant, how do you say? Sincere in his desire?"

"Yes."

Louise might have taken a secret, shameful pleasure in the grim cast to his jaw if she hadn't already tasted jealousy herself and found it bitter beyond words.

"I can't fault him for his choice," Daniel said, lifting a hand to draw a knuckle down the curve of her cheek. "All I can do is tell you he's not man enough for you."

As brief as it was, his touch seared Louise's skin. She savored the heat, took it into her heart. But when she saw the same emotions she'd battled just moments ago cross Daniel's face, the fist around her heart gave another cruel squeeze. It was the same for him. The hunger. The resentment. The vicious want.

No, not the same. He was the one chained by vows. How strange that Henri had offered her the chance to bed with other trappers and she'd refused. Now, the one man she desired desperately to take into her body was bound by his own brand of honor to a woman who could not give what Louise ached to so fiercely. Numbly, she turned away and groped for the bonnet she'd left lying on the table.

"*À bientôt*, Elizabeth. Goodbye, Daniel."

Daniel stood in the middle of the room, his fists balled at his sides. He hated the passions running loose and wild inside him. Hated this fierce hunger for what he couldn't have. Damning himself for a thousand kinds of a fool, he turned and felt a blow as swift and stunning as a rifle butt slamming into his chest.

His wife watched him. Her hands were still clasped loosely around the pewter tankard. She still sat silent as a shadow in her chair. But she'd fixed her eyes on him with what looked from this distance like a faint glimmer of reason.

"Elizabeth—"

He took a step toward her. Only a step. That's all it took to douse the light. Slowly, she turned her head back to the window and stared through the thick, wavy glass.

He'd found another.

The thought forced its way through the mists of Elizabeth's mind.

Daniel had found another. A young, vibrant woman who could give him a child, a babe like the one Elizabeth had seen carried on its mother's shoulder only this afternoon.

She couldn't bear the anguish, couldn't bear the grief. Slowly, she forced all thought, all pain from her mind until only the gray shadows remained.

13

"Do you have it, Simons?"

"Almost, Lieutenant. Almost."

Chin angled upward, palms planted on his knees, James occupied the stool in front of his dressing table. While his batman struggled with the folds of his starched linen stock, his gaze roamed over the rich crown moldings and ornate plasterwork decorating the ceiling. The owners of Belle Terre had spared no expense in building their home. It rivaled any plantation in Virginia or Maryland.

Normally, James would have taken quarters in town with the other officers in his company, but the recent death of his mother had moved the general to house him here, where father and son could assuage each other's grief. Which they might have done, if not for this damnable business with Burr.

Feeling much like a raccoon caught in a bear trap, James wondered how in Hades he would emerge from this disaster without having his neck stretched. He could hardly claim ignorance of the conspiracy now being trumpeted in every newssheet in the nation. His father had confided his grandiose dreams to his sons as early as the fall of 1805, after Colonel Burr's visit to St. Louis.

James gripped his knees and stared at a plump plaster cherub on the ceiling. They'd come so close, Burr and his father. So very close. How unfortunate the general had been forced to betray his friend to save his own neck. As a consequence, he was now pinning all his hopes on his younger son. The general's dreams of an empire hadn't died, James thought with a flutter in his stomach. They'd merely become centered on a new dynasty, one James himself was intended to found.

A sudden rap on the door to his rooms caused him to start, ruining the intricate knot the slim, somewhat dandified corporal who acted as his batman was trying to achieve.

"Enter," James called, while Simons smothered an oath.

The valet tugged the creased neck cloth free and tossed it onto the bed, where it joined a half dozen other discarded stocks. He had a fresh length of starched linen in his hand when the general strolled into his son's room.

The elder Wilkinson's brow lifted as he surveyed the litter on the bed. Shaking his head, he turned his gaze on his son. "Do I intrude?"

James gave a nervous laugh. "No, sir. Simons is merely experimenting with a new knot."

"It's called the 'cascade,'" the batman put in.

"Hmm."

The cool response had both officer and valet instantly abandoning any desire to achieve the complicated knot.

"Perhaps, Corporal, you'll be good enough to continue your experiment later. I'd like a word with the lieutenant."

"Yes, sir."

Gathering the discarded neck cloths, Simons beat a hasty retreat. James knew the general intimidated his batman almost as much as his own son. Uneasily James waited for the door to close behind his batman. He guessed what was coming.

Sure enough, his father went right to it. "How do matters stand between you and Chartier's widow?"

"They, uh, progress, sir."

"Has she accepted your suit?"

"Not yet."

Clasping his hands behind his back, the general fixed him with one of his unnerving stares. "Have you kissed her?"

"No, sir."

"Held her close in the dance?"

"I haven't felt it proper to attend any dances while in mourning for Mother."

"Well, have you done anything besides buy the woman bonnets and posies?"

"No."

"Contrary to your assessment," his father snapped, "matters don't appear to me to be progressing at all."

James dug his fingers into the tendons of his knees and fought to keep a tremor from his voice. ''It doesn't pay to press this particular female too hard, sir. She's very high tempered. Half savage, if you'll remember. You should have seen her go after Private Huddleston with a knife.''

''Damn it, I'm not suggesting you rip off her clothes and attack her. Unless—'' The general cocked his head, considering the matter. ''Do you fancy to have her that way? We can certainly arrange matters so she won't resist. A drop or two of laudanum or distillate of opium in her wine and she'll open her legs to you fast enough.''

Heat shot into James's belly. He could picture Louise Chartier spread-eagle on his bed, her blue eyes blurred, her slender body his for the taking. He opened his mouth to say yes, he would most definitely have her that way. Then, imagining her fury when she came out of her stupor, he shut it again with a snap.

''I don't think we have need to resort to such measures yet, sir. I just need a little more time to woo her.''

''We're fast running out of time! I shall have to leave soon to testify at Burr's trial.''

The general took a turn about the room, his hands still clasped behind his back. ''That fool, Jefferson, says I must explain my actions in this damnable tangle. As if I would give the prosecutors any further details and incriminate myself! But God knows what scurrilous countercharges Burr may level against me.''

He stopped his pacing and turned to his son. ''If I must hire lawyers and mount a defense, I shall need access to more funds than the paltry amount Spain has supplied. I want you to shorten the leash on this rich widow, James. Bring her to heel. Quickly.''

''Yes, sir.''

Satisfied his message had been delivered, he left his son to his thoughts and his crumpled neck cloths.

When Simons poked his nose through the door again, James snapped at him churlishly. ''Get with it, man. I've a widow to woo this night.''

Louise had just finished dinner with the Thibodeaux family when James was announced.

While at dinner Marie and Bertrice had chattered happily about their day, but their houseguest had contributed little to the conversation. She'd had no appetite for the chunky turtle soup or braised veal with mushrooms served at dinner, and merely picked at the lavishly creamed syllabub served in the parlor with cinnamon-sprinkled coffee.

Her meeting with Daniel's wife earlier that day had given her much to think about. As Marie treated her family to a selection of tunes on the flute, Louise settled onto a settee next to Bertrice and plucked at the ribbons adorning her long skirt.

She felt edgy and restless, and jealous of a woman who had done nothing to stir such feelings. Henri had taught her too well, she thought ruefully. She had tasted pleasure in his arms. Not always, and not without considerable effort on her part. Now she craved more than a mere taste. She hungered for this man who could not, *would* not, satisfy her yearning.

It was need, raw need, that made her breath catch when the sound of the knocker thumping against the front door echoed up the stairs. Perhaps Daniel had come to see her. Perhaps he, like Louise, was driven by the need for one more touch, one more word.

She'd twisted the delicate fabric of her skirt into a tight knot by the time the Thibodeaux's manservant came upstairs to announce the arrival of Lieutenant Wilkinson.

"He asks your pardon for the late call," Thomas relayed to Helene Thibodeaux, "but begs the favor of a few moments of private conversation with Madame Chartier."

Helene looked to Louise for guidance. Louise knew the merchant's wife thought the lieutenant exceptionally well mannered, but Louise had expressed some rather unflattering opinions of the young man when she'd first arrived.

"It is rather late for a call," the older woman commented. "I can make our excuses. Or do you wish to see him?"

"No. Yes. Oh, it matters not."

"Well, what word shall I send down?"

Louise blew out a long breath. "Tell him to come up."

"Escort the lieutenant to the Blue Salon and serve

him a glass of port," Helene instructed her manservant. "Madame Chartier will join him there."

Madame Thibodeaux had furnished the small parlor at the top of the stairs with every extravagance allowed a wealthy merchant's wife. Blue velvet window and wall hangings lavishly embellished with gold tassels gave the room its name. Paintings, portraits and miniatures framed in gilt adorned the walls and tabletops. Lieutenant Wilkinson sat in a graceful French rococo chair, his boots polished to a glossy shine and his uniform coat fitted tight across his shoulders. His expression could only be described as glum as he stared down into the glass he held loosely in his hands.

Louise stopped just outside the salon, no more enthused about this visit than her caller apparently was. Another long breath feathered out. Lifting her chin, she summoned a smile and joined him.

"You come late tonight, James."

He jumped up in his nervous way and issued an apology. "I'm sorry. I hope I didn't inconvenience you."

"No, we listen while Marie plays the flute. She is very good. Almost as good as the shaman in my uncle's village. That one calls the birds from the trees when he plays."

She seated herself on the striped settee and clasped her hands in her lap. Instead of retreating to his own chair, the lieutenant crowded beside her on the settee. Louise smothered a stab of annoyance and tugged her skirt from under his thigh before he crushed the soft kerseymere.

She'd no sooner pulled it free than he grasped her hands in both of his. His eyes as beseeching as those of a puppy, he begged her to open her heart to him.

"Tell me what I must do to make you agree to marry me."

"James—"

"I would see you're well provided for."

"Henri has done that."

"Chartier didn't give you children. I will." A touch of desperation colored his voice. "I don't wish to be indiscreet, but, well, I've fathered more than one babe. The latest was on one of my mother's house slaves, and a lusty, well set-up child it is."

"I don't doubt you are much a man," Louise lied. "Very much."

The grip on her hands tightened. Before she realized his intent, he'd dragged her across the settee. She sprawled half in his lap, her body twisted at an awkward angle.

"James, what do you—?"

His mouth came down on hers. Wet and urgent, his tongue pushed against her teeth. Louise set her jaw and resisted the probe, but couldn't pull her hands from his. She tensed her muscles, considered fighting and scratching her way free, but decided to simply wait him out. His actions were annoying, to be sure, but unlike with Private Huddleston, she felt no fear with James.

Nor any desire, she thought as his lips moved insistently over hers. He had not the skill of Henri. Nor the passion of Daniel.

Her womb clenched at the memory. One kiss under the stars, and Daniel had stirred everything that was female in her. One glide of his knuckle against her cheek, and her skin burned where he'd touched it.

She heard a small moan, not realizing it had come from her until James gave a grunt of triumph and raised his head. His cheeks wore a red flush. His pale blue eyes held a heat she'd never seen in them.

She was gathering her breath to flay him with a few well-chosen words when he set her away from him and slid off the settee onto one knee. His voice growing hoarse with urgency, he pleaded his cause yet again.

"Madame Chartier. Louise. I beg you to say you will be my wife." He rushed on, seeing the answer in her face, giving her no chance to voice it. "I have leave coming to me. I'll take you to our home at Dauphin Island. And to Europe, once this war between England and France is done. We'll travel to Spain and Italy and Greece, as far away from my father as we may get."

He caught himself. The flush on his cheeks deepened as he hurried to explain. "Far away from this damnable coil my father's become involved in, I mean. You'll like Italy. And the Italians will surely fall in love with you. They are so dark themselves, they'll take no notice of your skin."

It took her a moment or two to understand his

meaning. When she did, her back stiffened. "I have no shame for my skin."

"So you should not!" he said hastily. "I merely mention it because Sergeant Major Morgan made such an issue of your Osage blood when he came to see me yesterday."

"Daniel spoke of this?"

"Indeed, he did. He seems to think your mixed heritage presents an obstacle to our union, but I assured him my consequence is such that it will stand the test of marrying you."

Louise felt stabbed by a thousand small daggers. Daniel had said this? Daniel?

Her ready anger rose to add heat to the hurt, so hot and fierce that the force of it brought her to her feet. She rose so abruptly that she almost tumbled the lieutenant back onto his heels. Her eyes flashing, she twitched the skirts of her gown to straighten them.

"Perhaps," she said haughtily, "I do not wish to join with a man of *your* heritage."

"I beg your pardon?"

"Get up, James. You look beyond anything foolish on your knees, begging like a dog."

His cheeks, so red a moment ago, went pale at the insult. Louise had no care for his anger and no further patience with his clumsy attempts to woo her.

"Let us speak no more of marriage. I will call Thomas and have him show you out."

With a swish of her skirts, she turned on her heel and left him.

* * *

After providing Helene with a terse explanation for the lieutenant's abrupt departure, Louise retired to her bedchamber. She dismissed the maid Helene had assigned to help her with her toilets. She was in no mood to have creams rubbed into her face this night or to sit still with her hands folded in her lap while the maid pulled a brush through her hair one hundred times. Yanking the pins from the dark mass, she grabbed the comb, sank down on the bed and attacked it herself. With each pull, the lieutenant's words echoed in her head.

He would take her to wife despite her dark skin.

He had no care that her Osage blood tainted her.

The lieutenant's foolish notions bothered her not at all, but the idea that Daniel might consider her unsuitable to be a wife to James cut her to the quick. Could it be true? Had he said such things of her?

She might have adopted the dress and mannerisms of her father's people, but her mother was of the Osage. Louise knew well many whites held those with red or black skin in fear and some contempt. It was always thus with a people stronger or more devious than another. The Osage themselves disdained the more peaceful Wichita and had driven them south, far from their traditional hunting grounds.

Yet Daniel had given no sign that he held her in less regard because both French and Osage blood ran in her veins. On the contrary, he'd always treated her with dignity and declined to take her into his bed even after paying a bride price for her.

Now…

Now Louise couldn't help but wonder if his restraint sprang from his marriage vows to Elizabeth or from a hidden contempt for a woman of her "mixed heritage."

He wanted her. He hadn't been able to disguise his hunger these past months, any more than Louise had. Yet he didn't hunger enough to set aside his first wife and take Louise in her place, a small, angry voice inside her head insisted.

Not that she wanted him to!

Mouth set, she dragged the brush through her hair. She regretted now the impulse that had taken her to Daniel's quarters yesterday, regretted her rash promise to befriend his wife. She felt sorry for the woman, could see she walked between worlds…

As Louise herself did.

The angry strokes stilled. She sat staring at the gauzy netting draped from the iron ring above the bed.

Elizabeth walked a path between light and darkness. Louise walked a way between white and red. She belonged to both worlds, and to neither. Her mother's people had shunned her because of the curse of her eyes. As James had reminded her, there were many among her father's people who would shun her because of her skin.

Sighing, she laid the brush on the table beside the bed. She would keep her promise to Elizabeth. She would be her friend. But she would wait a few days to go again to Daniel's quarters. The hurt of the lieutenant's words was too sharp, the taste of her own jealousy still too bitter.

She changed into her nightdress, crawled into bed, drew the netting around the bed and stretched out on the sheets. The watchman passed by outside, crying the hour. Louise stared up at the darkness and tried to shut out the thoughts chasing around and around in her head, like a dog after its own tail.

She wanted Daniel with an ache that went deep into her bones, but she could not have him.

James wanted her, but she would not have him.

14

Three days later, Louise walked out into bright April sunshine and made her way to Bienville Street.

She found Elizabeth in the same chair by the window she always occupied. The towheaded child who sat with her during Daniel's absence clutched her rag doll and greeted the newcomer with big, solemn eyes.

"Hello, Tess." Louise loosened the strings of her drawstring purse and reached inside. "I have brought a sugar twist."

The girl's thumb went to her mouth, but she watched avidly as Elizabeth's visitor produced a paper cone filled with sugared candies.

"This is for you."

That was all the prompting Tess needed to dart forward and snatch the paper with a grubby fist. Smiling, Louise watched her scamper out before turning her attention to Elizabeth.

She looked better today, almost as bright as the spring day outside. Her hair was neatly braided atop her head and she wore what looked like a new dress. It was a simple gown of figured muslin, pale rose in color and tied with ribbons under her breast.

"I see you are already dressed and ready to go out," she said as she draped a shawl over Elizabeth's thin shoulders. "We will walk to the square in front of the cathedral, yes? Enjoy the flowers and this so-warm air."

Louise had fully intended to be gone when Daniel arrived home. She didn't want to deal with the jealousy she couldn't quite erase no matter how hard she tried. Or with her hurt at the idea he considered her an unsuitable bride for the lieutenant.

When she delivered Elizabeth back to her quarters, however, Daniel was already there. Still in full uniform, he was stuffing a change of linens into his haversack.

"You've returned," he said with relief, coming into the front room to greet them. "I was afraid I'd have to leave without saying goodbye to either of you."

"Where do you go?" Louise asked as she escorted Elizabeth to her chair.

"We're taking out two companies for firing drill. We march to a campsite outside town and will bivouac there tonight."

"How long will you be gone?"

"Three days. Possibly four."

"Shall I stay with Elizabeth?"

The offer came from her heart, but Louise couldn't

keep the stiffness from her voice. Daniel cocked his head and gave her a considering look.

"I thank you, but there's no need. Mrs. Tremayne down the hall has agreed to look in on her and help her to bed. If you would come by when you can, though, and take her out for a little air, I would be grateful."

"As you wish," she said coolly. "I'll leave you then, so you may finish what you do and return to your company. Goodbye, Elizabeth."

Lifting the latch, she turned to leave. To her annoyance, Daniel followed her out into the hall.

"Louise, what troubles you?"

"Nothing troubles me. Go back to your tasks."

He caught her arm and tugged her around to face him. "Is it Wilkinson? You don't need to worry on that account. I won't let him nag you or chivy you into an arrangement distasteful to you."

"Will you not?" Her chin came up. "Perhaps this arrangement is not as distasteful to me as it is to you."

He blinked in surprise. "Have you changed your mind about him?"

She was tempted to say yes, to tell him she'd decided to marry James, after all. The urge to fling his hurtful words back in his face was like a thorn under her skin, but it was not in her to lie or wear a deceitful face.

"No, I do not change my mind."

"Then, what the devil are you talking about?"

"James tells me what you say."

Her voice wasn't merely cool now, it wore a coat of ice as thick as the one that had covered the Arkansaw.

His eyes narrowing at her frigid tone, Daniel took another step into the hall and closed the door behind him. "Maybe you'd better tell *me* what James told you."

"Only that you do not consider me good enough to marry him."

Astonishment blanked his face. "I never said anything of the sort!"

"No? You did not tell him my Osage blood would be... What were his words? An impediment to our union."

"Of course not!"

"Does he lie to me, then?"

Scowling, Daniel rasped his palm across his jaw. "No, he doesn't lie, exactly, but—"

Her breath hissed in, swift and sharp.

"He put a twist on my words. I merely pointed out that the two of you come from different worlds."

"And so we do." Anger rushed through her veins, hot and fierce. "But James, he says he will have me despite my Osage blood. So generous he is. So kind. And so very eager to take me into his bed."

"I doubt he'd know what to do with you once he has you there," Daniel retorted, stung.

"Hah!" She tipped her chin another notch. "He is more a man than you think him. He pulls me into his arms and kisses me. Very hard and very earnestly."

"And you let him?"

"Yes."

Heat slashed into Daniel's belly as he remembered how this woman had kissed him. The thought of Wilkinson tasting those same dark delights had him balling his hands into fists. As angry now as she was, he stalked forward.

"Damn it, woman, you can't tell a man you don't want to marry him in one breath and use your tongue on him the next. You're playing with fire and you'd damned well better be prepared when he tries to fan the flames."

"I use my tongue on you," she taunted. "Or do you not remember, Daniel?"

He couldn't have wiped the image from his mind with a bucketful of rags. "I remember."

"You and I, we start a fire, but *you* did not fan the flames."

"You know why I didn't."

"Pah! Why do you not just say the truth? You want me, but not as James does. Not openly. Not honestly."

Her scorn was like a whip, slicing right through his guilt and anger and desire.

"I want you," he growled, backing her against the wall. "In every way a man can want a woman."

Her eyes widened. He saw surprise flicker in their blue depths, followed swiftly by a wariness he was long past heeding.

"Daniel—"

Her breathless warning came too late. Months of

wanting, weeks of hunger, exploded inside Daniel like a fusillade from a full battery of cannon. His blood drumming in his ears, he wrapped an arm around her waist, dragged her hard against him and crushed her mouth under his.

She didn't resist. Neither did she respond. She didn't have to. The taste of her, the feel of her against him, were all Daniel wanted. Or so he thought, until he shifted his stance and her hipbone rubbed against his belly.

The contact roused an instant, aching need. His mind emptied of all reason, all thought. Pressing hard against her, he savaged her mouth until she opened for him.

Louise felt their tongues mate, felt his body joined with hers at chest and belly and thigh. She tried not to answer the call of her blood. Tried to subdue the wild joy of feeling his mouth and hands and tongue on hers again. But her own needs defeated her.

He was all she remembered from their time together along the Arkansaw. All she'd ached for these many nights. So big, so strong, so hard and muscled. As greedy now as he was, she threw her arms around her neck and gave him mouth for mouth, breath for breath. His low, ragged groan sang in her ears like the wind through the canyons.

For that moment, he was hers.

Only hers.

Then he raised his head and ended it. She wanted to cry out, to pull his head back down and cover his mouth with hers again. The stinging regret in his face had her swallowing a curse.

"I'm sorry, Louise."

His breath was warm on her face, his mouth too near hers. She couldn't bear for him to see the want in her eyes. With a shuddering breath, she dropped her gaze.

"I, too."

They stood there in silence, willing their blood to cool, trying to drown their hunger. Daniel tipped up her chin with a gentleness that hurt far worse than his roughness of just moments ago.

"You have nothing to be sorry for," he murmured. "The fault was mine."

"Not all yours."

She couldn't let him take the blame for what she'd wanted as much as he. Sighing, she admitted the truth. "I spoke those heated words to wound you. And to goad you into doing just as you did. I wanted you to kiss me, Daniel. For so long, I have wanted you to kiss me."

A small, wry smile curved his lips. "For so long, I have wanted to do just that."

It should have given her great joy to hear him say the words. Instead, they sat like a stone on her heart. She had only to look at him to know the weight sat even heavier on his. Aching for him, for herself, for the woman he was bound to, she fumbled for a way to end this pain.

"I think perhaps I shall go away."

The smile left his eyes. "Go where?"

"I don't know. I—will have to think on this."

Where could she go? Not back to her mother's people. She wasn't welcome among them. Her father's people she knew not. Henri's family, if any still survived after so many lost their heads during the revolution in France, would not want a stranger in their midst.

She turned away to hide a swamping wave of loneliness. Like the current of a swift river, the sheer force of it almost dragged her under. She'd clung to Daniel since Henri's death, had depended on him for friendship as well as guidance. From now on, she would have to depend only on herself.

Perhaps once the monies from Henri's estate became hers, she would take ship and travel to those places James had spoken of. Spain. Greece. Italy, she thought with a curl of her lip, where her dark hair and skin would not be remarked on.

Remembering James's unintended slur to her heritage was enough to stiffen her back. "For now, I shall go back to the Thibodeaux house. Tell Elizabeth I will come to see her tomorrow, while you are gone."

He caught her elbow. "Louise—"

"Yes?"

He opened his mouth, shut it again. What words could he speak that had not already been said, after all? What could either of them say?

His hand dropped to his side. Louise left him standing in the hall.

The hot spring sun blazed down on her when she

went down the front steps. Intent on pushing her hurt to a far corner of her heart, she walked right past the fragile woman sitting in her chair by the window.

She wore her pain in her face.

And her love.

Elizabeth saw both as Louise rushed past. With a silent moan, she tried to blank out the younger woman's torment and let the shadows wrap her in their soothing mist. She couldn't bear the thought that Daniel loved this woman, as much or more than Louise loved him.

They fought so hard to hide their yearning from her. Daniel, with his gentle touch and soothing words. Louise, with her many small kindnesses. They couldn't know each touch, each kindness only added to Elizabeth's despair.

Nor could they know how much she ached to put aside her grief and be a wife to Daniel. But the thought of losing yet another child was like a spear through her heart.

She couldn't bury another babe! She couldn't!

Swallowing the sob that fought to rip from her throat, Elizabeth gripped her hands together and stared sightlessly through the wavy glass. So desperate was her need to lose herself in the beckoning grayness that she didn't notice the two men lingering in the dark alley across the street.

True to her promise, Louise returned the next afternoon. This would be her last visit to Daniel's quar-

ters. That much she'd decided during a long, sleep-
less night.

Rapping lightly on the closed door, she lifted the
latch and called out a greeting. "Hello, Elizabeth.
I've come to take you—"

She stopped on the threshold, frozen in place by
the sight of Daniel's wife held tight in the grip of a
swarthy male. The stranger had one arm wrapped
around her throat. His other hand was clamped over
her mouth. His fingers gouged white marks in her
cheeks, and above the brutal gag Elizabeth's green
eyes were wild and frightened.

Louise's first instinct was to throw herself across
the room and claw at the man's eyes. She had gathered her muscles and was ready to fly when she remembered the knife in her tasseled purse.

"Who are you?" she demanded sharply, stalling
for time while she jerked at the twisted strings of the
bag dangling from her wrist. "What do you do with
Elizabeth?"

He answered with a grin and a stream of Spanish.
Louise caught only a word or two. Henri had taught
her the language, and she'd spent enough time now
in this city of many tongues to have gained some
ease with Spanish words, but at this precise moment
her heart hammered too hard and too loud to make
sense of them.

Plunging her hand into her purse, she groped for
her knife. Her fingers had just closed around the handle when another figure leaped out from behind the
door. Louise caught only a glimpse of a thin black

mustache and the gleam of gold in one ear before she wrenched her skinning knife free.

"Aiyy!"

The blade sliced through his shirt, found flesh, left a thin line of red across his upper belly. He danced back, dodged another slash and shouted to his companion.

"Help me with this one!"

From the corner of one eye Louise saw Elizabeth's captor fling her aside like one of Tess's rag dolls. She went down, cracking her head on the ceramic tiles lining the fireplace, and landed in a crumpled heap beside the hearth.

"Bastards!"

Louise's fury burst into blinding rage. She wanted to plunge her knife into the man's heart, but he was more wary than his companion. He kept the table between them, circling to her right while the first danced just outside the reach of her knife.

They closed in on her, forcing her to stumble back against the wall. The mustached one came at her, drew a lunge, jumped back. The other swung a meaty fist and landed a crushing blow to her temple. Stunned, she went down on all fours.

A heavy boot stomped down on the bloodied blade. One of the men snarled something, but Louise was too dazed to catch his words. When she tried to free the knife, he reached down, took her arm in a brutal grip and yanked her fingers free of the handle. A swift kick sent the knife spinning out of her reach.

When he dragged her up, she used the force of his

pull to spring like a cat and shove her shoulder into his midsection. He staggered back, taking her with him, and managed to twist her arm behind her back. With a grunt, he wrenched it upward with a force that almost tore her bones apart.

"Dog!" she shouted over the blinding agony. "Son of a dog!"

Fighting the pain, she kicked back, hit his shin with her heel. Swearing violently, he gave her arm another brutal twist and bent her almost double.

Louise heard footsteps thud toward her, felt a hand fist in her hair. A vicious tug brought her head back, and a foul-tasting cloth was stuffed into her mouth. Gagging, she tried to spit out the wadded rag, but a length of rope went over her head and was jammed between her teeth like a bit. Another length of rope lashed her wrists behind her. Then a cloak or a blanket was thrown over her head.

Hot, smothering darkness closed in on her. She struggled frantically, twisting and kicking and trying to throw off the heavy covering, until a vicious blow between her shoulder blades sent her stumbling forward blindly.

"This one fights like a savage!"

The cloak muffled his words. Panting, straining against her bonds, Louise almost missed the next.

"Why does that surprise you? The bitch has as much Osage blood in her as French."

The reply hit her like another blow to the back. They knew her heritage. They'd been lying in wait for her here in Daniel's apartments.

The stunning realization had barely sunk in before something hard rammed into her middle. She felt herself lifted, slung over a shoulder like a sack of grain, left to dangle head down. Dizziness added to the burn of her bound wrists and the ache of thickly muscled bone cutting into her belly. Nausea rose up to fill her throat. She feared she would be sick and choke on her gag.

She was carried down the hall, out through the back garden. She heard the thud of her captors' boots on hard-packed earth, smelled the charcoal from the outdoor ovens. They were taking her by way of the back alleys, she reasoned while she could still think at all. They would not risk taking her down busy Bienville Street.

The agony in her stomach combined with the smothering blackness to defeat her. She could not keep the dizziness at bay. Her senses whirled. Bright pinpricks of light danced before her eyes. Her struggles became weaker, then ceased altogether.

Louise floated on waves of pain. Darkness surrounded her, no longer hot and suffocating but still so thick she couldn't pierce it. She tried to raise a hand to the throbbing ache in her temple, but didn't have the strength to lift her arm. The mere effort sent white-hot splinters through her skull. She heard a whimper, so feeble, so weak, like a small woodland creature after a futile struggle to escape one of Henri's traps.

Another sound emerged from the edge of the darkness. Faint, like the ripple of a stream. Low, like the whisper of the wind through a stand of birch.

"Drink this."

With the low murmur came the touch of something smooth and hard against her lips. Startled, she jerked her head to the side. The movement sent more pain splintering into her skull, and she knew this time the animal moan had ripped up from her throat.

"It will ease your pain." A hand slid under her neck, tilted her head back. "Drink it."

Lured by the promise of relief from this blinding hurt, Louise opened her mouth. A vile, chalky liquid slid down her throat. Choking, she tried to jerk her head away again. The grip on her neck tightened.

"More."

She resisted, revolted by the taste, but the smooth, hard object pushed firmly between her teeth. A bottle, she thought, her senses beginning to right themselves. She began to struggle in earnest, only to discover her wrists were still bound. And the darkness came not from the pain in her temple, but from a cloth tied over her eyes. Panicked now, she collected the bitter liquid in her throat, intending to spit it out the moment the bottle was removed.

"There. That should take the fight from you."

Before she could cough up any of the vile stuff, a firm hand clamped over her mouth. Retching, Louise had no choice but to swallow the whole mouthful. Over her violent heaves, she heard another speak.

"Nothing can take the fight from that one. The whore almost sliced open my belly."

Louise struggled to understand his words. Watery eyed from gagging and more dizzy than before, she could barely grasp one word in three. A strange lassitude was spreading along her limbs. The voices blurred, became distant, until they sighed like the wind through the trees. She was floating again. The ache had gone. The darkness had become her friend, filled with hazy images and vague yearnings.

Daniel. She saw Daniel in his dress uniform. So tall. So strong. A ribbon of warmth wound through her chest.

Helene was there as well, plump and pretty in her ball gown. And Bertrice. And Marie. And James.

A whimper rose in her throat.

The darkness gave way to dim light. James became his father, who became Henri, who became Daniel again. He smiled down at her, brushed a knuckle along her cheek.

"You feel no pain now, do you?"

No pain. Only a slow, gathering warmth. It swirled through her, rising and falling with every breath.

"You've caused me no end of trouble, my dear. That's behind us now, though, isn't it? A few days here, two or three more doses, and you'll be as eager for mounting as a broodmare in heat."

His words rippled through her mind like a distant echo in a vast, empty cavern.

"You rest here. Let the pleasure drift through you. Someone will be up in a few hours to give you another dose. As for you two— Get out. I don't want to see your faces again."

"We leave when you pay what you promised us."
"Here, take it and be gone."
The voices faded.

The tide carried her onto a great sea that swelled and swirled. She felt within her the power of a great shaman after a pipe ceremony. She called up visions, saw strange images. The bearded, half-remembered trapper who'd fathered her. Her uncle with his hand out, demanding payment. Henri, sitting beside the fire.

And Daniel. When the warmth built to a heat and the visions spun in her head, she called for Daniel. He came to her, loosened her bonds, removed her dress, her petticoats, her corset to make her more comfortable. Tipped back her head for her to drink from the bottle.

The drink didn't leave so vile a taste now. She knew what to expect, knew she would soon soar on the winds like an eagle and see all the colors of the sunset.

15

"**E**lizabeth?"

Propping his musket beside the door, Daniel shrugged out of his heavy haversack. After two full days and nights of field drill, alternating companies to assess their effectiveness, weariness ate into his bones. He wanted nothing so much as a hot supper, a good sluicing with a bucket of water and a bed to fall into.

He was pleased with the results of the drill, though. Very pleased. Company H's grenadiers had amply demonstrated their proficiency and his own Third Company, Second Regiment of Riflemen, had outgunned everyone else. The new dragoon squadron was manned with raw recruits who would need work, certainly, as would the militia, but at least Daniel now had a base against which to measure their progress.

Dropping the haversack on the floor with a *thump,* he searched the sitting room. A candle lamp chased back the night and showed Elizabeth's chair to be empty. Thinking perhaps Mrs. Tremayne had already helped her to bed, he went into the other room.

He found his wife lying in her nightdress, eyes closed, hands folded across her chest. His heart jumped into his throat. In the flickering light of the candle on the table beside the bed, she had the look of a corpse laid out for a viewing.

"Elizabeth?"

"She's sleeping." Tremayne's youngest scrambled up from the floor, her doll clutched in her arm. "She's been sleeping for nigh on three days."

"Three days!"

Daniel whirled back to his wife. Dread clutched at his insides. Had the shadows finally claimed her? Had she retreated into herself for good this time? Dear God, had he left her alone one too many times and snapped her fragile hold on her senses completely?

"Mam said to fetch her when you came home."

The girl scurried out, leaving Daniel racked with guilt and worry. He sank down on the side of the bed, took Elizabeth's hand in his. It felt cool to the touch, almost clammy, despite the heat of late afternoon.

"Wake up, sweeting."

A faint crease formed on her brow, sending his hopes soaring.

"Open your eyes, Elizabeth."

She made a small sound deep in her throat, not quite a moan but close enough to carve out a piece of his heart. She was in pain, a kind of pain he couldn't cure or take from her, no matter how much he wished to.

"Open your eyes," he repeated, more harshly this time, as if he could command her obedience as he did that of his men.

The sound of footsteps brought his head around. Polly Tremayne came into the bedroom, looking every bit as tired as Daniel felt. Her dark hair flew out in untidy wisps and a weary resignation lined her small, birdlike face.

"I couldn't get her to wake, either," she told Daniel. "She's been like this since I found her lying on the floor. She must have tripped on her skirts or caught her foot on the floorboards. I'm guessing she hit her head when she went down. There's a lump the size of a bird's egg on the back of her head."

"You should have sent for me."

"And you would have done what? Deserted your post and rushed back here to bathe her brow?"

Her face softened. Like many army wives, she'd spent years at frontier posts where medical assistance was limited, if available at all. Women had to depend on each other in their husbands' absences.

"There's nothing you could have done for her I didn't do, Sergeant Major."

He hated to admit that was the truth, hated even more this feeling of absolute helplessness.

Tremayne's wife must have sensed the feelings ripping his insides apart. With a sympathetic cluck, she laid a hand on his arm.

"I'm thinking you should just let her sleep. Time and the Good Lord will tell her when to wake. Why don't you come with me? I've got corn bread rising and a stew bubbling and you've the look of a man who needs something hearty in him."

He couldn't bear to leave Elizabeth lying so still and waxlike. "I thank you, but I'm not hungry."

"If you change your mind, there's plenty for all."

She bustled out, leaving Daniel to unbutton his uniform jacket and tug at his neck cloth. He'd unpack his haversack, he decided, wash the gunpowder and smoke off his face, then try again to wake Elizabeth.

That was when he spotted the knife. It was lying almost hidden under the dish cupboard, with only the end of its handle showing. Frowning, Daniel slid it out.

For the second time in less than an hour, his heart jumped into his throat. He recognized the bits of red yarn woven into the rawhide handle. Recognized as well the long, lethal blade Louise had almost gutted him with.

His thumb went to the reddened tip. The blood had dried to a dark rust. There wasn't much of it, only enough to show the knife had been used. Recently.

His jaw tight, Daniel thrust the knife into his cartridge pouch and grabbed his shako.

"I've got to go out for a while," he called to Elizabeth, driven by a need greater than that of his wife's right now. "I'll ask Mrs. Tremayne to look in on you."

* * *

Daniel!

The cry rose in Elizabeth's throat, fought to tear free. Panic pierced her safe, gray cocoon.

She had to warn him, had to tell him about the men who'd hurt her. She could feel their rough hands on her. Hear their coarse laughter. Despite her terror, despite her confusion, she'd known the moment Louise walked in the door they'd been waiting for her.

They meant to hurt her. Why, Elizabeth couldn't begin to understand. But she had to tell Daniel, had to send him in search of the woman who'd shown her so much kindness.

The woman Elizabeth knew he loved with all his being.

With a low moan, she forced her eyes to open. Dark shapes loomed in front of her. Terror almost sent her fleeing into the grayness again, but the dark shapes became shadows dancing on the wall.

Panting with fear, with a pain that stabbed into her head, with sheer desperation, she gripped the quilt with trembling hands and shoved it aside. When she tried to rise, her nightdress tangled around her ankles. She flung out a hand to steady herself, caught the edge of the bedside table, tilted it onto one leg. The candle tipped over, spilling hot wax and its one, small flame.

The burning wick caught the edge of Elizabeth's sleeve and fired the fine lawn. Jerking her arm back, she beat at the tiny, dancing flames.

* * *

Daniel hurried through the warm April night, his long legs eating up the blocks to Doumaine Street. Ten minutes later, he rapped on the Thibodeauxs' door and inquired for Madame Chartier.

"She's not here," Helene Thibodeaux's manservant answered gravely.

"Where is she?"

"Don't know, sir. We none of us does."

A cold weight settled in Daniel's gut. "Is Monsieur Thibodeaux at home?"

"No, sir, but his missus is. If you'll follow me upstairs, I'll tell her you're here."

Daniel waited impatiently until Helene Thibodeaux hurried into the parlor, a crumpled linen handkerchief clutched in her plump fist.

"What's this about Louise?" he demanded before the matron got out so much as a word of greeting.

"We don't know where she is. She went out three days ago, saying she was going to visit your wife. We waited until evening, and when she didn't return, Bernard went to your quarters to enquire. Someone—a neighbor—said her daughter had seen Louise earlier that afternoon, but not since."

Tears spilled from Helene's worried eyes. Distraught, she dabbed at them with her handkerchief.

"Bernard's notified the watch. He wanted to send word to you, but the captain at the *cabildo* said you were on maneuvers and couldn't be recalled. Wherever can Louise be?"

He shook his head, started to tell her he had no idea, when Louise's last words cracked like rifle fire in his mind.

She'd said she might go away.

He hadn't allowed himself to think about that possibility these past few days. Thirty-six straight hours of firing drill had helped keep the thought at bay. Now, he had no choice but to face it.

No. That wasn't Louise's style. She wouldn't be so thoughtless as to slip away without letting Thibodeaux and his wife know she was leaving. Nor did that explain the bloodied knife.

"This is so distressing," Helene murmured into her handkerchief, "so very distressing! Coming on top of that unpleasantness with the lieutenant, I'm sure I don't—"

"What unpleasantness?"

The sharp question brought the matron's nose out of the damp linen. "I'm not one to spread gossip," she sniffled, "but— Well—"

"Tell me, Helene!"

"Lieutenant Wilkinson tried to force his attentions on Louise. Right here, in our Blue Salon! I was never so disappointed in a man, although Louise did say she could not hold him in very high regard."

Hell and damnation! Another layer piled on top of the guilt that all but bowed Daniel over. He'd accused Louise of leading Wilkinson on, was sure she'd played the same games with the lieutenant she had with him. From the sound of things, she'd practically had to fight the man off.

Suddenly, he could almost see the stubborn determination on the lieutenant's face when Daniel had confronted him. Wilkinson had made it clear he wanted Louise—or the wealth she stood to inherit.

Did the lieutenant have something to do with her disappearance? With that bloodstained knife? Daniel damned sure intended to find out.

Night cloaked the city by the time he tracked Wilkinson down.

He'd ridden first to Belle Terre, where he learned the general was preparing to leave for Richmond the next morning to give testimony in the Burr trial. The lieutenant, he was informed, had just this afternoon moved into rooms in town with his fellow officers.

His sense of urgency mounting with every mile, Daniel returned to town and searched out the Royal Arms. Unlike the sparsely furnished apartments allotted to the enlisted personnel on regimental staff, the Royal Arms offered meals served in a luxurious taproom graced by gleaming brass candle sconces and rack upon rack of French and Spanish wines. Carved oak stairs led up to the second-floor landing, where a passing chambermaid directed Daniel to the lieutenant's rooms.

The corporal who served as Wilkinson's batman answered his knock. "Yes, sir?"

Frowning, Daniel searched for his name.

"Simons, is it?"

"Yes, sir."

"Sergeant Major Morgan to see Lieutenant Wilkinson."

"I'm sorry, Sergeant Major. The lieutenant is preparing to go out and doesn't wish to receive visitors at this time.''

''Tell him I'm here and need to speak to him on a matter of some urgency.''

Puffed up with his own importance, the corporal shook his head. ''You'll have to come back another time. Tomorrow, perhaps?''

''Tomorrow be damned!''

With a hard hand Daniel knocked the door back against the inner wall.

''See here!'' Sputtering with indignation, Simons dogged his steps as he crossed the room. ''You can't just charge in like a drunken dragoon. The lieutenant—''

''Will see me tonight,'' he growled, skimming his glance over heavy, dark furniture. ''Where is he?''

''He's at his toilet, but—''

At that moment, the door to the bedroom opened and Wilkinson appeared. His face was flushed and his eyes held a glitter that suggested the glass of wine in his hand wasn't the first he'd downed.

''Morgan!''

The high color drained from his cheeks, but he looked more frightened than surprised. With his sudden pallor, a grim suspicion settled in Daniel's gut.

Wilkinson had some hand in Louise's disappearance. What's more, the man had expected to be called to task for it.

Typically, the lieutenant tried to hide his nervousness in bluster. Straightening his shoulders under his frogged uniform jacket, he scowled. "What the devil do you mean by entering my quarters uninvited?"

"I want to talk to you."

"You will show a proper respect when you address me, Sergeant Major."

"Any man who would force himself on a woman, as I'm told you did Madame Chartier, deserves no respect."

"Force myself?" His face, so flushed a moment ago, now blanched. "I didn't— I haven't had to—"

"Don't try to deny it. Madame Thibodeaux told me about your visit to her house a few nights ago."

"Oh, that!" His breath rushed out on a nervous titter. "That was a misunderstanding. Nothing more. Madame Chartier, uh, encouraged me. I fear my ardor overcame my manners."

Disgust rippled through Daniel. Louise would never have encouraged this fop. And someone or something, he reminded himself grimly, had bloodied her knife.

"No harm was done," the lieutenant continued. "Madame Chartier is a widow, after all, and well used to the ways of men." He gave a knowing wink. "Very well used."

The leer snapped Daniel's restraint. Under other circumstances, he might have gone to the *cabildo* and laid the knife before his superior, along with his growing suspicions that Wilkinson was somehow involved in Louise's sudden disappearance. But fear for her safety shattered the restrictions that had governed his life for the past fourteen years,

Striding across the room, he caught the lieutenant by his lapels. "Where is she?"

"Morgan! Are you mad?"

"Tell me, damn you!"

Simons rushed forward and made a grab at Daniel's sleeve. "Think what you're about here, man! You can be court-martialed for laying hands on an officer!"

Swatting the batman away like an annoying gnat, he took the lieutenant's linen stock in a stranglehold. "I intend to do more than lay hands on you. If you don't tell me where Madame Chartier is, I swear I'll beat you to a bloody pulp."

"You cannot! You dare not! Striking an officer will get you the whip! Or the gallows!"

He was beyond caring. "Tell me what you know, you whining, useless turd."

"I—I know nothing!"

The small, telling hesitation hardened Daniel's suspicions into absolute certainty. Wilkinson was holding something back. Something that frightened him more than the prospect of taking a beating. Coldly determined now, Daniel tightened his choke-hold on the linen stock, brought his other arm back and plowed his fist into the lieutenant's stomach.

The man doubled over, gasping, only to be yanked upright again by his neck cloth.

"Tell me!"

James couldn't tell him anything! He didn't dare open his mouth and let out so much as a whimper. He hadn't known what his father intended, could hardly keep from pissing his pants when he'd learned what had been engineered.

But who would believe him? Who would agree he was only a pawn in a dangerous game? He was in this now every bit as deep as his father and knew only one way out. He had to play the hand he was dealt.

"Tell me, damn you!"

James took a second blow, was yanked upright again with another cruel twist of his stock. Terrified, he clawed at the brutal hold.

"I...know...nothing."

Daniel looked into his eyes, saw stark fear in their depths. At that moment, he knew the lieutenant would take whatever secrets he held to the grave with him. His fist bunched, tightening the noose around Wilkinson's neck. Every muscle strained with the urge to beat the man to a quivering, whimpering pulp.

The lieutenant flailed at his hand, his blows weaker by the second. His eyes rolled back in his head. He went limp.

With a disgusted growl, Daniel released him. The man sank like a stone and lay on his back, twitching and gasping. Daniel stood over him for a moment, his chest heaving, then swung around to the orderly.

The corporal stood his ground, but his face flew ruddy flags of color at the sergeant's approach.

"What do you know of your lieutenant's affairs?"

"Nothing! All I do is lay out his uniforms and clean his boots."

"Don't shovel that horseshit on me, man."

"I swear, he never discusses his personal affairs. His father won't allow it."

A muscle ticked in the side of Daniel's jaw. He had to think, had to bring order to his chaotic thoughts. "When you answered the door, you said the lieutenant was preparing to go out. Where?"

"To meet some of his fellow officers, he said."

"At what place?"

The batman hesitated, threw a glance at his still-gasping superior. Loyalty often forged the bond between servant and master into a thick chain. Just as often, it ran as thin as water, particularly in the ranks, where being selected for valet duty often subjected the chosen one to jeers and insults from his peers. In army parlance, batmen were known as dog-robbers, pitiful half-soldiers who stole scraps from the table that would otherwise be thrown to household pets.

Daniel would never know whether it was a secret satisfaction at seeing his superior brought low or the desire to save his own skin that loosened Simons's mouth.

"I think," he whispered, "the lieutenant may have made mention of a tavern down by the river. I don't remember the name."

Daniel found Louise in the dark hours after midnight.

Pistol in hand, he crashed through the door of an upstairs room in the riverfront hovel that billed itself as the Hounds of Orleans. The first thing he noticed was the sickly sweet scent of opium that hung in the small room like a cloud.

The second was the figure on the bed. She lay on her back, sprawled across the mattress. Long, tangled black hair spilled over her shoulders. Her gown lay on the floor beside the bed and her chemise was unbuttoned in the front. The light from the near-gutted candle gleamed on the smooth, swelling mounds of her breasts.

"Son of a whore!"

He fought the rage pulsing through him in hot, red waves. Shoving his pistol into his belt, he ducked his head to keep from hitting the low-hanging eaves and went to her.

"Louise…"

Her eyelids fluttered up. Her glazed eyes showed only a small rim of blue surrounding the huge, dark pupils.

"Daniel."

A dreamlike smile curved her lips. She lifted her arms in slow, languorous invitation.

"I knew you would come to me."

16

With murder in his heart, Daniel stood over the woman sprawled on the bed. He'd kill Wilkinson! Gut the whoreson with his own sword. If the lieutenant had brought Louise here and left her in this state, he wouldn't live to see another dawn.

Setting his pistol on the crude wooden shelf above the bed, Daniel sank onto the dingy sheets. When he gathered her into his arms, her head lolled back and her vague smile cut into his heart.

"I call to you." Her words were so thick he could hardly understand her. "Always, I call to you."

The fat tavern keeper downstairs claimed she'd come in with two men. Two Spaniards, who'd paid him well for a room and a bed where they could play their games with the whore they'd brought in from the streets. Yes, the whore had a tumble of black hair. No, the barkeep hadn't seen her eyes. She'd been too drunk to keep them open.

Not drunk, Daniel saw now. She hadn't been drunk.

He was no stranger to the effects of opium. It could be bought at any apothecary shop. Men and women alike drank laudanum to cure any number of ailments, from nervous tremors to birthing pains. When mixed with tobacco leaves, opium extract provided pipe smokers with temporary release from all cares.

Daniel had seen troopers resort to the restorative often enough among the ranks, had seen as well the havoc it wreaked on military discipline. That was why smoking opium while in uniform had but recently been forbidden. And why he knew the next few hours would take their toll.

Gathering Louise against his chest, he rocked her back and forth. "I've got you, sweeting. I've got you."

Instead of soothing her, the soft murmur roused her from her stupor. She squirmed around and frowned up at him.

"You will not...call me this." Dragging her tongue along her dry, cracked lower lip, she struggled for the words. "It is...it is how you call Elizabeth."

Dear God! She was near enough to stupor as made no difference, yet she recognized him, recognized as well the woman who stood between them.

"Call me as I am," she mumbled. "Wah-shi-tu."

He remembered the first time she'd told him her Osage name, saw again the clean white snow, the sky so blue above stands of blue spruce and dark pine. Tucking her head under his chin, he rocked her gently.

"Wah-shi-tu," he echoed. "What does it mean?"

She slumped into his chest, her whispered reply almost lost against his uniform coat. "The accursed one."

Christ's foot! No wonder she'd chosen to use the name Henri Chartier and the priest had given her. "Maybe that's what it means in Osage," he told her softly, fiercely. "In my reckoning, it means the brave and beautiful one."

She didn't answer. Her breath coming slow and shallow, she sagged bonelessly against his chest.

Daniel was clutching her tight when he heard the *thud* of a heavy tread on the stairs outside the door. Untangling his arms, he laid her on the mattress and dragged the sheet over her.

He was on his feet, his pistol in hand, a second later. He ached for Wilkinson to show his face. Or one of the Spanish bastards who'd hired this room. All any of them had to do was show his face...

To his knifing disappointment, it was the tavern keeper who puffed to the top of the stairs. Red-faced and wrapped in a stained leather apron the size of a two-man tent, he hooked a thumb at the woman on the bed.

"She's the one you seek?"

"She is."

His massive shoulders lifted in a shrug. "It's no matter to me if you want to take another man's leavings, but you'll have to pay for the use of the bed if you've a mind to take a tumble with her yourself.''

Disgusted, Daniel lowered the pistol. "Tell me what you know of the Spaniards who brought her here."

"What is there to tell? They paid me with copper *maravedies,* they spoke the Viceroy's tongue and they promised there'd be no screams except of pleasure. Now I know why." He sniffed the air, his nose wrinkling at the sweet stench. "Opium eater, is she?"

"What about the other? The one you told me came after the Spaniards?"

"Never saw his face. Kept a fancy silk handkerchief to his nose, as though the stink of the riverfront was too much for him."

"Did he wear a uniform?"

"If he did, his cloak covered it. Wrapped in the thing from neck to knees, he was. The kitchen slut thinks she saw a flash of gold lace once, but she's taken too many blows to the head and says whatever she has a fancy to."

Daniel smothered an oath. He'd find no reliable witnesses here to take to the captain of the guards. Either the tavern keeper told the truth, or he'd been bribed well to keep his mouth shut. Daniel dismissed him with a curt order.

"Tell the kitchen wench to bring a bucket of water."

When the man had waddled out, Daniel returned

to the bed. His mouth grim, he unbuckled his cartridge belt, dragged off his uniform jacket and rolled up his sleeves.

"Take another drink."

Keeping a firm grip on Louise's shoulders, he held the dipper to her lips.

"No more. Please!" She squirmed in his hold. The sheet he'd wrapped her in twisted around her thighs. "My belly swells now like a buffalo's bladder."

"Better your belly swells than the opium stays in your blood. Drink the rest."

"I cannot!" she snapped, shoving his hand away.

The fire was back in both her eyes and her voice. Relieved, Daniel tossed the dipper into the wooden bucket the kitchen maid had brought up.

Holding the sheet with one hand, Louise pushed back her tangled hair with the other. Her gaze traveled around the small, hot room under the eaves as if seeing it for the first time. Her glance lingered on the stained floorboards, the soot-streaked timbers in the sloped ceiling, the chair Daniel had propped against the door to hold it shut.

"How long have I been here?"

"Three days, best I can tell."

Her jaw set. She sat silent for a long moment. He could only imagine what thoughts sifted through her mind.

"It shames me," she said finally. "Greatly."

"No!" Taking her chin in his hand, he turned her face to his. "You're not to blame for whatever happened here."

"But I am to blame for what happened at your quarters."

In mumbled fits and starts, she told him of the struggle in his apartments, of seeing Elizabeth held in a brutal grip, then thrown aside, of her own fierce battle to escape.

"How in God's name can you think any of that was your fault?"

"Me, I let them take me too easily. I should have used my knife. I should have kept them from hurting Elizabeth."

"Listen to me, Louise. You did all you could and more. You bloodied at least one of the scoundrels who attacked you and Elizabeth."

"Better I cut out his entrails!"

Daniel would take care of that. "Tell me again what you recall of them."

"One has a mustache and a ring in his right ear. I tell you that already. They spoke in the Spanish tongue."

"You say they were waiting for you there in my quarters?"

"Yes. They knew my habits, knew also of my Osage blood. One—the one I cut—says I fight like a savage."

"Did they make mention of any name?"

"Not then, but later I hear yours."

"My name? How was it spoken?"

"I cannot remember. Perhaps—"

"Perhaps what?"

She wet her lips, staring up at him with huge, bruised eyes.

"Perhaps," she said slowly, "I hear it only in my head. Perhaps I want so desperately for it to be you who comes to me here, I say your name to myself."

With an ache that went bone deep, Daniel gathered her into his arms.

Louise buried her face in his shoulder. She had not thought she could feel such shame. Not because of what those pigs had done to her. She would settle with them in her own time and her own way. But because Daniel had found her like this, so weak, so helpless, so eager to spread her legs for him.

He'd cleaned her. Clothed her in her soiled chemise. Used the same gentleness with her he used with Elizabeth.

That had humiliated her even more.

"You say you went to James? You think he's the one who had me brought here?"

"If he didn't, he knows who did. He'll pay for his part in this, Louise. I swear to you, he'll pay."

That was what she feared. Daniel would avenge her and, in the white man's way, he would hang for it. Already he faced retribution for the beating he said he'd given James. Sick at heart, she knew of only one way to save him.

"Listen to me, Daniel. You must think with your head, not your heart. If you take vengeance on James without proof, they will hang you. And if that happens, what will become of Elizabeth?"

His head snapped back. "For the sake of God! Do

you think I need to be reminded of my responsibilities to my wife?''

''Yes! Me, I take care of myself. Always I have done so. But Elizabeth—''

Eyes blazing, he gripped her arms. ''What kind of a man do you take me for? Do you really believe I'd turn a blind eye to what was done to you? Is that how I'm to honor my vow to Chartier?''

''Henri is dead. I do not want you dead also!''

He would have wrenched away in disgust, but Louise clung to him, desperate to make him understand.

''I know you are brave, Daniel. I know a warrior's heart beats in your breast. I could not ache for you as I do if this were not so.''

''You picked a fine way to show it.''

''I don't ask you to ignore what was done to me, only to bide your time. Find this proof you say is needed, have a care to Elizabeth until it is done.''

''And in the meantime, we're to let the dogs who snatched you have another chance at you?''

It was an idea she hadn't considered. She could offer herself as bait, lure James out of the shadows— if he was the one who'd had her taken, the one who'd crawled between her legs. As hard as she tried, she couldn't separate the blurred images swirling around in her mind.

One image, only one, was clear and sharp. The one before her now. She'd carry the memory of his wide shoulders, strong jaw and gray eyes with her wherever she went.

"No," she replied quietly. "I do not want to let them have another chance at me. I go away from New Orleans. Today."

"That's probably for the best. You'll be safer away from here. I'll see you settled and—"

"You do not understand." Gripping the sheet, Louise rose onto her knees. "I go far away. To France."

"France?"

"I spoke with Bernard Thibodeaux before... before this happens. I tell him to book me passage on the next ship that leaves."

A retort rose in Daniel's throat. He couldn't protect her with an ocean between them. The bitter realization that he'd done a piss poor job of protecting her here in New Orleans sent the protest back down his throat.

Chances were he'd be brought up on charges for assaulting the lieutenant. If Wilkinson had a hand in Louise's kidnapping, he'd be counting on the fact that no one, her included, could identify him or in any way tie him to the men who'd taken her. They'd dosed her all too well. Even the tavern keeper would swear she was an opium eater, awash in a sea of her own imaginings.

Daniel's word would be discredited, as well. He'd attacked a superior, assaulted him in his own quarters. His only defense was a suspicion that Wilkinson had some knowledge of Louise's abduction. A suspicion he still couldn't prove, despite doing his damnedest to choke the truth out of the man.

The only hope of connecting the lieutenant to the kidnapping was to find those Spaniards. Until he did, Louise was safer away from here.

"What will you do in France?" he asked, struggling to accept the idea that she'd be gone from him.

"Speak with the lawyers who settle my claim. Seek out my husband's people. Leave you to Elizabeth."

He opened his mouth to argue.

"I must go," she said softly, gripping the sheet with a white-knuckled fist. "I can't bear to see you torn between the two of us, any more than I could bear to see you hang."

"Louise—"

"I ask only one thing of you before I leave you." Her sad, beautiful eyes smiled into his. "Kiss me, Daniel. Just once more."

He knew before he lowered his head that it wouldn't end with a single kiss. Louise had refused to let whatever happened here break her, had fought her way through the drugging mists with the same ferocity she'd battled every other enemy. She was awake now, fully aware of what she asked for, and as hungry for him as he was for her.

He moved his mouth over hers. Slowly at first. Gently. As if to store up her touch and her taste in his memory. After the first kiss, he craved more than a taste. His hand cupped her shoulders, drew her close. Her arms lifted to lock around his neck.

The sheet dropped. Like stones toppling from a wall, every restraint fell with it. The gnawing need he'd denied for so long burst its chains. Daniel shut his mind to any thought of his wife. All he could think of, all he wanted to think of, was this woman.

Her skin was like warm honey, smooth where he touched it, salty sweet where he tasted it. Savoring the flavors, he trailed kisses along her cheek, over her chin, down the line of her throat.

Her head went back. Eyes closed, Louise reveled in the feel of his hands and his mouth on her body. She'd ached for his touch for so long. Had imagined he would kindle little sparks under her skin, just as he now did.

The fear and confusion of the past days and nights seeped out of her bones. The blurred images faded completely. She'd wanted his kiss to drive them from her mind. Now, she wanted him.

Bringing her head forward, she fumbled at the ties to his linen shirt. The skin beneath was warm to her touch. She slid her palms under the linen and peeled it back, gliding her fingers over hot flesh and hard muscle.

A smile feathered her lips. "Your skin is brown from the sun," she murmured, dropping kisses on his shoulder. "More brown than mine. Perhaps you should come with me and we will go to this place where no one will notice our dark skin."

"I would give my soul to come with you."

She tipped her head back, saw he spoke from the heart. "But you will not," she said softly.

"No."

"Because of Elizabeth."

"Because of her. And because I'm no deserter. I still wear a uniform. I don't know for how much longer, after last night, but..."

"We will not speak of last night," Louise said fiercely. "For what time we have left together, we will not speak at all."

His fingers fisted in the linen and dragged it over his head. The shirt caught at the cuffs. She tugged at it impatiently and muttered a curse when the buttons wouldn't give.

"Here, let me."

Sinking back on her heels, Louise caught her breath as he discarded the shirt and went to work on his boots and trousers. His sheer beauty made her blood sing and her pulse soar like a hawk in flight.

He was more muscled than the men of her mother's people, and dusted with hair. Light brown and curling, it swirled across his chest and down his belly. His shaft hung from another nest of brown.

Her womb clenching in anticipation, Louise closed her fingers around it. The skin was hot, the veins rigid. One slow, sliding squeeze, and he grew thick and hard as a tent pole.

Whatever, whoever had come before lost all significance. Henri. Elizabeth. The nameless, faceless men who swam in the shadows of her mind. None of them mattered. There was only this tall, bronzed warrior she'd hungered for all these months.

When he joined her on the bed, she lifted her mouth to his eagerly. And when he kneed her legs apart, she opened for him joyously.

Daniel tried to go slowly. He worried she'd been hurt by the men who had used her, feared the feel of him pushing into her would drive the pleasure from her face and bring on panic.

His fear was for naught. Her mouth was welcoming under his, her hands urgent on his back. She clenched muscles around him, drawing him in, wrapping him in hot, wet flesh. His breath coming hard and fast now, he drove into her.

All too soon, he felt his body harden. His blood pounded like a drum in his veins. He pushed up, bracing himself on his elbows.

"Louise."

She arched under him, panting.

"Louise, look at me."

"Daniel—" It was a wail, a plea.

"Look at me!"

Her lids raised. As he had the very first day he'd encountered this tangle-haired creature, Daniel saw himself in the clear, shimmering blue of her eyes.

He flexed his hips, and with a hard, sure thrust, he sank home.

17

Louise lay in Daniel's arms, her head nested on his shoulder, her legs tangled with his. She didn't have any idea of the hour, guessed it was some time yet before dawn.

"We'd best get you out of here."

The quiet words shattered the stillness. Louise nuzzled her face into the warm skin of his neck and pretended not to hear. Everything in her cried out for another hour. Just one. Despite what she'd endured in this small, hot room, she'd give every penny of Henri's fortune to stay huddled on these dingy sheets.

Daniel pushed up on one elbow, the straw mattress sagging under him. The movement rolled Louise onto her back. Sighing, she stared at this wide-shouldered, square-jawed man she'd come to love more than she'd ever thought it possible to love. His brown hair stood up like a partridge's ruff where she'd thrust her hands through it. His cheeks and chin showed the shadows of a new beard, and the look in his eyes told her he'd accepted what she had not.

Their time together was done. This stolen hour would have to see them through the months and years ahead.

"I will carry you always in my heart, Louise Therese."

"And I you."

Giving in to the urge to touch him one last time, she cupped his cheek. He turned his head and pressed a kiss against her palm.

"Will you send word of how you fare when you reach France?"

"I will. And you will let me know how you and—"

She broke off, silenced when Daniel frowned and raised his head.

"What is it? What do you hear?"

"It's not what I hear." The slash between his brows deepened. "It's what I smell."

Louise sniffed, but with him leaning so near to her, all she drew in was the sharp tang of their sweat and the yeasty scent of their loving.

"That's smoke," he muttered, "and not from cook fires."

Rolling off the bed, he reached for his trousers. "Get dressed."

She scrambled up and dug through the pile of discarded clothing. She could smell the smoke now, too. A faint whiff drifted in through the eaves.

Ignoring her corset, she pulled on the muslin chemise and grabbed her soiled walking dress. By the time she'd fumbled with the buttons that closed the dress at the neck, Daniel had stamped into his boots. Louise was reaching for her ribboned leather shoes when she heard the tramp of feet on the wooden stairs.

Her glance flew to Daniel. "Could it be the men who took me?"

A feral gleam came into his eyes. "I surely to God hope so."

Snatching his pistol from the shelf above the bed, he checked the firing pan for powder, then gave her a quick shove.

"Get over there, behind the door."

The chair Daniel had propped against the broken lock wouldn't keep anyone out for long.

"I wish I had my skinning knife," Louise muttered as she scurried across the room. "I would peel the hide from those two Spaniards."

With a small grunt, Daniel tipped up the flap of his cartridge pouch. "Happens I have it with me."

A flick of his wrist sent the long-handled knife across the room. The blade became buried in the wooden door. Louise wrapped her hands around it and felt the blood rise in her veins.

One glimpse of a gold earring. That's all she needed. Just one glimpse.

Her fingers fisted around the hilt, she flattened herself against the rough board wall. A sudden hammering mere inches from her ear had her biting down hard on her lower lip.

"You in there! You and the wench!"

"It's the tavern keeper," Daniel grunted, kicking aside the chair.

"There's a fire," the man huffed. "They're calling for all able-bodied souls to man the bucket brigades."

Louise came out from behind the door. The fat, puffing tavern keeper didn't spare her so much as a glance.

"I'm going myself. Last time fire swept through the city, it damned near took this place and me with it."

Daniel's stomach clenched. Fire was a constant threat, especially in crowded cities like this. Wooden shingles and old timbers went up in a flash. Leaping flames consumed whole districts. The *cabildo* and the cathedral next to it had burned to the ground and been rebuilt a number of times.

And he had left Elizabeth alone!

"Where is this fire?"

The tavern keeper had already started back down the stairs.

"I don't know how far it's spread," he called over his shoulder, "but they're saying it started over in Bienville Street."

What should have been a twenty-minute race back to the regimental staff quarters became a journey through hell.

The streets were jammed with people, some running frantically to the river with bundles of possessions in their arms, others toward the fire. The stench of smoke grew stronger with every turn. Scorching heat rolled through the narrow streets. Nearer the old quarter, whole blocks were ablaze and flames turned night into day.

Eyes watering, lungs heaving, Daniel shoved through crowds and dodged barricades. Someone shouted at him to grab a bucket. A frantic woman caught his sleeve and begged his help lifting her husband's portrait onto a cart. He yanked his arm free, heaved the portrait atop the other furnishings in the wagon and ran on.

Louise kept up with him, panting and cursing the high wooden heels on her shoes. She lost one, didn't dare run through the dark streets without it.

"Daniel! Wait!"

She raced back, jammed her foot into the shoe, came pelting after him again. The flames forced them west, then north. In a desperate attempt to get around the conflagration, they cut through back alleys and clambered over gates.

Finally they reached Rue de Duc Bourgongne, some blocks above Bienville. The flames were well south of them now and moving toward the river. What remained behind were charred, blackened skeletons of buildings.

Some walls still stood. Others had caved in under the weight of collapsed roofs. Fire brigades were hard at work, throwing bucket after bucket of water on sizzling timbers to kill any remaining sparks. Women and children with faces blackened and wide, ghostlike eyes clutched whatever meager possessions they'd managed to save from the flames.

Louise's stomach roiled when she stumbled over a dog lying in the gutter. The stench of its charred fur filled her nostrils. Stables and chicken coops had gone, too, as had the swine penned in backyards. She could only pray Elizabeth, little Tess and the others in the apartments housing the regimental staff had escaped the terrible flames.

When they reached what used to be the apartments, she thought at first her prayers had been answered. The building was a smoldering mass of fallen timbers, but a frantic search of the crowd standing numb with shock a safe distance away gave her a clutch of hope.

"Daniel!"

She tugged on his arm, tried to turn him from the burnt timbers. He couldn't be moved. He stood like one turned to stone.

"Daniel, it's Tess! Over there!"

He turned then, and the despair on his face hit her like a blow.

"It's Tess," she said again, digging her nails into his sleeve. "The little one who stays with Elizabeth."

His wife's name pulled him from the dark place where he'd gone. He spun around, shook Louise off like a pesky fly and raced toward the girl.

"Morgan!"

A burly figure separated from the rest. Artillery Sergeant Tremayne was as big and barrel-chested as his wife was small and birdlike. Leaving his daughter to the care of her brothers, he strode forward.

"Elizabeth?" Daniel asked urgently.

"She's alive, or was a few hours ago," the sergeant told him, his voice raw and hoarse from the smoke. "She was badly burned when my Polly found her."

Louise put a fist to her mouth. Her glance flew to Daniel. His face could have been carved from the gray granite in the hills above the Arkansaw.

"How did it happen?"

"A candle toppled over. The missus smelled smoke and ran to your apartments. She found the bed ablaze and Elizabeth's nightdress alight."

"Mon Dieu!"

Both men ignored Louise's agonized whisper. "Polly dragged her out of bed and tried to smother the flames with a blanket," Tremayne continued grimly, "but the whole room had already gone to smoke. It was all she could do to get Elizabeth out and sound the alarm."

"Where's my wife now?"

"They took her to the hospital. Sisters of Charity, over on Canal Street, I think."

Daniel wheeled and set off at a run. Louise started to follow, but he threw a harsh order over his shoulder.

"Stay with the Tremaynes."

"No, I come with—"

"Stay with the Tremaynes," he snarled.

* * *

He was drenched in sweat and black from smoke by the time he reached the cluster of brick and mortar buildings that housed the Sisters of Charity Hospital.

A nun swathed in stained white robes met him at the entrance to the main building. Her eyes widening at his wild appearance, she hurried forward.

"Are you badly burned?"

"Not me," Daniel ground out. "My wife. Elizabeth Morgan. They brought her here."

"I don't know. We have so many—"

"Thin. Blonde. Green eyes. Wearing a muslin nightdress—or what remained of it."

"Ah, yes. She's in the women's ward. I'll escort you, but—" Her brown eyes filled with sympathy. "You must prepare yourself."

The wooden rosary hanging from her rope belt rattled as she led him down a short hall awash with the odors of camphor, eucalyptus oil and charred flesh. The women's ward occupied a long, open hall. Cots crowded the room, every one occupied. Heat rose in palpable waves and mingled with the stench from the slop buckets. A half dozen or so sisters tended the injured. Blood and vomit stained the aprons they wore over their white robes.

"Your wife is there," the sister said, gesturing to a cot placed halfway down the hall. "The netting helps keep the mosquitoes from the fluids seeping through her bandages."

Agonizing images of an injured Elizabeth had haunted Daniel all the way to the hospital, but not even the worst of his imaginings compared to what he saw when he lifted the netting.

Bandages stained to a pale pink swathed her head, her shoulders, her entire body. Even her face was covered, leaving only small slits for her nose and mouth. A few charred strands of hair—her once beautiful, moonlit hair—showed through the bandages.

"The only mercy is that she feels no pain," the sister said quietly. "She's not awakened since they brought her in. Nor will she, until God decides she's strong enough to bear the agony. *If* He so decides," she added. "Her lungs were seared. Each breath comes harder than the last."

She spoke the truth. Daniel could hear the shallow rasp over his own labored breathing.

"Do you wish to stay with her?"

"Yes."

She moved to the next cot, returned with an empty bucket. Too numb to voice any thanks, he upended the wooden bucket and sank down.

He ached to reach for Elizabeth's hand, to stroke it as he so often did, but he kept his clenched fists in his lap. He'd seen his share of oozing, festering blisters, had heard the howls of pain from troopers who'd set their tents too close to campfires or been set ablaze by barrels of burning pitch flung over palisades. Remembering their shrieks, he could only sit and damn himself with each slow, rattling breath that his wife drew into her tortured lungs.

He shouldn't have brought Elizabeth to New Orleans. Shouldn't have left her with only Polly Tremayne to look in on her.

And he surely to God shouldn't have spent that stolen hour with Louise in a squalid tavern by the river.

Slumping, he propped his elbows on his knees, covered his face with his hands and prayed his wife would forgive him.

Elizabeth died two hours past dawn.

She didn't wake, didn't so much as stir. Daniel was beside her cot, listening to every tormented breath, branding each one on his conscience until the terrible rattling ended.

He sat on the upturned bucket, staring down at her bandaged form, until another sister came and stood with him. Over the moans of the other patients, she fingered her beads and murmured a quiet prayer.

"We must move her," she said after a moment. "The injured still arrive. We need the cot."

Like an old, bent man, Daniel pushed to his feet. "Give me time to build her coffin."

"Of course. We'll wrap her in clean linen and say prayers for her soul. Come and claim her when you're ready. It must be soon," the sister warned gently. "Today, if possible. The heat, the flies, they will grow worse."

His jaw working, he nodded.

Daniel walked outside to a dawn made gray by smoke and low clouds. Thunder rumbled across the river. Rain drizzled down to mingle with the sweat and soot on his face and send stinging rivulets into his eyes.

Most of the flames were out, he noted in a distant corner of his mind. The rain would soon finish the job the volunteer fire brigades had begun. Weary men and women streamed past, carrying buckets and pails and tubs. The fire had threatened every home, brought every citizen running. Merchants in waistcoats and shirtsleeves, some in nightcaps. Streetwalkers decked in gaudy stripes and scorched feathers. Soldiers, rivermen, voodoo sellers with red-rimmed eyes and bright kerchiefs wrapped around their heads.

Even, Daniel thought as his entire body went taut, Spaniards with thin black mustaches and gold rings in one ear.

His fury when he'd found Louise sprawled naked on a bed in a hot, stuffy attic chamber didn't begin to compare to the rage that exploded inside him now. This man—or one who looked much like him—had invaded his quarters, kidnapped Louise, put hands on his wife.

With a savage cry that sounded much like the scream of the panther that had ripped out Henri Chartier's throat, Daniel lunged through the straggling crowd. Nightcaps went flying. Pails clattered against the cobbles. Shouts and curses followed him.

The dark-haired Spaniard heard the commotion, glanced over his shoulder as Daniel charged straight for him. Any doubt he was one of the men who'd stalked Louise to the regimental staff quarters vanished when he dropped his bucket and ran.

With the speed and single-minded determination of a panther hard on the heels of its prey, Daniel chased the Spaniard across the square and into a narrow alley. He thought about pulling out his pistol and bringing the man down, but didn't reach for his holster. He wanted his hands around the man's throat.

He wouldn't strangle him. Not until he'd learned why he'd laid hands on Elizabeth and taken Louise. But he'd make the bastard beg for every gasp.

He could taste the revenge, felt the juice of it stir in his mouth. His lips curling back, he pounded out of the alley hard on his quarry's heels.

The Spaniard sent a look over his shoulder, swore viciously and plowed through a group of schoolgirls in gray dresses and soiled white pinafores. One went down. Another squealed in fright. Daniel dodged around them.

The Spaniard raced on, leaping a wooden barricade, trying to lose his pursuer in the smoking ruins. The half-burned timbers spearing through the tumbled brick and masonry fired Daniel's rage. So much destruction. So much pain. The Spaniard would pay for his part in it, whatever that was.

Daniel jumped a tumbled black iron cooking pot, almost lost his footing in the rubble, and suddenly, swiftly, skidded to a halt. His prey had run himself into a corner.

Caught up short by the smoking remains of what was once a baker's shop, the Spaniard whirled and dropped into a crouch among the still glowing timbers. Knife in hand, he spit out a stream of words. With a feral smile, Daniel sidestepped a timber burned down to a sharpened stake.

"No *comprendre,* you slit-nosed son of a whore."

He stalked him, inching closer. He could smell the man's fear over the stink of smoke, see the sweat pearl on his face and mix with the rain. The Spaniard slashed the blade from side to side and lunged.

Dancing to one side, Daniel brought his hand chopping down on the man's wrist with all the force in his powerful body. The bone snapped like a dry twig.

With a howl of rage and pain, the Spaniard grabbed the knife in his other hand, twisted around in the rubble and lunged again. This time, Daniel's fist smashed into his face and shattered the bridge of his nose. Blood gushed out in great crimson spurts. An animal howl ripped from the man's throat.

"That was for Louise."

The blood roaring in his ears, Daniel doubled his fist.

"This is for Elizabeth."

He put all his fury, all his grief, into the vicious swing.

The uppercut snapped the Spaniard's head back. He staggered a few paces, tripped over the blackened pot, fell. Arms flailing, he landed on one of the still-glowing timbers. The charred, jagged tip drove through his back and out through his stomach.

"Aaaaiii!"

His agonized scream ripped through the streets. Impaled, he writhed frantically on the hot stake. The scent of burning, sizzling flesh mingled with the stink of smoke.

His scream rose to a long, ear-shattering shriek. Before the echoes of it died, he flopped his arms and legs once, twice, then lay still.

Slowly, the red mists of Daniel's rage parted. His one regret, his only regret, was that he hadn't choked the information he wanted from the man before he died. Ignoring the wide-eyed bystanders who'd been drawn to the scene by the Spaniard's cries, he climbed over the rubble, reached down and tore the gold ring from the bastard's ear.

18

Troops moved in and established order in the ravaged section of the city with military efficiency. A cordon was set up to keep out looters, with street blocks at every corner. Guards stopped Daniel twice before they recognized his soot-stained uniform and allowed him through.

He found Louise where he'd left her. Skirts blackened, hair hanging in a wet tangle, she worked side by side with the Tremaynes to pick through the ruins for the few possessions that had survived the flames.

A small corner of Daniel's mind not numbed by grief and guilt felt a sort of detached wonder at her resilience. Despite all that had happened, she refused to succumb to despair or the weariness etched in every line of her body. Both ate at him with every step.

Polly Tremayne was bent over beside Louise. Her hair, too, hung in rattails. Her small, thin frame slumped with fatigue. She picked up a melted, misshapen object and rubbed a hand over it. Fighting tears, she turned to toss the object into a cart filled with what remained of her home, and spotted Daniel. A murmured word brought Louise's head up.

Their gazes found each other's above the mounds of rubble. She made a small keening sound, her blue eyes flooding with the same guilt and sorrow Daniel knew he would carry for the rest of his life.

It was left to hulking Sergeant Tremayne to clamber over the debris and put the question into words.

"Elizabeth?"

Daniel shook his head.

"Ahh, man. I'm sorry."

Tremayne's wife joined him. "She would have suffered so for her burns. It's for the best."

Daniel wanted to believe her, but he hadn't come to that point yet. "I thank you for what you did for Elizabeth."

"I'm only sorry I didn't find her sooner."

"You got her out," her husband said gruffly, laying an arm across her shoulders. "Her and the rest. You did all you could, Missus."

Daniel's gaze went past them to the remains of what had once been their home.

"I've not drawn all my wilderness pay," he told Tremayne. "It won't replace everything you lost, but it will help get you and your family back on your feet."

The beefy artillery sergeant scratched the bristles on his cheek. "Well, I won't deny we could use a bit of help. But won't you be needing the funds yourself? You've got a coffin to buy and a wife to bury."

"I'll build her coffin myself."

"Lumber may be hard to come by right now," Tremayne warned. "With so much rebuilding to do, pine boards will be dearer than gold."

A muscle jumped in the side of Daniel's jaw. "I'll find the boards."

"Bernard Thibodeaux sells lumber," Louise said quietly. "If the fire did not take his shop, he will give you what you need. Come, we will go to him now."

They picked their way through the rubble, watching for rusted nails and sharp objects until they gained a clear stretch of undamaged banquette. Unspeaking, Louise walked beside Daniel. She knew no words of hers could ease the burden he now carried.

He blamed himself for Elizabeth's horrific death. She'd seen that in a single glance. He'd held to his vows to his wife for so long. Had cared for her with such gentleness. Yet he would remember none of what went before, only that he'd been in bed with another woman while flames consumed Elizabeth.

Would he ever think of their time together without shame?

Would Louise?

A sick feeling rose in her stomach, adding to the bitter taste of remorse and grief. She'd done this. She'd caused this pain. She'd all but begged Daniel to lie with her last night, had done all she could to tempt him from his vows to his wife.

Like the blue-eyed woman of the legend, she brought nothing but disaster to those around her.

They met Bernard Thibodeaux at his shop. Stoop-shouldered and red-eyed, he and several of his hired help were just returning from a night of manning the buckets. While his shop clerks and house servants went wearily to their various tasks, Louise gave him a brief recount of her abduction and Elizabeth's death.

"A bad business," the portly merchant muttered, shaking his head. "A very bad business all around. I sorrow for your loss, Sergeant Major."

"Thank you. I came not only to bring Louise home but to purchase planking for my wife's coffin."

"Of course. There's good, solid oak in the storeroom. Nails and tools, too. You're welcome to whatever you need." He shook his head again. "Will you take her home for burial?"

"We have no home."

Thibodeaux blinked at the stark pronouncement. Daniel couldn't tell him of the many posts the army had assigned him to, of how Elizabeth had withdrawn into the shadows a little more each time he packed her up and moved her to another unfamiliar place.

"My wife's parents settled in North Carolina, but are gone now. I'll have to see what arrangements I can make here in New Orleans."

"My family has a vault in a cemetery not far from

here. If you wish to make use of it, your wife will sleep peacefully there.''

''I... Thank you.''

''Let me wash and change, then I'll see to the funeral carriage and cortege.''

''I, too, must wash and change,'' Louise said as the merchant went up the stairs. ''I'll leave you to your task, unless... Do you wish me to help you?''

''No.''

''I did not think so.'' She hesitated, worrying her lower lip. ''Daniel, my heart weeps for Elizabeth and for you. I know you hate me for what happened between us this night. Always I will hate myself for causing such hurt to you and your wife.''

Her torment pierced his own. He'd been so lost to his own misery he hadn't spared a thought for her. ''You're not to blame for any of this.''

''But I am! They spoke the truth when they named me, no? The accursed one.''

She would have turned away, but he caught her elbow. Guilt and grief filled every corner of his soul, so much so that he'd almost forgotten the Spaniard.

''I brought you something.''

He shoved a hand into his pocket. When she saw the glint of gold in his palm, a savage satisfaction sprang into her eyes.

''The mustached one! When did you find him?''

''After I left Elizabeth.''

''Did he admit to striking her or taking me?''

''No.''

"At least tell me he suffered greatly when he died," she begged.

"He did."

"Good!"

She claimed the gory trophy, just as she had the claws Daniel had brought her so many months ago.

"I will pray to the God of the whites and the spirits who guide the Osage," she said fiercely. "May the crows pick the eyes and strip the flesh from the bones of the one who wore this."

The provost marshal and a troop of armed guards came for Daniel an hour later.

He'd removed his filthy uniform jacket and was working with sleeves rolled up in the quiet of the storeroom. The clean, sharp smell of sawdust blotted out the stink of smoke as he measured cuts, sawed boards and planed the oak to a smooth, hard finish. The work had occupied his hands. Thoughts of Elizabeth had filled his mind. So lost was he in memories that he looked up blankly when the door to the storeroom banged open.

"He's in here."

Thibodeaux's wide-eyed clerk stepped aside and a blue-jacketed lieutenant strode in. A detachment of guards crowded in after him. Rifles at the ready, bayonets gleaming dully in the dim light, they took up positions on the lieutenant's flanks.

"Sergeant Major Morgan?"

"Yes."

"I'm Provost Marshal Lieutenant Cappingham. It is my duty to place you under arrest."

The clerk gasped and slipped out. Daniel heard him pounding up the stairs as he straightened and laid aside the plane.

"On what charge?"

"The charges will be read to you at the *cabildo*."

He'd expected this. He knew he'd have to answer for the death of the Spaniard, but with all the confusion from the fire, he hadn't thought the military police would come after him this soon.

He'd also have to answer for pummeling Lieutenant Wilkinson, he remembered belatedly. Everything else that had happened since he'd stormed into Wilkinson's rooms had all but pushed that incident from his mind.

Assaulting an officer was no light matter. If done during a mutiny or in the face of the enemy, it was a hanging offense. More than one officer had taken his licks during drunken barracks brawls, however. Given Daniel's years of service and spotless record to date, he'd most likely be sentenced to the lash.

He'd take the strokes. He had no choice. But he wasn't done with Wilkinson yet.

"You will surrender your weapons, Sergeant."

He'd hooked his cross belt with its cartridge case and leather holster over the end of a sawhorse, just out of reach. Mindful of the leveled bayonets, he let his hand hover over the holster. In all his years of service, he'd never asked for a personal favor. He asked for one now.

"I'll surrender the pistol, Lieutenant, but I beg an hour to attend to personal affairs."

"I have no authority to—"

"I must bury my wife. She died of burns from the fire."

"I'm aware of that, Sergeant Major," the lieutenant said coldly. Nodding, he sent one of the guards forward. "Take his weapons."

The man kept a wary eye on the would-be prisoner as he retrieved the cross belt.

"Attach the shackles," Cappingham ordered.

The rattle of the chains had Daniel curling his fists. He wasn't marching off to the *cabildo* before he buried Elizabeth. He'd always despise himself for leaving her to suffer agonizing burns. He'd be damned to hell and back before he'd allow strangers to claim her body.

Tensing, he waited for the guard shaking out the shackles to take one step, just one. He'd snatch the irons out of the man's hands, wrap the chain around his throat and use him to—

A clatter on the stairs broke into his black thoughts.

"What goes on here?"

Huffing, Bernard rushed into the storeroom. Louise pushed in right behind him. Instantly, Daniel abandoned any idea of taking the guard hostage. He would have risked his own skin against a troop of armed men, but he couldn't risk hers.

"Who are you?" the merchant demanded.

"I'm Provost Marshal Lieutenant Cappingham. Identify yourself, sir."

"I am Bernard Thibodeaux. This is my shop."

Cappingham's gaze narrowed on Louise. "And this woman?"

She'd changed into a clean gown and scrubbed away the soot, but her hair still fell in damp tangles over her shoulders and, Daniel saw, she clasped her skinning knife in one hand.

"This is Madame Chartier," Bernard answered. "What goes on here? Why are you and these soldiers in my shop?"

"We've come to take Sergeant Major Morgan into custody."

"But why? What has he done?"

"The formal charges will be read to him at the *cabildo*."

"But his wife," Louise protested. "She dies and must be buried this day."

"Someone else will have to attend to it."

With a low growl, Daniel cursed the officer's callousness, but the very coldness of his reply had roused instincts dulled by grief and rage. Something wasn't right here. No military man would deny another the chance to bury his dead. Wilkinson was behind this, Daniel guessed with a sudden tightening in his gut. Or his father.

"I'll answer to whatever charges have been laid against me," he told Louise urgently, "but I want you on that ship to France and gone when I do."

"Daniel—"

"I'm afraid Madame Chartier won't be allowed to board any ship," Cappingham interrupted. "She's been named as a witness to give evidence at your court-martial."

"Madame Chartier wasn't present when I struck Lieutenant Wilkinson or fought with the Spaniard," he said tersely. "She has no firsthand knowledge of either event."

"You mistake the matter, Sergeant Major. You're not being charged with assaulting Lieutenant Wilkinson, and I know nothing of any Spaniard."

"Then what the devil is this about?"

"You are to answer for the fire that caused the death of your wife."

He felt as though the heavens had opened and God had hurled a thunderbolt at him. They knew he'd left Elizabeth alone, knew she'd been unable to tend to herself. They blamed him for her tragic death, just as he blamed himself. He couldn't refute the charge, couldn't speak a word of denial.

Louise experienced no such restraint. Raging, she confronted the lieutenant. "What you say is beyond anything incredible! This man would not harm the woman he has loved and cared for all these years!"

The provost marshal looked her up and down again, this time with insulting thoroughness. He was too well trained to sneer, but the sound of it was in his voice.

"As I understand the charges, Madame Chartier, it is now believed the sergeant major decided to rid himself of one wife in order to take another."

The flat statement dragged Daniel from the depths of his own private hell. They weren't accusing him of neglect, but of murder! Of deliberately causing Elizabeth such suffering and torment.

Fury rose hot and swift, and he had to fight the animal urge to leap forward and wrap his hands around the lieutenant's throat. Savagely, he beat his rage into submission. He wouldn't help himself or Louise by adding to the crimes already leveled against him.

"What evidence is there to support this charge?" he demanded.

"You'll be made privy to the evidence when you're brought before the court, but I'm told there is a statement to the effect that you and Madame Chartier engaged in adulterous conduct while traveling together."

Wilkinson! That could only have come from Wilkinson. It wasn't true, but what court would believe that now? Especially if the fat tavern keeper attested to the fact that Daniel and Louise had spent hours together last night in that small, dim room.

"There are also statements indicating you objected to the order to bring your wife to New Orleans," the lieutenant continued coldly. "Reliable witnesses have stated that you were closeted privately with Madame Chartier in your quarters several times after your wife's arrival, and that you flew into a jealous rage when Lieutenant Wilkinson began paying court to her."

Christ! Someone had spun a fast web to gather all this evidence so quickly.

"Then there's the matter of her pending inheritance," Cappingham said, his lip curling. "Reports are it's considerably more than a sergeant major draws in pay."

The web had not only been spun fast, Daniel realized grimly, it had been spun fine. And it was beginning to look as if it might yet be woven into a noose.

Lieutenant Wilkinson couldn't have pulled all these strands together. Not this swiftly. Or this ruthlessly. He might have the brains but he didn't have the guts. There was more going on than Daniel grasped, but for the life of him, he couldn't figure out what or how Louise played into it.

He needed time to think matters through. Needed to force his mind past the shock and grief over Elizabeth. Right now, it looked as if the only place he'd have that time was in the *cabildo* prison.

"Stay here with the Thibodeauxs until I sort this out," he told Louise tersely. "Bernard, see that you mount a close guard over her."

"I will."

"Daniel!"

Her nails dug into his arm. Her eyes reflected confusion and a mounting fear, but she put both aside to make him a fierce promise.

"I shall see to Elizabeth. I swear to you she shall be taken care of. And I shall have the lawyers Bernard hires to press my claim come to the *cabildo*.

They can speak for you, tell whoever makes these charges how absurd they are.''

The lieutenant was out of patience. ''Guard, fix the shackles.''

Louise claimed Elizabeth's body and buried her that same afternoon.

Bernard apologized several times for the procession that wove its way through the rain-damp streets. He'd done his best on such short notice, but worried that the funeral lacked the color and style of a typical New Orleans burial.

Since Elizabeth was not of the Catholic faith, he hadn't paid for a mass to be said, but had arranged for a priest to accompany the cortege and say a few words at the cemetery. A hearse drawn by four horses with black plumes attached to their halters carried the plain oak coffin. Louise, the priest and the Thibodeaux family walked behind the hearse, the hired mourners walked ahead. Their keening turned heads and drew curious glances, but none of the bystanders joined in the procession, as so often happened. They'd seen enough funerals this day.

Helene Thibodeaux had loaned Louise the proper mourning clothes. The high-waisted black jersey gown hung loosely on her small frame. Its skirts trailed the wet, damp cobbles and its long mitten sleeves covered all but the tips of her fingers. A heavy veil, draped over the brim of her hat, shielded her face as well as her thoughts.

The burial ground where Bernard's ancestors

rested was a strange place, shaded by moss-covered oaks and crowded with raised marble crypts that held many coffins. Like the Osage, the people of New Orleans did not put their dead into the ground. But neither did they put them on high biers to shorten their journey to the spirit world. As Bernard quietly explained, they raised them above the ground so the water just under the surface of this city built on silt would not seep into their coffins and wash away their bones.

The tombs lay so close together that the carriage could not proceed beyond a certain point. The hired mourners took Elizabeth's coffin from the carriage, lifted it onto their shoulders and followed Bernard through the maze. He halted before a marble vault mounted by an angel with great, spread wings. The cemetery keeper was waiting. Hobbling on his one leg, he unlocked the tomb's iron gate. Louise stared into the darkness of the crypt as the priest said a few words. When he finished, Elizabeth's coffin was carried into the darkness.

The mourners pocketed the coins Bernard handed them and dispersed. The priest took a generous contribution and left as well. Helene shepherded her daughters down the path.

"It's done," Bernard said quietly.

"No," Louise whispered. "Not yet. I have words to say to Elizabeth."

"I'll wait for you with Helene and the girls, then."

She heard his boots crunch on the shell, heard the

clip-clop of the horses' hooves as the carriage drove away. Still she stared into the darkness.

A breeze sighed through the moss hanging from the oaks. As if called by the spirits, she stepped inside the dank darkness of the tomb, reached into her pocket and laid a gold earring atop the oak coffin.

"Your husband avenges you, Elizabeth. I give you this to take into the spirit world with you."

She backed out of the crypt and stood silent while the cemetery keeper limped over. The iron gate clanged shut. The key rattled in its rusted padlock.

Still it wasn't done. She had one last vow to make.

"This I swear to you. I will not rest until Daniel is free to mourn you properly."

Nor would his wife, Louise thought as another breeze whispered through the moss.

19

Restless and consumed with worry, Louise fretted through the next four days. Bernard attempted without success to obtain a pass for her to visit the *cabildo* prison, while his lawyers hemmed and hawed over the matters to be presented to the military court that would try Daniel.

"They say the evidence is rather daunting," the merchant told Louise when he joined her and his family for dinner the evening of the fourth day. Candles flickered in their holders and the scent of braised pork and mushrooms set his ample stomach to rumbling. Waiting until he'd been served a generous portion and the servants had left the family *en table*, Bernard picked up the thread of his thoughts.

"The tribunal is scheduled to convene in a week. The woman who cared for Elizabeth... I forget her name."

"Polly Tremayne."

"She'll likely be called to give witness. As will you."

"Me, I will not speak against Daniel," Louise said hotly. "Nor will Mistress Tremayne."

"Not willingly perhaps, but her husband wears a uniform and, well, there's no denying the woman found Elizabeth ablaze shortly after Daniel left her."

Louise sat silent, her hands tight in her lap, while Bernard sopped up some gravy with a piece of crusty bread.

"A good many people lost all they owned in the fire," he said between bites. "Public anger runs high against the man many are now saying started it to be rid of his feebleminded wife."

"How can they say this! It is not true."

She could tell from the quick glance he shared with his wife that there was worse to come.

"I haven't showed the newspapers to you," Helene admitted, "but they're calling for Daniel to be hanged from the nearest street lamp."

Louise sprang up, sick at hearing her worst fears spoken aloud. "No! No, I tell you! I will not let such a thing happen."

"What can you do?" Helene asked. "Your association with him has already called your credibility into question."

"I—I must think on this!"

She pushed away from the table and retreated to her room. The alcove bed and privy closet that had so fascinated her when she'd first arrived held no interest now. All she could think about was the military tribunal that would convene within a week.

Skirts swirling, Louise paced the room. Her low-heeled slippers sank into the rose-patterned carpet. The oil in her bedside lamp had burned low when she finally decided on a plan of action.

She would go to see James. If he was the one behind her abduction, if he wanted to marry her so much that he would resort to such desperate measures, she would barter herself in exchange for Daniel's freedom.

And if James lacked the authority to arrange his release, his father certainly did not. The general commanded all the troops in Louisiana Territory. His word was law. He could dismiss these absurd charges against Daniel. He must.

Shoulders slumping, Louise dropped down on the patterned silk coverlet. So much had happened so very swiftly that she could scarcely recall a time now when she wasn't sick with worry and regret and shame. Could hardly remember the time before she'd opened the door to Daniel's quarters and seen Elizabeth held in the brutal grip of the Spaniards.

At least one of them had paid for that!

Her brief spurt of satisfaction gave way to the troubled thoughts that now followed her like a shadow. Daniel had not yet been charged with the Spaniard's death. He'd given her no details of what had occurred, but surely someone had seen the two men fight and could identify, by his uniform, the one left standing. A second charge would only add to the difficulties he faced.

She flopped back onto the coverlet, threw an arm

over her face and tried to shut out the image of a knotted rope swinging from a gallows.

She rose with the dawn, hollow-eyed and fixed in her determination to go to James. She could see no other path to take. When she announced her desire to speak with him, Bernard and Helene both objected strenuously.

"Daniel said you were to stay here until he sorted matters out."

"How can he do this in prison? Each day that passes tightens the rope around his neck. No, I must plead with James to intercede. Bernard, will you send Thomas to tell him I must to speak with him? Make sure he tells James it is most urgent that I see him."

The Thibodeauxs' manservant returned an hour later with word that Lieutenant Wilkinson very much regretted that military duties precluded a meeting with Madame Chartier until seven o'clock this evening. He'd be honored to call at Doumaine Street at that hour, or receive her at his quarters should that prove more convenient. Deciding that what she had to say to the lieutenant was best said away from Helene and her daughters, Louise sent word she'd visit him at his quarters.

She dressed carefully for the meeting. The finest silk stockings. Garters trimmed with lace. A gown of cherry-striped muslin, with delicate embroidery bordering the cuffs and square neckline. Deliberately, she tugged the bodice lower to show more of her breasts. After tying the ribbons of a bonnet lavishly trimmed with feathers, she pulled on lace mittens. As a final thought, she slipped her skinning knife into her drawstring reticule.

Bernard ordered his coach to carry them to the Royal Arms. Thomas and another well-muscled servant accompanied them. The house servant stayed with the carriage, but Bernard insisted the other come upstairs with him and Louise.

"I must speak with James alone," she said, her nerves as taut as a bowstring now that she was here.

"That's all well and good, but first I'll make sure he knows I'm here."

The servant who answered his knock looked surprised to see such a gathering at the door. "Lieutenant Wilkinson returned late from parade. He's just washing the dirt from his hands. Will you come in and take a glass of wine?"

"My man and I will wait downstairs in the taproom. Louise, send word when you're ready to leave."

She nodded, her throat too tight for speech.

The corporal showed her into a sitting room made comfortable with a scattering of books and various personal items.

"I'll inform the lieutenant you're here."

He closed the doors to the bedroom behind him. Strung too tight to sit, Louise wandered to the fireplace. A carriage clock ticked on the mantel beside a collection of miniatures in folding leather frames. She recognized Major General Wilkinson in full dress uniform and had just glanced at the woman in the other frame when James came into the sitting room.

He was still in uniform, she saw when she turned to greet him, and even more nervous than she. He tried to put on a friendly smile but it barely creased his cheeks.

"Madame Chartier. Louise. I did not hope to see you again after our last meeting."

"Which meeting do you speak of, James?"

"Why, the one in the Thibodeauxs' parlor, of course. Will you take a dish of tea or glass of wine?"

"No."

He fingered his neck cloth, wilted from his long day in uniform. "I was told you wished to speak to me on a matter of some urgency. May I ask what it is?"

She'd thought it would be so easy to make the bargain. Now that the moment had come, she had to force the words. "I have decided I will marry you."

The blunt declaration dropped the lieutenant's jaw. He gaped at her, agog, until Louise had to bite back a sharp request that he close his mouth.

"What...? When...?" He gulped and tried again. "Why have you changed your mind?"

"Because of Daniel."

"Sergeant Major Morgan?" A stunned look came over his face. "Morgan sent you here with this...this proposal?"

"Daniel does not know I come."

She crossed the room to stand before him, wanting

him to know the terms of their bargain, needing to
see his eyes when he understood. "But if we are to
marry, you must see he goes free."

"I can't do that!"

"You can. You must. You know him. You traveled many miles together. He cared for you when
you were sick with fever. He wiped your face and
spooned broth into you. You know he would not
harm his wife."

"No, I don't," the lieutenant protested weakly.
"He came to my quarters. He assaulted me. I didn't
lay charges against him because, as you said, he gave
me great service during the expedition. But now
that his negligence in the matter of his wife has
been—"

"I will hear no buts," Louise said fiercely. "Do
you want me, James? Do you?"

Sweat popped out on the lieutenant's brow. He
hooked a finger in his cravat again, tugging at the
linen as though it choked him.

"Yes, I do."

"To have me, you must set Daniel free."

"I can't," he said again. "I don't have the authority."

"Your father does."

"My father is not here. He left New Orleans the
day after the fire. He's on his way to Richmond to
give evidence at the Burr trial."

Staggered by the news, Louise pressed the heel of
her hand against her forehead and tried to think. She
didn't know this place called Richmond. Was it a

great distance from New Orleans? Dropping her hand, she pinned the lieutenant with a glare.

"You will send a messenger after him, tell him Daniel must be freed."

"It will take weeks for a letter to reach my father. Morgan is to be taken before a court in six days' time."

"Delay this court. Tell them you write to your father. Tell them they must wait until you receive word back from him."

The suggestion penetrated the welter of thoughts clamoring around inside James's head. He'd been in a sweat since receiving word that Louise wanted to speak with him this afternoon, had been sure she'd come to accuse him as Morgan had when he'd stormed into these same apartments.

James hadn't slept except in fits and starts since. The fire had brought him running into the streets the first night, and word that Morgan had found Louise Chartier naked and drugged had haunted his every waking moment after that.

He hadn't laid the charges against Morgan for the death of his wife. Those had come from his father's chief of staff, Colonel Matthews, after hearing the circumstances of Elizabeth Morgan's death and assessing the devastation caused by the fire. Someone had to answer for that. Someone had to satisfy the howls of outrage from citizens who had lost so much. James had breathed a secret sigh of relief when Matthews decided that that someone was Morgan.

And now this!

Desperately, James tried to decide how to respond to Louise's remarkable demand. Perhaps he *should* talk to Matthews. Ask him to delay the court-martial. Buy some time to write to his father and get the general's guidance on how to proceed with this startling change of circumstances.

No, he didn't need guidance. He knew what his father would say. Despite betraying Aaron Burr to save his own neck, the general hadn't given up his dreams of carving an empire for himself out of the vast Louisiana Territory. The woman standing before James now represented his father's last hope for that empire.

She was rich, or would be when the damned lawyers finished with their endless letters. She combined both French and Osage blood and could, he hoped, rally those peoples to her cause. She claimed ties, however remote, to royalty.

And, he admitted, his glance straying to the swell of her breasts, she was very much a woman. Swiping his damp palms down the sides of his uniform jacket, James took a deep breath.

"I would be honored to take you in marriage."

"And you will see that Daniel is released?"

"I'll see that his trial is delayed" was all he would promise. "Until I hear back from my father."

Her breath escaped in a little hiss. For the life of him, James couldn't tell whether that signified anger or agreement. He curled his hands to hide the sweat pooling in his palms and stood stiffly until she nodded.

"It is done." She turned away and started for the door. "I leave you to make what arrangements you must."

"It's not done yet."

"What do you mean?"

James wet his lips. He'd never know where he got the daring for what he was about to propose. "I mean you should stay and watch me write the letter to my father. That way you will know I keep my word. And in return, you must show you will keep yours."

She cocked her head, her eyes wary. "How am I to show this?"

"By coming to my bed. Tonight. And staying here with me until we marry."

She stood silent for so long, James was sure he'd overplayed his hand. Nervously, he cleared his throat.

"You must understand my position. You rejected me most embarrassingly that night in the Thibodeauxs' parlor. I'm only seeking to make sure—"

"Yes."

"I beg your pardon?"

"Yes, I will bed with you."

Not sure he'd heard her right, he demanded confirmation. "Here? Now?"

"Here," she said stonily. "Now."

"And you'll stay with me until we're wed?"

"Yes."

By God, he'd done it!

"Write this letter to your father," she said, her

voice flat. "I shall go down and tell Bernard I do not go back to Doumaine Street with him."

When she walked out, his elation went up like a puff of smoke. She wouldn't return. He'd bet his last copper penny she'd change her mind and scurry away. Either that or Bernard Thibodeaux would come pounding on the door, pistol in hand. If so, he'd better be prepared.

Calling to his batman, James strode into the bedroom.

"Simons! Lay out my pistol. And my frogged dressing gown," he added, just in case.

Louise expected Bernard to object to the bargain she'd struck—and he did. Long and vigorously. Drawing her into a private corner of the taproom, he laid out argument after argument against the scheme.

Wilkinson had not promised to release Daniel, only to delay the trial. Daniel might still hang.

If Louise went to the lieutenant's bed like this, he could well decide not to marry her, but keep her as a mistress.

And if they did marry, she would be tied to the man for life. Was that what she wanted? Was it?

"No, but it is what I must do."

"He'll have control of your fortune. Of you."

"He is weak. If we marry, I will arrange matters to suit me."

"He may be weak, but his father is not. I tell you, Louise—"

She gripped the agitated merchant's arm, stilling

him. "I am no untried maiden who has never shared a man's blanket. I know what I do here."

"Daniel would not agree!"

No, he would not. Daniel didn't believe in the legend, wouldn't accept that one cursed such as she brought only disaster to those she loved. Nor would he agree Louise owed this to him—and to Elizabeth.

"This is not Daniel's decision," she said quietly. "Nor is it yours, Bernard."

"A wheelbarrel full of difference that will make!" the red-faced merchant retorted. "Morgan will have my head when he hears I was the one who brought you here."

"If you had not, I would have come alone." She squeezed his arm and stood up. "I thank you for all you have done for me. You and Helene and your so kind daughters. Now I must ask you to leave. Send my things to me here, if you will."

He made a final, desperate plea. "Louise, this is madness. Will you not reconsider?"

"No."

When the servant answered her knock for the second time, his eyes were as round as moons. He craned his neck and searched the hallway in either direction before stepping aside to allow her entry.

James stood beside the mantel, nervously fingering a pistol that lay within easy reach. He'd exchanged his uniform jacket for a dressing gown and his boots for felt slippers, but still looked as though his linen stock choked him. When his servant shut the door behind Louise, the lieutenant's breath escaped on a low, whistling sigh.

Relief that she'd returned? she wondered. Or regret?

She walked to the center of the room and stood silent while James studied her face. Whatever he saw there seemed to reassure him. Waving a hand, he dismissed his servant.

"That will be all for tonight, Simons. You may return to your quarters."

"Yes, sir."

When the door thumped shut, James seemed at a loss over what to do next. Finally, he reached out to relieve Louise of the cashmere shawl draped over her elbows. Carefully, he folded it across the back of a chair.

"Shall I take your hat? And your bag?"

Wordlessly, Louise untied the ribbons of her bonnet. She handed him the feathered creation, which he laid beside the shawl. When he took the reticule, however, the weight of it drew a surprised glance.

"What do you carry in here?"

"A handkerchief. Some coins. My skinning knife."

His cheeks lost their color. "I'll put it on the mantel, shall I? Out of the way."

Shoving aside the pistol and leather-framed miniatures, he made room for the bag. When he returned, she asked whether he'd written the letter he'd promised.

"Yes. It's there, beside my writing desk." With a

little flourish, he indicated the small wooden box with a slanted lid.

She'd seen him use it many times during the journey down the Arkansaw to write notes in his journal. Its lid was propped up, revealing a supply of papers, quills and ink. A page filled with writing lay beside the box on the table.

"Do you wish to read it?"

She wouldn't admit that she could not. She didn't trust him not to go back on his promise and change the wording.

"I do not need to read it. You must know I will use my knife on you while you sleep if you do not hold to your end of our bargain."

"I'll hold to it. Will you?"

"Yes."

He hesitated several moments before bending his head. His lips were dry with nervousness. His breath carried the flavor of brandy.

Opening her mouth to him, Louise used her tongue in the way Henri had taught her.

James was young, but not as strong as Daniel. And, she soon discovered, nowhere near as skilled as Henri at bringing a woman to pleasure.

He escorted Louise into the bedchamber and stripped both her and himself down to their small clothes with fumbling haste. He didn't take the time to remove her chemise. Yanking the straps down to her elbows to bare her breasts, he suckled eagerly. His teeth tugged too hard on the nipple, but she made no complaint. Nor did she protest when he rolled her onto her belly, found the slit in her drawers, and rammed into her from behind.

Two thrusts and he was groaning.

Five, and he was done.

He fell atop her, grunting. His body was damp with sweat, his breath hot in her ear. She lay under him, pressed into the bedsheets by his weight, until he slid off and flopped onto his back.

She lay awake, staring into the darkness, long after he began to snore.

20

The batman, Simons, arrived the next morning with rich, steaming chocolate and sugar-dusted beignets fresh from the inn's kitchens. Avoiding Louise's eye, he laid out a small table by the wavy-paned window in the sitting room.

"Sit here, my dear."

James held a chair for her. Louise smoothed the wrinkles from her blue gown, accepted a cup of chocolate, but refused the pastries. She could not eat now if a whole roasted deer sizzled on the spit.

The lieutenant suffered no lack of appetite. He devoured his in two bites and reached for another. "You really should eat one of these cakes."

"I have no hunger."

"They're quite delicious." He ran an indulgent eye over her. "And if truth be told, you could use a bit more meat on your bones."

"Were you not satisfied with my bones?" she asked coolly. "You made no complaint last night when you spilled your seed in me."

Flushing, he shot a look at the valet, who quickly went to busy himself in the bedroom.

"You must learn to be more circumspect in your speech when we are married," the lieutenant admonished when the door had closed behind his aide.

"What is this, 'circumspect'?"

"More careful. One doesn't speak of, er, bedroom matters in front of the servants."

"Mmm."

Toying with the handle of her cup, Louise studied the man she'd given herself to. She'd seen him at his worst, sick with fever and lying in a pool of his own sweat. Now hale and healthy, he looked almost handsome. He'd brushed his hair back in a neat queue and tied it with a black ribbon. His white linen shirt molded shoulders that, while not wide and well muscled, were well proportioned to his frame. It was the intricately tied neck cloth he and his manservant had fussed over for so long that gave him something of a dandy's air, she decided.

"Why do you marry me?"

"I beg your pardon?"

"Why do you marry me? My skin is dark. My words are not careful. I have no strong affection for you, nor, I think, do you for me."

"You mistake my sentiments. I have a great regard for you."

"For me or for Henri's money? You may speak honestly," she added when he began to bluster. "I have made a bargain with you and I will keep it. I just wish to have the truth between us."

"The truth?"

He gave a small huff. But not of laughter, Louise thought as he poured himself another cup of cocoa.

"I will admit your inheritance adds to your appeal," he said after a moment. "What man would not rather take a wife who brings him great wealth than one who does not? Henri Chartier's ancestry is also a benefit."

She leaned forward, frowning. "Why do you care so much for Henri's ancestry?"

"You were wed to someone with ties to royalty. That makes you a duchess by marriage in the minds of some. As for your Osage blood—"

He looked away from her, his glance fixing on some point across the room. "He'll use that, as well."

"Who?" She followed his gaze, saw that he looked to the leather-framed portraits on the mantel. "You speak of your father?"

"Yes."

"I do not understand. Tell me how your father makes use of my Osage blood."

"He thinks our union will bind your people to his cause."

"Pah! It will not bind my uncle. You saw how eager he was to be rid of me. And what is this cause you speak of? My uncle has already granted your father land for an outpost deep in Osage country. What more does he want?"

His mouth twisted. "He wants it all."

"All of Osage country?"

"Ha! If only he'd be satisfied with that. No, you're the key to the empire he thought was lost when—when other plans came to naught."

Confused, Louise struggled to understand his meaning. Did the general think to claim all the lands hunted by the Osage? Or did James refer to this so absurd Indian Removal Plan? Perhaps his father supported the notion of moving Cherokee and Choctaw and other eastern tribes to lands beyond the Mississippi. Could he really believe a union between Louise and his son would reconcile Big Track to such a scheme? Before she could ask any further questions, James pushed away from the table and called for his servant.

"Simons! My uniform jacket and sword, if you please."

The batman helped him into the blue coat with its red facings. Rolling his shoulders to settle the cloth, James buckled on his cross belt with its attached sword and sent his man for his shako.

"I dislike leaving you, my dear, but I must attend to my military duties. I'll return as soon as possible."

"You will speak with Colonel Matthews before you attend these duties," Louise reminded him sharply. "And send the letter you wrote to your father."

"I'll go right to the *cabildo,* where the colonel has his office."

And where Daniel was being held.

She must see him, tell him about the bargain she'd made before he heard of it from Bernard. Shoving back her chair, she crossed the room to scoop up the bonnet and gloves James had relieved her of last night.

"I will accompany you."

"There's no need for that. I gave my word I would speak to Matthews and so I shall."

"While you speak with him, I shall speak to Daniel. You must write me a pass."

The lieutenant's head snapped around. "I'll do no such thing! Your name has already been linked with his in connection with his wife's death. I can't have you consorting with him any further."

"I know not this 'consorting,' but I must speak with him."

"I cannot allow it."

This one would learn, Louise thought as she jammed the bonnet over her hastily woven coronet of braids and tied the ribbons. Just as Henri had learned.

"When we are married," she informed him coldly, "you soon discover I am used to following my own mind."

"Louise, I insist you—"

"Daniel must know it is my choice to stay here with you," she snapped, impatient now to be gone. "If he does not hear this from my own lips, he will think you feed me opium to keep me here. Again."

He blanched. "I didn't— I never— I swear, I knew nothing about—"

He lies, Louise thought disdainfully. And he fears. Although he tried to pull a mask over his face, she saw the panic ripple over him like the shadow of a cloud passing over the earth.

She had no concern for his private fears. He could drown in them for all she cared. She'd come to this place with one purpose, and that was to save Daniel. She only hoped he would agree to be saved.

"You will write a pass for me, James. Now, if you please."

He drew himself up. "I'll write it, if you promise me this is the last time you'll go to Morgan. You must leave me some pride."

She'd already made her bargain with the devil. This was but an extension of it.

"You have my word."

Louise showed the pass to a succession of officials.

Once she was granted entry to the prison, a guard escorted her past the jailer's quarters and the offices of the city's police guard to a dank tunnel secured by two separate gates. She yielded her purse along with the skinning knife and a substantial bribe at the first, waited while it was locked behind her, then proceeded to the second. This one opened onto a roofed-in courtyard at the rear of the prison.

"She's come to see the bugger what burnt his wife," her escort informed the guard at the gate. "Sergeant Major Morgan."

The guard held out his hand, palm up. She dropped two more coins into it. He bit down on each coin to test it, pocketed them and twisted an iron key. The spiked iron bars creaked open, and she walked into a cesspit.

Never had she seen such a foul place. The walls surrounding the yard contained two tiers of cells. Most looked too small for a man to stand upright, and the odors spilling through their iron grates were so fetid, Louise almost retched. Swine and chickens rooted in the filth littering the yard. They shared the crowded space with the prisoners allowed out for exercise. Debtors, vagrants, runaway slaves and the insane rubbed elbows with military men awaiting trial, serving sentences or pending execution.

Male and female prisoners mingled with the animals in the yard. Clumps of men were gaming, using limestone marbles as counters. Others puffed on clay pipes. One scarecrow-thin female with matted hair and oozing pustules on her face was servicing a hulking male prisoner right under the avid eye of the others. Another sat in a wallow alongside a fat-bellied sow, cradling a piglet in her arms and crooning to it like a mother to a babe.

"You're allowed fifteen minutes," the guard warned, clanking the gate shut behind her. "Mind where you put your feet."

Holding her skirts high, she picked her way across the yard. The gamblers ceased throwing their bones. The woman cradling the piglet looked up, hollow cheeked and hopeless. A bald giant with a livid scar running from temple to chin dug an elbow into his companion's ribs.

Louise felt the hairs on the back of her neck rise

as the two men began to drift toward her. Other inmates followed. New odors rose with each shuffle of their feet, along with a chorus of murmurs.

"Fresh meat."

"Fancy lookin' piece, ain't she?"

"If no one claims her, she's mine."

Louise raised her chin. These mangy dogs couldn't drag her kicking and screaming into one of those foul cells. The guards were within earshot. Surely they'd intervene. She pinned her eye on the giant.

"I have come to speak with Sergeant Major Morgan," she stated firmly. "Where is he?"

"What do you want with that one, *cherie?*" Grinning, the giant splayed a hand over his crotch and jiggled. "Big Jean has what you want right here."

"Where is he, if you please?"

She heard a stir of movement behind her and spun around, half expecting an attack.

"What are you doing here, Louise?"

If he hadn't spoken, she might not have recognized Daniel. His once-white linen shirt and trousers had been stained with soot from the fire when he'd been arrested. Now they were black with grime and filth. The beginnings of a beard furred his cheeks and chin. A great bruise purpled one side of his face, and his left eye was swollen shut.

"*Sacre bleu!*" She reached up a gloved hand. "Did the guards do this to you?"

"No." He jerked away from her touch. "Why are you here?"

He knew about James. She saw it in his face, heard it in his voice.

"Bernard Thibodeaux has already spoken to you?"

"He came last night, after he left you at the Royal Arms. It cost him a fortune in bribes, but he got the guard to call me to the gate."

She refused to look away. "I will not plead with you to understand. Nor will I beg you to believe I sold myself to James to save you. You know that."

"Yes," he ground out. "I do."

"And you hate me for it. So it must be. But you will—"

"You little fool!"

Wrapping a fist around her upper arm, he hauled her through the ring of onlookers. Her skirts dragged the dirt. Mud and excrement squished into her shoes. She tripped over a squawking chicken that didn't get out of the way fast enough and would have gone down if not for Daniel's bruising hold. He yanked her upright, dragged her to a corner of the wall and pinned her against the brick.

"I don't hate you!" he raged, his one good eye blazing. "How could I hate you for what you did? I know it was done for love, or from this misguided belief that you're somehow to blame for what happened."

"Who else is to blame? Me, I caused you to dishonor your vows to Elizabeth. I brought heartache to you and destruction to—"

"Damn it, Louise! You didn't cause anything."

His grip brutal, he brought her up until they were almost chin to chin.

"*I* broke my vows. *I* left Elizabeth alone. *I* didn't protect her or you. *I* sent you to Wilkinson's bed."

"No!"

"Yes! I despise myself more with every breath I breathe."

The bitter bile of fear rose in her throat. He was so ready to take the blame for Elizabeth's awful death that he might well disregard the bargain she'd struck with James and willingly climb the gallows steps.

"Listen to me, Daniel. Please. Perhaps— Perhaps we must both carry this burden of grief and guilt. Perhaps we will never find forgiveness or peace within ourselves. If that is our punishment, we must accept it."

His hands loosed their vicious hold. The rage went out of him and left only desolation.

"I have."

He would have turned away from her then, but Louise pulled him back.

"Then you must also accept this bargain I make with James. Swear to me you will not protest if they delay this tribunal. Swear you will not object if General Wilkinson agrees to lift the charges against you."

"I'm to live with the hell of knowing you spread your legs for his son every night, is that it?"

She didn't so much as flinch. "Yes."

* * *

As promised, James convinced Colonel Matthews to delay the trial by court-martial until General Wilkinson was apprised of the charges laid against Sergeant Major Morgan and provided written guidance as to how to proceed.

The colonel dispatched a courier with orders to catch up with the general. Days stretched into weeks. April gave way to May, then to June. With the resilience of a city plagued regularly by flood and fire, New Orleans covered its blackened scars with new buildings, new squares, new gardens.

News from Virginia gradually pushed the fire to the back of people's minds. On June 24, 1807, Aaron Burr was arraigned before Supreme Court Chief Justice John Marshall, who also presided over the Fourth District Court in Virginia. Marshall's narrow interpretation of the charges and his instructions to the grand jury allowed Burr to evade a charge of treason, but he was indicted for conspiring to invade a nation at peace with the United States.

General Wilkinson was called to give testimony before the grand jury and barely escaped being bound over for trial himself. The vote was close—nine to seven against indictment—and the resulting flood of revelations about his role in the conspiracy led New Orleans newspapers to paint the man they'd once hailed as the city's savior as a villain of the first order. Presses turned out broadsheet after broadsheet detailing the general's lucrative fur dealings and his close partnerships with many of the men who had supplied soldiers and equipment for Burr's private army.

They also reported Wilkinson's many dealings with Spanish officials, including a meeting right in New Orleans between the general and the governor of Spanish-held Florida, the same governor who later sold Wilkinson Dauphine Island, off the coast of Mobile, for a paltry sum. Reward, the newspapers asked in blazing headlines, for the general's role in the scheme to return the vast Louisiana Territory to its former Spanish masters? Or for betraying Burr and thus keeping him from invading Texas and Mexico?

With each inflammatory article, James became more agitated. Pleading a nervous disorder, he begged to be excused from his military duties and took to his bed. To Louise's profound relief, he couldn't bear to have anyone near him except his batman. She had a small trundle bed moved into his quarters and spent her days and nights alternately wondering whether she'd done right or wrong by Daniel and waiting for the general's reply to his son's letter.

In the midst of the agonizing wait, she received a visit from Bernard Thibodeaux. A ship had arrived with letters from France. Henri's first wife had died two years before he married Louise. His fortune was hers to claim. When she advised James of the news, he nodded weakly and said he'd send another letter to his father immediately.

He could send what additional letters he wanted. Louise cared only about the answer to his first.

* * *

The reply arrived on the last day of June. James dragged himself from his sickbed to advise her of its contents. Gray faced and sweating, the lieutenant relayed that the general recognized Sergeant Major Morgan's long and faithful service to his country and could personally attest to Morgan's devotion to his wife.

Daniel would not hang, but neither would he escape punishment for the negligence that led to his wife's death and the devastating fire. He was to receive one hundred lashes. If he survived the whip, he would be dismissed forthwith from the United States Army.

The sentence was carried out two days later in the public square fronting the *cabildo*. James professed himself too unwell to attend, but Louise stood among the spectators who'd gathered for the show.

She didn't look away when Daniel was stripped to the waist and chained to the whipping post. She didn't flinch when the first stripes were laid across his back. She didn't count the strokes along with the noisy, boisterous crowd.

But with each lash of the whip, she bit down harder on her lower lip. By the fiftieth stroke, it was a raw, pulpy mass. By the eightieth, she'd chewed through her own flesh. Blood ran down her chin, dripped onto the bodice of her dress. Drawn by the feast, flies swarmed about her face and neck. She blinked them away and stood unmoving as the attending physician checked the unconscious prisoner and declared him hale enough to take the final twenty strokes.

After the last stroke, the physician stepped forward again and examined the prisoner. When he signaled that Daniel was still alive, a disappointed howl went up from the crowd. Ignoring a chorus of shouts and hisses, a uniformed officer came forward and read the order dismissing Sergeant Major Morgan from the Second Regiment of Infantry, United States Army. The chains were removed and the former soldier was left to lie in the pool of his own blood.

As Louise had begged him to, Bernard Thibodeaux claimed Daniel's lacerated body. She watched, stony eyed, while the merchant's servants wrapped the unconscious man in blankets and lifted him onto the wagon bed. The wagon drove off, its wheels rattling on the cobbles, and the crowd drifted away from the plaza.

Louise stood unmoving until the last rattle died away, then turned and made her way back to the Royal Arms.

21

Pressing a bloodstained handkerchief to her mouth, Louise let herself into Wilkinson's quarters. The curtains were drawn despite the heat. The smothering gloom, along with the rise and fall of voices in the other room, told her the lieutenant still lay abed.

She was too sick at heart to speak to him right now. Closing the door behind her with a quiet *click,* she sought refuge in a chair wedged into a dim corner beside the fireplace and laid her head back to staunch the blood still trickling from her lip. She squeezed her eyes shut, but couldn't block the horrific image of Daniel's back laid open to expose weeping muscles and glistening bone.

How could she have done this to him? Had she known what punishment the general would prescribe, would she have stood back? Let Daniel face the tribunal? Mount the steps to the gallows? She didn't doubt he would wish himself dead when he regained his senses.

If he regained his senses.

Louise had seen far less grievously injured animals lie down in the snow and wait for death. Daniel might well succumb to his wounds, and her bargain with James would have been for naught.

With a tiny whimper, she fought hot, stinging tears and paid no attention to the voices in the next room, until one grew sharp with anger.

"I tell you, Lieutenant, I won't let your father make a scapegoat of me the way he did Burr!"

She didn't recognize the speaker. It wasn't the valet, Simons. But she had no difficulty identifying the one who mumbled a reply. James's petulant whine had come to rasp on her nerves like the bone scraper she'd once used to clean deer and beaver pelts. Whatever he said didn't seem to satisfy his visitor.

"Hogwash! I received a letter from Daniel Clark. He says the general suggested in his testimony to the grand jury that Clark and I were in collusion with Burr."

James roused himself enough to answer more clearly. "You and Clark *were* in collusion with Burr."

"At your father's specific behest! He sent Burr to me with letters of introduction. He gave coded instructions for funds to be deposited to the man's account. He exhorted me to recruit others to our cause."

Their cause, she thought wearily. Always they speak of this cause.

"I have a bill drawn on Daniel Clark in favor of

P. V. Ogden. If necessary, I will produce it in court and show it was your father who masterminded this whole scheme.''

The names meant nothing to Louise, but she grasped well enough the import of what she'd just heard. According to James's visitor, the rumors were true. General Wilkinson was as deep in the plot to set up a separate nation west of the Mississippi as Burr.

She couldn't bring herself to care. She was long past the point of pretending any interest in James or his father. Sucking on a slow trickle of blood, she tried to close her ears to the exchange, but James had become as agitated as his visitor and would not be shut out.

''You will not be called on to produce anything, I promise you. I've received letters, too. My father assures me these rumors are absolutely untrue. He didn't speak against you or Clark. He's too much in your debt.''

''He'd best not forget that.''

''He won't. He can't.''

Louise could picture James in bed, nightcap askew, his face streaked with sweat, as he tried desperately to placate his visitor.

''You must know the debts you incurred will be repaid many times over. When this business with Burr is finished, the general will regroup and press forward once again. He has the Spanish squarely behind him. Once I'm wed, he'll use my wife to sway the French and the Osage to our side.''

Louise jerked upright. With the red-stained handkerchief pressed against her lip, she listened while James made clear the plans he'd hinted at to her.

"My father will use my wife's inheritance, as well," he was saying. "It will more than pay to replace the arms and boats that were seized in Ohio. He'll have his empire yet, and you'll be part of it."

His impassioned speech evidently calmed his visitor's fears. Their voices dropped to muted murmurs. Some moments later, the man showed himself out. He didn't notice Louise tucked in her dim corner and she saw only his profile. He was a stranger, a wealthy banker or merchant judging by his cutaway frock coat and snowy white linens.

When the door shut behind him, she let her head drop back against the chair once more. She couldn't summon any concern over the general's plans for her or for her inheritance. The general, like his son, would learn that what Louise had, she held.

Closing her eyes, she let her mind take her back to a hot, jammed square and the vicious *crack* of a lash.

Daniel lay facedown on cool sheets, wrapped in a sheath of pain. He told the passage of hours by the number of times he swam in and out of consciousness, the passage of days by the number of times he endured the agony of having his wounds dressed.

Helene Thibodeaux tended to him. Her hands were gentle and skilled, but her lightest touch set his back afire. Gritting his teeth, he thought of what Elizabeth must have suffered and welcomed the pain. Thoughts of what Louise was now enduring kept him alive.

Three days passed before he could draw in a full breath. Six, before he could pull on his clothes. A servant found him clinging to the bedpost, one leg in the pair of trousers Bernard had purchased for him, and scurried out calling for Helene.

The mistress of the house bustled in a moment later. She'd put off her silks and lace caps while she nursed him. Clad now in a sensible broadcloth skirt and calico blouse, she looked more like a drayman's wife than the cherished spouse of a wealthy merchant.

"Daniel! What can you be thinking of? Your back is still a mass of welts. You must return to bed immediately and let the scars heal over."

"They've healed enough."

The effort of pulling up the trousers caused waves of blinding pain. Black spots danced in front of his eyes and sweat dampened his temples, but he got the damned things up and buttoned.

"If you break open those cuts and bleed all over my carpets," Helene warned tartly, "I shall be quite annoyed with you!"

"I'll try to spare your carpets." Unclenching his jaw, he forced a smile. "Someday I'll repay the kindness you and Bernard have shown me. If you'll help me with that shirt, I'll stand even more in your debt."

"Daniel—"

"Please, Helene."

Lips pursed, she gave him grudging assistance. By the time he had the shirt over his head and both arms in the sleeves, sweat drenched his whole upper torso and burned like the fires of hell in his wounds.

"This is absurd," she protested when he grabbed for the bedpost with both hands to keep from toppling over. "You're so weak you can scarcely stand."

"Two turns about the room and I'll have my feet under me."

"Two turns about the room and you'll be flat on your face again!"

"All I need is a strong shoulder to lean on. Call Thomas, if you would."

Grumbling, she picked up her skirts and left. She returned not with the sturdy house servant, but with her husband. Bernard took one look at Daniel's determined face and swallowed whatever admonishments he'd been instructed to deliver.

"Fetch Thomas, Helene. Between us, we should provide sufficient support for your patient."

Sheer will kept Daniel on his feet. Every muscle in his body screamed and sweat poured down his face, but he made two turns around the room with assistance, two more without. Despite Helene's insistence that he return to bed, he lowered himself into a chair.

He shook all over. Each tremor pulled at the half-healed welts. Ignoring the nausea that rose in his throat with every breath, he begged some beef and ale.

"You're not ready for beef *or* ale," Helene protested. "Gruel, perhaps. Or soup. Cook has fixed a tasty ratatouille and—"

Bernard stilled her with a pat on her shoulder. "He knows what he needs, wife."

Scowling, she muttered something about the pigheadedness of all men. Thomas left the room with her to assist in the preparation of a tray.

When the door closed behind them, Daniel blinked the sweat from his eyes and looked to Bernard. "I would beg something of you, too."

His face grave, the merchant cocked his head. "A pistol?"

"Yes."

"Should you not wait until you're stronger to go after her?"

"I have the strength for what I must do."

"You escaped the gallows once, Daniel. If you put a bullet through young Wilkinson, you'll not escape the rope again."

"Dueling is still legal in New Orleans."

Thibodeaux's jaw dropped. "You're going to challenge the lieutenant to a duel? Damnation, man, you can scarce hold yourself upright. How do you expect to march twenty paces, turn and hit your target?"

"You forget I'm an army—" He stopped. His jaw working, he corrected himself. "I *was* an army sharpshooter. I've brought down many a deer and wild turkey at a hundred yards. I won't miss at twenty paces. Will you act as my second?''

It was the merchant's turn to sweat. Dragging out a handkerchief, he mopped his forehead.

"I know nothing of duels. I trade in beeswax and beaver pelts, for God's sake!''

"All I require of you is to provide the pistols. And,'' Daniel added with a grimace, "accompany me to the Royal Arms this night.''

He found Wilkinson in the luxuriously appointed taproom. The lieutenant had joined a group of his fellow officers to bend an elbow and share the latest barracks gossip over ale and wine.

The lively conversation flagged, then died away completely when Daniel and Bernard walked in. Most of the officers recognized the former sergeant major instantly. Those who did not were quickly apprised of his identity.

Daniel faced the sea of blue coats and for the first time really knew himself to be an outsider. Men who had once treated him with respect now regarded him with mingled contempt and scorn. The army to which he'd given most of his life had completely, unequivocally shut him out.

Willing his tortured body not to fail him, he wove a path through the tables and stopped at Wilkinson's. The lieutenant drew courage from his brothers in arms. Raising his flagon, he took a long, deliberate swallow before addressing the man standing before him.

"What do you want, Morgan?"

"I've come for my woman."

His tankard hit the oak boards with a *clank.* "*Your* woman, as I recall, died of burns."

A cold rage curled around Daniel's heart.

With a sneer, Wilkinson dug the knife in deeper. "If you refer to Madame Chartier, she's soon to be my wife. *My* wife, Morgan."

"Not unless I sell her to you."

"The devil you say! She's no slave to be bought and sold on the auction block."

"No, she is not. But Osage blood runs in her veins. I paid her uncle a bride price, which she agreed to. According to the laws of her tribe, she's mine."

"See here, man!" a mustached captain protested indignantly. "You're not in the wilds of Osage Country now. You can't hold to the customs of those savages."

"Then, I'll hold to the customs of our society." His eyes flat and cold, he turned back to his prey. "Name your second, Wilkinson. Bernard Thibodeaux will act as mine. We'll settle this here and now. Swords, pistols, knives or tomahawks. You choose."

Every vestige of color drained from the lieutenant's face. He'd shared months in the wilderness with Daniel, was all too familiar with his skills. Wildly, he looked to his brother officers and found no relief there. They were bound by a gentleman's code of honor that demanded retribution for even the slightest insult. Shoving back his chair, Wilkinson tried to bluster his way out of the situation.

"I won't lower myself to duel with a common criminal. Get out of here before I lay a whip to you."

He knew before the words were out of his mouth that he'd said exactly the wrong thing. He stared into Daniel's eyes and saw death smiling back at him.

"I've already had a whip laid to me, you puling little prick. I've taken a hundred lashes and will take a hundred more if necessary. Before I do, I'll have what's mine. Name your second."

The captain standing at Wilkinson's elbow snorted. "He's weak as a kitten, man. Shaking where he stands. Choose a weapon and be done with this."

"I think—" Gulping, Wilkinson hooked a finger in his neck cloth. "I, uh, think we should let Madame Chartier decide this."

With a little hiss of disgust, the captain turned away. The lieutenant flushed but stood his ground.

"We both want the lady, but neither of us would force her into our bed against her will. Let's go upstairs and settle the matter once and for all."

Daniel wanted it settled right there. Images of Louise in this man's bed, opening herself to him, had tortured him far worse than the cuts on his back. Only the bitter knowledge that she'd gone to Wilkinson voluntarily kept him from shoving a pistol barrel in the bastard's mouth.

"You stay here," he growled at the whey-faced coward. "I'll bring her down so she can speak her piece in front of these witnesses. Bernard will stay, as well. Not that I think you would put a bullet in my back, mind you. Just to keep you company.''

The damnable truth was that he didn't want the lieutenant to see the sweat it took for him to mount the stairs. If Wilkinson knew how weak he really was, the bastard might decide to go for swords, after all. At this point, Daniel wasn't sure he could lift a sword, much less swing it.

His torn muscles screamed with agony by the time he reached the second floor. Blood seeped through the bandages onto his shirt, plastering the linen to his back. He paused outside Wilkinson's rooms to suck in a deep breath.

As he had the last time Daniel hammered on the door, the batman answered. He looked surprised when he recognized the man on the threshold.

''The lieutenant's not in quarters.''

''I know. I just spoke with him down in the tap-room. It's Madame Chartier I've come to see.''

''I'm sorry, Sergeant Maj— Uh, sir. Madame Chartier is not receiving visitors.''

''Yes, she is.''

With a *thump* of his fist, Daniel sent the door banging back against the wall. The batman jumped away and looked to Louise for guidance.

She sat as stiff as a pine plank in a chair tucked into the alcove beside the fireplace, wearing a lilac gown frilled with blonde lace, and an expression of pure anguish.

"Get out," Daniel ordered the batman, not taking his eyes off her.

"But the lieutenant—"

"Now!"

He slammed the door shut behind the man. Louise didn't so much as blink at the *thud*.

"You must leave, Daniel. I promise James I will not see or speak with you again."

"James sent me up here."

Surprise blanked her face. "Why would he do such a thing?"

"He had little choice in the matter."

"Why do you come?"

"To take you away," he said bluntly.

She closed her eyes for a moment, drew in a ragged breath. "I struck a bargain. I will hold to it."

"The bargain is invalid."

"What is this, 'invalid'?"

"It has no teeth."

"I do not understand. What do you say?"

"As Bernard explained it, you agreed to give yourself to James if he stayed my court-martial and pleaded with his father to make sure I didn't hang. Do I have the right of it?"

"Yes."

"The problem is, you weren't free to give yourself. I paid your uncle a bride price. You belong to me."

She sprang up, shock chasing the torment from her face.

"But you could not— You did not—"

"Take you to my bed?"

"Take me to wife. You were already wed to Elizabeth."

"You told me yourself it didn't matter. That many trappers kept both white and Indian wives."

"Yes, but—"

"We spoke no formal words of marriage, such as you did with Henri, but you belong to me as surely as you did to him."

"Why do you do this! You can't want me. Not after all that has happened. There is too much hurt between us, Daniel. Too much hate."

"I told you at the *cabildo*. I don't hate you."

The whip had laid more than his back open. The raw, blistering pain had stripped away guilt, remorse, even grief. All that remained was the need to tell her what was in his heart.

"Elizabeth was my first love, Louise. God willing, you'll be my last."

He had to touch her. Lifting a hand, he brushed the edges of a puffy, bite-shaped sore on her lip. The effort cost him more strength than he wanted to admit, but the thought that Wilkinson had put that mark on her sent fury and absolute determination surging through his veins.

"Pack what things you want to bring with you. You're coming with me."

Hope leaped into her eyes. "James agrees with this?"

"Yes."

As quickly as it had come, the hope died. Hugging her arms to her chest, she turned away from him.

"I cannot go away with you. You choose to ignore the curse I was born with. I cannot. Me, I bring you nothing but heartache and grief."

"You've brought neither."

"But think how you have suffered since that day we met. Think of what Elizabeth suffered."

He didn't try to argue, as he had so many times before. He'd learned by now that her fears and beliefs went too deep to be shrugged aside.

"I've had time aplenty to think these past weeks. Perhaps it was your destiny to come into my life that day, just as it was mine to find you. It doesn't matter whether the meeting was the work of the Almighty or the spirits you believe in or happened by mere chance. What's done can't be undone. But I do know this. If you deny your heart now, you'll only cause more suffering to us both."

She pressed her lips together. She couldn't refute his last argument. But the legend that had followed her all her life still haunted her.

Daniel settled the matter by curling a knuckle under her chin and tipping her face to his.

"I'm not leaving this place without you."

22

Torn between joy, relief and the nagging worry that she and Daniel tempted fate, Louise let her heart overrule her head. She would go with him. Wherever their paths led, they would walk them together. Whatever storms arose, they would brave them together.

Her blood singing, she rushed into the bedchamber to gather her things. She'd acquired a considerable wardrobe of gowns and fripperies since her arrival in New Orleans. They were carefully packed in the leather-bound trunk Bernard had delivered to the Royal Arms.

She had no thought for silks and cashmere now. Frantic to be away from the two rooms that had become her prison, she pawed through the neatly folded shawls, pantaloons and chemises to the bottom of the trunk. There she found the buckskin leggings and tunic she'd cleaned and packed away soon after her first shopping expedition with the Thibodeaux women. Those, a change of underlinens and the lace-trimmed lilac dress she was now wearing were all she'd take with her. The rest James could dump in the river for all she cared.

Clutching the few items against her chest, she searched the bedchamber for something to carry them in. An army-issue haversack hung from a peg in the clothespress that held James's extra uniforms, but it was too large and too heavy for her needs. She decided instead on the leather pouch that contained his writing desk.

Snatching the pouch from the shelf, she dumped the wooden writing box on the bed. Quills, papers and a stoppered horn spilled out. The plug came off the horn and a stain of black ink spread across the coverlet. Louise paid no attention to it as she crammed her few things into the leather bag. Grabbing up a bonnet and shawl at random, she thrust her hand through the strings of her reticule. The reassuring weight of her skinning knife bumped against her thigh as she hurried into the sitting room.

"I'm ready."

Daniel turned at the sound of her voice, but not before Louise saw the red spotting the back of his shirt. Her glance flew to his face. Deep grooves were carved into his cheeks. Sweat beaded his temple.

The joy singing through her veins stuttered and died. She could only imagine the pain he still suffered. Slinging the pouch over her shoulder, she crossed the room and slid her arm around his waist.

"Come. Let's leave this place."

Daniel leaned on her going down the stairs, but when they turned into the taproom, he squared to his full height. His arm stayed across her shoulders, protective and possessive. Louise huddled close to his side, made wary by the sight of so many blue coats and gold epaulets. She searched for James and found him standing tight-lipped beside Bernard Thibodeaux.

The lieutenant didn't notice the leather pouch, hidden as it was behind her back, but the fact that she wore her bonnet and shawl was enough to put twin spots of red in his cheeks.

"So, you're leaving."

"Yes."

"I suppose I was foolish to think a slut such as you would hold to her promise."

Daniel started for him. Louise clung to his waist to hold him back and rushed into speech.

"I said I would marry you, James, and so I would if you really wanted me."

"The hell you would," Daniel countered savagely.

Ignoring the furious outburst, Louise hurried on. "What you want—what your father wants—are Henri's name and his fortune. I cannot give you his name, but I give you his fortune. It is yours. All of it. Bernard, you will sign the papers?"

The merchant looked ill at the thought of turning the funds he'd worked so hard to secure for Louise over to the lieutenant.

"Is that what you really desire?"

"It is."

He looked to Daniel and found no support.

"Those monies are hers to do with as she pleases."

With a long sigh, Bernard came to join them.

"Well, we have enough witnesses here to swear that's your wish. I'll take care of the matter."

James opened his mouth, and for a fleeting moment Louise wondered whether he would throw her gift back in her face. He snapped it shut again, swallowing whatever he'd intended to say, and turned his back to her.

She didn't spare him another glance. Digging her fingers into Daniel's side, she all but pushed him out the door of the Royal Arms and into the warm June dusk.

Daniel handed Louise into Bernard's carriage, climbed in behind her and dropped his head back against the squabs. She sat on the edge of her seat, but couldn't draw in a full breath until the vehicle had rolled away from the inn. When it rounded a corner and she saw the last of the Royal Arms, she felt as though a great weight had been lifted from her chest.

"Where do we go?"

"To Doumaine Street," Bernard answered. "While Daniel's wounds heal, I'll speak with the lawyers and arrange for—"

"Not Doumaine Street." With a grunt, Daniel raised his head. "I don't trust Wilkinson."

"Where do wish me to take you? Another inn? I know a quiet place on Canal Street where you could hide away for a few days or weeks."

"I want you to take me to the cemetery where you buried Elizabeth. I want to see where she lies. Then—" He groped for Louise's hand and threaded his fingers through hers. "If you will, take us to a church. That business about the bride price carried us through tonight, but the lieutenant—or his father—may decide to challenge my claim. It's best to make it legal in every way."

"You want to be married?" Bernard exclaimed. "Tonight?"

"Yes."

"But your back bleeds!" Louise protested. "Your knees wobble and shake like those of a babe. You need to be abed, not rattling about in a coach."

"And so I will be. After we're married."

The joy that had gripped her earlier returned, fierce and hot. They'd traveled so many miles together, she and Daniel. Faced so many dangers. Shared so many sorrows. He was in her heart, in her every thought. Now she would take him to husband and stand with him against the world if it came to that.

"All right, we will marry this night. But me, I will not be surprised if you fall on your face at the church."

"It's all well and good to talk about being married," Bernard protested, "but you cannot decide one minute and wed the next. The bans must be cried and the proper documents drawn up."

"Pah!" Louise said with a shake of her head. "A gold coin took care of the bans when I married Henri. And we need no documents but the marriage lines. Find us a priest."

"If you think I'll take you to a church without stopping first at Doumaine Street, you much mistake the matter! Helene would have my head on her best china platter if she did not stand witness with me to your marriage."

When apprised of the plans, Helene promptly bundled herself into a bonnet and shawl. Bertrice and Marie begged to be allowed to come, as well. Rather than crowd everyone in one carriage, Bernard suggested he take Louise and his family to the Church of the Immaculate Conception and make the necessary arrangements for the marriage ceremony, while his servant drove Daniel to the cemetery.

"I go with Daniel," Louise said, keeping her hand threaded through his. "We meet you in thirty minutes, yes?"

When the carriage drew up to the cemetery entrance, Louise climbed out first and offered her shoulder to Daniel.

He'd regained some of his strength during the short ride, and walked without leaning on her, but the spreading stain on his back worried her. Frowning, she took her lower lip between her teeth. Pain arrowed through her and she loosed the still healing flesh instantly.

"This way," she murmured, tasting blood.

Their footsteps crunched on the crushed-shell walk and echoed through the quiet. Although the spreading oaks cast much of the burial ground in shadow and made the hanging moss look like long fingers reaching from the graves, a summer moon shed enough light for Louise to find her way among the marble crypts and statues. Kneeling figures with arms lifted to the stars in supplication and prayer guided her. An angel with widespread wings beckoned.

"The gate is locked," she told Daniel when they approached the tomb where Elizabeth lay. "You cannot go inside, but I will show you which shelf holds her coffin.''

Nodding, he let her lead him to the iron grate. Barely enough light filtered through the bars for her to make out the dim shapes inside.

A glint of gold caught her eye. The trophy she'd given Elizabeth to take with her into the spirit world lay where she'd left it, but the soft sigh of a breeze through the moss whispered its own message.

Yes, Louise answered silently. *I've kept my promise. I've brought Daniel to mourn you properly.*

Easing to one side, she made room for him at the bars.

''There. Do you see? The moon shines on the oak boards you cut and nailed.''

''I see.''

''I'll leave you, then, to say what prayers you will for her.''

Retracing her steps, she stopped in the shadow of a weeping mother bent over a cross and a lamb. Face lifted to the stars, Louise offered her own prayers.

Give him peace, Elizabeth.

He loved you greatly and with honor. Any pain that comes because of what we do tonight, give to me. Any guilt that must be born, let me bear it.

Please, give him peace.

23

Daniel and Louise were married in a side chapel of the Church of the Immaculate Conception. Votive candles flickered in red glass containers. The faint perfume of incense drifted on the dank air. Bernard stood with Daniel, Helene with Louise. Bertrice took everything in with wide eyes and Marie cried softly into her handkerchief.

A donation of five gold louis to the orphans' fund ended the priest's objections to performing the ceremony without having the bans read. Since Daniel was not Catholic, no mass was sung, but he was required to pledge that any children born of the union would be baptized and raised in the One True Faith.

That formality taken care of, the black-robed priest recited the Latin phrases that held no meaning for either Louise or Daniel. His soft chants echoed through the stillness of the church and, oddly, their very strangeness brought Louise a slow, spreading comfort.

She would not have thought all those months ago,

when she looked up from the bloody beaver pelts and watched Daniel stride into Henri's camp, that she would one day stand beside him and take him to husband. She couldn't have imagined the twists and turns their journey together would take before it led them to this place, this time.

Perhaps Daniel was right. Perhaps he was her destiny and she was his. Perhaps God or the spirits or mere chance had brought them together. Perhaps they'd each had to suffer greatly before they could bind their hearts as the priest now bound their bodies and souls.

The simple ceremony took its toll on Daniel's strength, so much so that Louise grasped his arm when they walked into the deserted square outside the church. The two carriages were where they'd left them to enter the church, their coach lanterns flickering like beacons in the still, warm night.

"I ordered a wedding supper to be laid out and waiting for us when we return," Helene told the small party. "It won't be as lavish as I would have liked, but..."

"Monsieur Thibodeaux!"

Startled by the shout, Daniel grabbed Louise and was about to thrust her behind the carriage when the Thibodeauxs' manservant, Thomas, pounded out of a side street. His broad chest heaving, he skidded to a halt before the small group.

"Lieutenant Wilkinson's at the house," he panted. "He done brought a whole squad of soldiers with him. They's after Miz Louise. I slipped out through the back and come running to tell you.''

Bernard blew out a slow, hissing breath. ''You were right to insist on a wedding this night, Daniel.''

''They's wanting to search the house,'' Thomas said, getting his wind back. ''The lieutenant is sayin' Miz Louise is a thief who done stole from him.''

''I stole nothing! All I take away with me is a change of linens and the leggings and tunic I arrived in.''

''He's fussed 'bout some bag. A leather pouch, I think he said.''

''But I leave my trunk! All my gowns and hats and shoes. They are worth more than an old, scratched pouch.''

''The man is pulling at the hairs of a mange-ridden dog,'' Bernard said, his mouth tight with anger. ''He didn't have the grit to face Daniel down at the Royal Arms. Instead he brings this trumped-up charge of thievery against Louise!''

''Trumped up or not, it could land her in the *cabildo* prison,'' Helene put in worriedly.

''Not while I still breathe,'' Daniel said in a flat tone that left no doubt in the matter. ''Where is this pouch?''

''It is there,'' Louise told him, ''in the carriage.''

''Get it out. We'll empty it of your things and send it back with Bernard and Helene. In the meantime, you and I will take to the road. I'm not giving him or anyone else a chance at you.''

"Daniel! You cannot travel tonight. Your back—"

"Get the pouch."

She scrambled into the coach and retrieved the bag from the corner of the seat. The carriage lanterns threw enough light for Daniel to recognize the engraved initials on the flap.

"It's the same one Wilkinson carried on the expedition. He used it to tote his writing box with his journal and circumferentor."

"I empty everything in the bag onto the bed! I do not take his journal or any surveying tools."

His jaw locked, Daniel dumped Louise's few belongings onto the floor of the carriage, then ran a hand inside the pocket of the flap to make sure he hadn't missed anything. The pocket was empty, but his probing fingers discovered a slight bulge behind the lining. Scowling, he carried the pouch closer to the flickering light and felt inside again.

"What is it? What do you find?"

"I don't know. Feels like folded paper. It's down behind the lining."

"I'll wager it's a wad of banknotes," Bernard guessed. "Louise probably made off with his private stash, all unknowing. No wonder he's after her."

"I give him Henri's money," she exclaimed indignantly. "Me, I take no banknotes!"

Thoroughly incensed, she let loose with a spate of epithets concerning James Biddle Wilkinson's person that widened the eyes of Bernard's womenfolk. Daniel interrupted her in mid-curse.

"They're not banknotes." Drawing a sheaf of folded papers through a thin slit in the lining, he unfolded the top sheet. "They're letters."

"Pah! Throw them back in the bag and let us be away."

"Hold on a moment. Look at this, Bernard."

The merchant peered around his arm. "I can't read it. Hold it up to the light."

Daniel obliged, his face set in tight lines.

"I still cannot make out the words. Or these strange symbols."

"Looks like a special cipher, wouldn't you say?"

"I believe—" His glance shot from the paper to Daniel's face. He swallowed hard. "I believe you may be right," he finished on a faint note.

"What is this, 'cipher'?" Louise wanted to know.

"It's a special kind of writing," Daniel answered, flipping open another sheet to find it filled with the same code. "Secret symbols. Aaron Burr used them in the letter he wrote to General Wilkinson."

"The letter the general turns over to President Jefferson? The one everyone speaks of?"

"Yes."

Frowning, she studied the strange symbols. "Do you think this traitor Burr writes to James?"

"Could be. Or the letters could be from the lieutenant's father. For all we know, the general was the one who devised the code he and Burr used to communicate with."

Louise shook her head in disgust. "It is all anyone talks of, this business with Burr. The day of your beating, a man comes to see James. This man, he worries that the general will betray him as he betrayed this Burr. James says he will not, but he sweats like a pig when the man leaves and again when I ask him about his father's schemes.''

Daniel spun around, his eyes narrowed. ''You asked Wilkinson about his father's schemes?''

Taken aback by his tone, Louise tried to recall the brief conversation. ''I ask James why he wants to marry me. He says his father now makes a new plan. One that uses my name to bind the French, my blood to bind the Osage and my monies to buy the arms he needs.''

''Dear God above!'' Bernard gasped. He threw a look around the quiet, moon-washed square. ''This is not the place to speak of such things!''

Daniel heartily concurred. The hair on the back of his neck was standing straight up. Thinking hard and fast, he whirled to Bernard.

''Go back to your home. If Wilkinson is there, tell him that you and Helene and the girls came with us to the church and you parted with us here.''

The merchant nodded. He, like Daniel, recognized the dark waters rising about them all.

''If he asks about the pouch?''

''You can say Louise had it with her but—'' Grasping the bag by the strap, Daniel spun it over his head and let fly. It sailed through the night and landed in the shadows across the square. ''But she threw it away outside the church. If he searches for the damned thing, he might just give us time to get out of the city.''

''And the letters?''

He looked Thibodeaux square in the eye. ''What letters?''

''What letters, indeed? You'd best take the carriage.''

Reaching into his frock coat, the merchant pulled out his purse. He pressed it into Daniel's hands, refusing to listen to his protest. ''I'll deduct the monies from Louise's inheritance. You'll have to send word what you want done about that, by the by.''

Confused by the swift exchange, she frowned. ''I already tell you what to do with it. You must give it to James.''

The two men exchanged looks. ''Send me word,'' Bernard said again.

Nodding, Daniel wrenched open the carriage door and all but tossed Louise inside. She landed on the velvet seat in a flurry of petticoats and had barely righted herself before he instructed the driver to take the old Spanish post road north and climbed in beside her.

''Now,'' he said grimly as the carriage began to roll, ''tell me about the conversation between Wilkinson and this visitor of his.''

By the time the carriage had passed through the outskirts of the city, Daniel felt much like a man sitting on a powder keg. The coded letters he'd found in the pouch just might be the fuse. Louise was most definitely the tinderbox.

His gut twisted into a tight knot as he assessed the significance of what she'd overheard in James Wilkinson's quarters. An unknown person had stated flatly that the lieutenant's father was the mastermind behind the traitorous scheme Burr was about to stand trial for. This same person claimed to have evidence in the form of a letter from Wilkinson. Moreover, the general's son had as much as admitted that his father had planned to use Louise's heritage and her inheritance to further a new scheme after his other plans *came to naught.*

Daniel's one, driving instinct was to get Louise as far from the general's intrigues as he could, as fast as he could, but the damned letters burned like a brand inside his shirt. Wilkinson had incriminated Burr by sending his letter to President Jefferson. Had he incriminated himself in one of these letters to his son?

The imbroglio weighed more heavily on Daniel's mind with each mile the carriage traveled along the rough, rutted road that had once stretched from the Spanish possessions in Florida to their capital in Mexico. Finally, he leaned forward and called to the driver through the front opening.

"Pull up."

"Here, sir?"

"Here."

The empty darkness outside the open window

drew a puzzled glance from Louise. "Why do we stop?"

"We need to talk about which road to take. If we follow the Old Spanish highway west, it will carry us to New Iberia and Lafayette and on into Texas."

"Is that not where you wish to go?"

"I'm thinking," Daniel said slowly, "that maybe we should leave the carriage, buy a couple of horses and head east until we pick up the Federal Road."

"Where does this Federal Road lead?"

"It cuts through Mississippi Territory and Creek Country in Alabama, then goes north to Richmond."

"Richmond? It is the place where they hold the trial of this Aaron Burr. Why do you wish to go there?"

"So I can deliver the letters tucked inside my shirt and you can tell the barristers conducting the trial what you heard."

She stared at him in surprise, her face a pale blur in the wash of moonlight coming through the side window.

"If General Wilkinson *was* the mastermind behind Burr's scheme," Daniel said, "he needs to answer for it."

"Do you think to take vengeance on him for ordering you to be whipped?"

"No, I would have ordered the same given the circumstances."

"I do not understand. If you seek no vengeance, why do you care about the general's schemes? He can spin whatever webs he wants. They mean nothing to me."

"They mean something to me. I wore an army uniform for fourteen years. I can't close my eyes to a plot to destroy the frontiers so many of my friends and comrades shed blood to defend."

"Pah! The army strips you of your uniform. It almost strips the flesh from your back. You owe nothing to the soldiers who stand by and watch it happen."

She was right. He owed nothing to the army that had drummed him out of its ranks, nothing to the country he'd served for fourteen years. He had no reason to involve himself in the doings of men like Wilkinson and Burr—except one. He still called himself an American.

"If I go with you and speak to these barristers," Louise said determinedly, breaking into his thoughts, "I do so only because you ask it of me. It will be my bride gift to you."

Wondering how many other men had received testimony at a traitor's trial as a wedding gift, Daniel could only grin.

"You'd best change into your buckskins and moccasins. We've a long road ahead of us."

They sent the carriage back to the city and spent their first night as husband and wife alone together under the stars.

Daniel insisted on getting well away from the road. He carried the carriage blanket the driver had offered up along with one of the coach pistols. Louise rolled her few possessions up in her gown and tucked them under her arm. Leaving the rutted road, they went deep into a stand of eucalyptus. The branches, with their peeling bark, gleamed like old bones in the moonlight. The scent was strong, wrinkling Louise's nose, but she didn't complain. She knew the camphor odor would help keep the mosquitoes at bay.

Daniel spread the blanket close against one massive trunk. "Tomorrow we'll find a hostelry where we can buy horses and supplies."

"First," she said firmly, "we will collect spiderwebs with the dew still wet on them so I may make a poultice for your back."

He didn't argue. He hurt from his neck to his knees. Gingerly, he eased down onto the blanket, but Louise stopped him before he could plant his shoulders against the trunk.

"You must lie flat, on your stomach."

His mouth curved in a wry grimace. "I'm not going to spend our wedding night with my nose in the dirt."

"Lie on your side, then, and I will lie with you."

When she stretched out beside him, Daniel pillowed his head on one arm and hooked the other around her waist to draw her bottom against his belly. Her scent came to him over the stink of the eucalyptus. Incense from the church still clung to her hair, mixing with the faint tang of lye soap and the earthy sweat raised by the June night.

"I did not think we would ever lie like this again," she murmured, cradling her head on her bent elbow.

Nor had Daniel. During those dark days in prison and the agonizing nights after the flogging, the need to get her away from Wilkinson had almost eaten him alive. But until tonight, he hadn't thought beyond that need.

Now he had her in his arms again and was too damned mauled to act like a man, much less a man who'd just taken a woman to wife.

He'd have just a taste of her. One taste. That much at least he'd give himself. Ignoring the scream of his back, he leaned forward and nuzzled the warm skin of her neck.

He should have known one taste wouldn't be enough. All too soon, his groin ached almost as fiercely as his back. Sliding a palm down her hip, he found the edge of her tunic.

Her breath hitched. "What do you do?"

"I'm thinking if I don't make too many sudden moves we could turn this into a wedding night after all."

His hand found the warm flesh above her waist. When it closed around the soft swell of her breast, she stiffened.

"Easy, darling," he murmured in her ear.

She made a low, throaty sound of exasperation. "Daniel, this is beyond anything foolish."

"You're right, it is. Just lie still."

She doubted he had the strength to do more than

touch, but she couldn't ignore the lance prodding at her backside. Or the hand he reached down some moments later to find the slit in her leggings. When his fingers slid inside her, she was already wet for him.

She told herself she was submitting merely to spare him more hurt to his back, but his skilled fingers soon made a mockery of that untruth.

"Easy," he murmured again, his breath hot in her ear. "Just lie easy."

It was a new experience for Louise to be pleasured without pleasuring in return. Henri had needed much work to bring him to hardness, and James— She shut her mind to his swift, clumsy mountings.

She couldn't shut her mind to Daniel's touch, though, or the words he whispered to her.

"I dreamed of you, Wah-shi-tu. Every night in that cesspool of a prison. Every day when I couldn't think for the fire in my back."

She held herself rigid, afraid to move for fear of hurting him, thrilled by this strange sensation. She did nothing but shiver to the sound of his voice and the sly, clever movement of his fingers.

"I wept for Elizabeth," he confessed, easing his knee between hers, "but I dreamed of you."

He entered her slowly, deliberately. Just as slowly, he withdrew. She felt every hard ridge, every smooth stretch of skin.

"I dreamed of you, as well," she whispered. "And of this."

Deliberately, she tightened her muscles. His breath left on a swift rush.

She would not have believed she could take—or give—so much with so little movement! One clench of her belly and heat began to swirl through her lower body. She made herself go slowly, so slowly, yet her breath came fast and hard. Clenching, unclenching, she drew Daniel into her a little more each time, until her blood pounded in her ears and he filled her completely.

They used no hands, no teeth, no tongue, just joined their bodies in a slow, sensual ritual older than time. Pleasure began to spiral, to swirl through her like a slowly gathering storm. Louise stiffened, locking her legs, her back, her belly and felt a groan rise up in her throat.

He moved then, cinching his arm around her waist, ramming his hips up, taking her with him in a swift, shuddering, straining climb to the peak.

Louise awoke to a hazy dawn and the chirp of crickets greeting the day. Daniel had already scouted out a marshy stream and hunkered down patiently on the bank while Louise washed her face and tended to her personal needs. Only then did he let her peel off his shirt and unwrap the stained bandages.

She'd thought herself prepared, but couldn't hold back a gasp at the sight of his lacerated flesh. From his shoulders to the curve of his buttocks was nothing but a mass of livid, still-weeping cuts and half-scabbed welts. When they healed, he'd be scarred forever.

If they healed. Wishing fervently for the stock of dried herbs and medicines she'd always carried when running the trap lines with Henri, Louise washed the cuts as best she could and made Daniel sit unmoving while she searched for spiderwebs. Still dewed from the night before, they shone silver-bright in the morning sun. She found enough to form a stretchy, gauzelike skin for the worst, open cuts. The welts that had already started to scab she left alone.

"I will wash the blood from your shirt, but you should not put it on until the webs dry or they will stick to the linen instead of your cuts."

"It won't take long to dry in the sun."

"I'll walk behind you," Louise told him, gathering her bundle and his shirt, "to keep the flies and gnats from your back."

"It could be a long trek," Daniel warned. "I'm not sure how far it is to a hostelry where we can buy horses and supplies. After that it will be a long, hard journey to Richmond. We'll have to travel fast. Lieutenant Wilkinson may well come after us."

"I have traveled with you before. Always I keep pace. So will I this time."

Her utter nonchalance over the hardships ahead kicked up the corners of his mouth. He had a feeling he'd be the one hustling to keep pace.

24

August 9, 1807
Richmond, Virginia

Daniel and Louise arrived in the bustling city on the James River just before dusk. They'd kept a constant watch for signs of pursuit. If Lieutenant Wilkinson had picked up their trail, they'd managed to outrun him.

As they discovered soon after riding into Richmond, thousands of people had poured into town to observe the sensational trial now in full swing. There wasn't a hotel room, a boardinghouse bed or a pile of hay in a stable loft to be had. After being turned away for the fourth time, Daniel came out of a riverfront inn and almost bowled over a young man on his way in. He was a small man, delicate in appearance, wearing a gray frock coat, embroidered white vest and blue small clothes. He waved aside Daniel's apology with a winsome smile.

"No apologies necessary, sir. One can hardly walk the streets of Richmond these days."

His glance went to Louise, astride the dappled mare that had carried her from Louisiana. Like Daniel, she was wearing buckskins. He'd purchased his at the start of their journey. Hers were the same tunic and leggings she'd worn on the expedition down the Arkansaw. With her startling blue eyes and hip-length hair worn loose and rippling down her back in the way of the Osage, she made a striking picture.

"Are you just come from beyond the mountains?" the young man asked curiously.

"We rode up from New Orleans," Daniel replied. "Before that we were in Osage Country."

Interest leaped into his eyes. "I've but recently returned from a tour of Europe, which I found most enlightening. After reading the stirring accounts published by Captains Lewis and Clark, though, I now wish above all things to visit the lands beyond the Mississippi. May I take your direction and call upon you while you're in Richmond to hear more about your journeys?"

"I'd give you our direction and gladly, if we had one. It appears there isn't a room to be had in town."

"Nor out of it, either, I'm afraid. Many folks have had to make do with pitching a tent or sleeping in the back of a wagon."

"We saw the colonies of tents and wagons as we rode in," Daniel admitted, rubbing a hand across his jaw. After weeks on the trail, his beard had come back and was itching like the devil in the summer heat. He wanted nothing more than a bed, a bath and a shave. If he couldn't manage the bed or the bath, he'd at least scrape away his whiskers. They'd begun to leave red patches on Louise's cheeks and belly.

The mere thought of those patches spread a warmth through his veins. These weeks on the road had eased much of the sorrow that haunted them both. Gradually, he'd come to think he might be allowed some happiness despite his guilt and grief. She'd stopped insisting she brought disaster to those she loved and almost—*almost*—believed the silly words he whispered in her ear each night. If they hadn't been pushing so hard to reach Richmond, they might have stopped earlier each night, slept later each morning.

Now they were here, and Daniel could only hope he'd done right dragging her over a thousand miles of narrow traces and dirt roads. Recalled to the urgency of his mission, he turned back to the young man.

"Are you here for the trial?"

"Yes. I'm reporting the events for the New York *Gazette.*" He thrust out a hand. "My name is Irving, by the way. Washington Irving. I'm a scribbler of stories when I'm not dabbling in the law or newspapering."

Daniel folded his calloused hand around the younger man's. "Can you tell me where we might find the one who's collecting the evidence in this trial?"

"You mean George Hay, the lead prosecutor? Or Chief Justice John Marshall?"

"I'm not sure who I mean. We've got information we want to present."

His eyes lighting up like a ship's lanterns, Irving made haste to offer his assistance. "Why don't you come into the tavern? I'll buy you and your lady dinner, and you can tell me what information you want to present. I'll be more able to direct you to the right man then."

Daniel shook his head. "I'd best find George Hay. Do you have his direction?"

Reluctantly, Irving gestured to a broad avenue that led up a steep hill. "He has a plantation on the river, but the trial has so consumed him that he's putting up with his cousin here in Richmond for the duration. Mrs. Charlotte Durham, I believe her name is. She and her husband have a home one block up, on Franklin Street."

"I thank you."

"I'd still like to talk with you about Osage Country," the young man said hopefully as Daniel gathered his reins. "Perhaps after you've met with Mr. Hay?"

"Perhaps."

Louise spoke up for the first time. "Before I meet with anyone, I must wash my face and change my dress."

Daniel glanced over at her. "Why? You look fine to me."

More than fine. She'd grown more beautiful to his

eyes with each dawn that had shed its light over her face and lithe, slender body.

"The one you seek is more likely to listen if we don't stink of mud and horse," she said with a wry smile.

Daniel suspected all the attorney would need was one glimpse of those letters to sit up and listen to anything they had to say, but he understood her need to scrape off the road dirt. So, apparently, did young Irving.

"I say, you're welcome to use my room here at the inn to refresh yourselves. I'm sharing with two other fellows, but they're off dining with friends tonight."

Faced with his open, eager generosity, Daniel accepted graciously. While Louise swung down, he untied their saddle packs, slung them over one shoulder and retrieved his musket from its perch atop the rolled blanket. A few copper pennies pressed into the grubby palm of the boy who served as the inn's stable hand won instant assurances the horses would be watered and fed and brought around again whenever Daniel sent word.

The taproom was dark and hot and smelled of sawdust, sweat and the rack of lamb sizzling on the spit in the fireplace at the far end of the room. Daniel's stomach rumbled at the tantalizing scent. He placed orders with the tavern keeper for two dinners and seats at the long pine plank table when he and his wife had finished washing.

"Will you join us?" he asked Irving, as much to

repay his kindness as to gain a better understanding of the trial they'd heard about only in snatches as they'd traveled these past weeks.

"I will," the newspaperman said eagerly. "I'll show you to the room, shall I, and have the kitchen maid bring hot water, then wait for you here."

Daniel stood aside to let Louise follow Irving's willowy form down the narrow hall that led off the taproom. Her easy smile had disappeared, he noted. Frowning, she chewed down on her lower lip. Wondering what troubled her, he scanned the room, but saw nothing suspicious or untoward.

Her frown had deepened to a scowl by the time Irving lifted the latch to his room and executed a little bow. The chamber was small and crowded, with an extra mattress laid out on the floor beside the bed. Shirts and neck cloths spilled haphazardly out of satchels. Shaving mugs littered the pine dressing table.

Louise brushed by Irving with barely a word of thanks. Daniel followed with the saddle packs, closing the door behind him. His stomach clenched when his wife came to an abrupt halt in the middle of the room, wrapped both arms around her waist and moaned.

"What is it?" he asked, the skin prickling on his arms. "Who did you see in the taproom to alarm you?"

"No one," she managed to say through clenched teeth. "It was the smell. That meat roasting on the spit— Oh!"

Shoulders heaving, she sank to her knees and began to retch. Daniel dropped the saddle packs and grabbed the chamber pot from beside the bed. Louise snatched it out of his hands. He could do nothing but wait as she emptied her stomach of their meager noon meal of coffee, corn cakes and smoked venison.

Finally, she shoved the chamber pot aside. Daniel found a strip of linen toweling beside the water pitcher and dampened it. Hunkering down, he offered her the towel. She took it gratefully, scrubbed her face and sat back on her heels. Her expression was grave as she met his gaze.

"Three times this past week I have been sick."

"I know."

"After the second time, I begin to— I wonder—" Her brow creased. She twisted the strip of damp linen. "I have not had my woman's flow since before we left New Orleans. I think perhaps I carry a child."

"I think so, too." Daniel spoke quietly, gently, keeping a tight rein on the welter of conflicting emotions that had gripped him since he'd begun to suspect Louise was pregnant.

His first reaction had been the instinctive joy of a man who'd long wanted a son to carry his name or a daughter to warm his heart.

His second, the suffocating fear that Louise would suffer as Elizabeth had. Each miscarriage had added to his first wife's sorrow. The last, final stillbirth had sent her into the shadows. The memory of her silent agony brought back Daniel's familiar, swamping sense of guilt and regret.

But only for a moment. Even as he ached for Elizabeth, he took fierce joy in the woman who was now his wife. Louise was so strong, so courageous. She walked in shadows of her own—that damned legend haunted her still. Yet she refused to succumb, refused to retreat before her fears. She faced them now, squarely, as he'd anticipated she would.

"I do not know who fathered this babe, Daniel. You or James."

Curling a knuckle, he brushed it along the curve of her cheek. "It doesn't matter who fathered it. All I hope is that it has its mother's heart and bright, beautiful eyes."

"Oh, husband, do you truly feel so?"

"Yes, wife, I do. Any child born of your body will have my name and my love."

A sigh feathered out of her lips. Shoulders slumping, she leaned forward and rested her forehead against chin. They remained thus for a few moments, each lost in their separate dreams.

Daniel's dream was of a distant place where he could keep Louise safe and watch the babe she carried grow strong and tall. A place far from intrigue, where they could lift their faces to the sun and walk proud among friends.

The dream hovered in Daniel's mind for long, tantalizing moments. Then harsh reality forced him to tip Louise's face to his once again. His face grave, he issued a cautious warning. "We'd best not let it out you're with child while we're here in Richmond.

I wouldn't want General Wilkinson to get wind of it.''

Louise grasped his meaning instantly. "Do you think he would say the babe was his son's? Use our child in these so-grand schemes of his?" Louise's eyes flashed. "Pah! Let him but try."

Let him, indeed. Daniel suspected a snarling grizzly defending her cub would strike less terror in a man's heart than Louise protecting her own. Nor would she stand alone. Daniel would allow no one, be he general or private, to harm his wife and child. Hiding the utter implacability of his determination behind a smile, he dropped a kiss on Louise's nose.

"I'll scrub up and stand Mr. Irving to an ale in the taproom. Join us when you're ready."

Irving shared not only a round of ale with Daniel, but a wealth of information on the trial he'd been writing about for the past few months.

"It's a very complicated affair, more about politics than treason, I would say. Burr has hated Jefferson since they both ran for president back in '01 and tied for votes in the Electoral College. The issue went to the House of Representatives, where Jefferson won the presidency due to Alexander Hamilton's vigorous efforts on his behalf. Burr was then forced to serve as vice president for four years to a man he despised."

"I'd say Burr got a measure of revenge when he killed Hamilton in that duel a few years back," Daniel drawled. "Not enough, it would seem."

"Not nearly enough. Burr railed against Jefferson's Republican tendencies all the while he served with the man. His arguments struck a chord with many, including our Supreme Court chief justice, who's a staunch Federalist—has been since his days in the Virginia legislature."

"You're speaking of John Marshall, the judge who's presiding over Burr's trial?"

"I am. He and Jefferson have been at odds for years. More to the point, Burr and the chief justice are old friends. They dined together at the home of a mutual acquaintance here in Richmond only last week. Rumor has it George Hay nearly went into a fit of apoplexy when he heard about it. You know Hay is son-in-law to our current vice president James Monroe."

"No, I didn't."

"With both Jefferson and Monroe involved, you can imagine how much direction poor Hay has been getting from Washington on the conduct of this trial. Jefferson is determined to bring down his nemesis once and for all. For that reason, some speculate, the president sold his soul to that wily old devil Wilkinson, and agreed not to prosecute him if he'd testify against Burr."

His mind racing with the implications of what he'd just heard, Daniel eased back in his chair and gave the young journalist a hooded glance. "Has the general done so?"

"Loudly and at length! He's the personification of outrage, mortally wounded that anyone could think him a traitor to his country. He insists he merely pretended to go along with Burr's schemes to gain information about the plot.''

"What do you think?"

"I?" Irving snorted. "That the man's a scoundrel of the first order. I doubt we'll see that proved in court, though. He's gotten away with more than—" He broke off, his eyes widening. "I declare! Is that your lady?"

Daniel threw a glance at the woman weaving her way through the taproom. Her lilac gown was sadly wrinkled from being crammed into a saddle pack and a wreath of stray tendrils escaped from her hastily pinned-up hair, but she moved with a lithe grace that caught the eye of every man in the room.

"Yes," he murmured, his voice rough with pride. "That's my wife."

"She's quite astonishingly beautiful. I thought so when I first saw her outside. Do you think she'd allow me to sketch her?"

The tight line to Louise's mouth as she approached told Daniel she had no desire to risk her uncertain stomach once again to the heat and heavy odors of the crowded taproom.

"You'll have to ask her. But some other time, if you please. We have business to conduct with Mr. Hay."

"You're not staying for dinner, after all?"

"Not this night." Rising, he gathered his saddle pack and musket and gave Irving his hand. "I thank you again for the use of your chamber."

"You're more than welcome. I very much hope I shall see you and your lady again. Perhaps at the courthouse?" the journalist probed delicately.

"Perhaps."

Sweat shone on Louise's temple and her mouth had taken on a grim cast. Relieving her of her pack, Daniel slung it over his shoulder atop his, slipped a hand under her elbow, and steered her outside. She gulped in the muggy evening air gratefully.

"I begin to think the next months will be a test of my fortitude," she muttered.

"I don't doubt it," he said with a rueful grin. "Shall I have the hostler bring the horses around or can you walk? The hill looks steep."

"Not as steep as the mountains we have crossed these past weeks. Come, let's be done with this business."

They found the Durham house easily enough. It was a three-story brick mansion with a white-columned porch encircling the second level. Candle-light lit the windowpanes and threw a golden glow into the gathering dusk.

A uniformed manservant answered their knock, took their names and showed them into a small parlor off the black and white tiled foyer. Disdaining the sofa and chairs scattered about the parlor, Louise paced the polished oak floorboards until the man they'd come to see hurried across the hall. His hair was neatly clubbed back. He wore the buckled knee britches of a wealthy planter and a wary expression that could only have come from having been at the forefront of a bitter legal battle for months now.

"Mr. and Mrs. Morgan?"

Despite the stripes on his back and the weeks that had passed since he'd been drummed out of the army, Daniel still found it odd being addressed by Mr. instead of by his military rank.

"I'm George Hay." The lawyer took in Daniel's buckskins and Louise's wrinkled dress in a quick, assessing glance. "Did I understand the manservant correctly? You have evidence to offer in the Burr trial? New evidence?"

"We think so."

"May I ask what this evidence is?"

Daniel produced the folded sheets of parchment that had traveled with them from New Orleans. "These letters were written by General Wilkinson and sent to his son, Lieutenant James Biddle Wilkinson. They're in cipher, same as the letter from Burr to the general."

Hay's eyes bulged. "Do you know their content?"

"No."

He looked from Daniel to Louise again and reached out an eager hand. The sheets crackled as he unfolded them one by one and skimmed their contents.

"I shall have to refer to the cipher key," he muttered, his voice low and heavy with excitement. "I should have it inscribed in my heart by now, but some of these symbols are unfamiliar to me."

"There's more," Daniel said quietly.

"More?"

"My wife overheard a conversation between Lieutenant Wilkinson and an unknown companion. In this conversation, the man indicated he had proof General Wilkinson masterminded the entire conspiracy. She's also received some indication from the general's son that his father has not abandoned his plans to set up a separate state west of the Mississippi."

"Good Lord!" Clearly stunned, Hay swept a hand toward the sofa. "Please, be seated, and tell me what you know and how, precisely, you came by this information."

The telling took longer than either Daniel or Louise had anticipated. Hay had not served in the Virginia legislature and been elevated to attorney general of the United States without reason. His mind was as prickly as a briar patch. He extracted every detail, from Louise's recollection of the trappers' talk about a Spanish agent intending to reclaim the Louisiana Territory for Spain to James's admission he'd courted her with intent to use her name and her funds in one of his father's schemes. He also delved delicately into the relationship between James, Louise and Daniel. The fact that Sergeant Major Morgan had been cashiered from the service gave the prosecutor some pause. Daniel didn't doubt that Hay, like Louise, wondered whether he wanted revenge on the man who'd ordered his flogging and subsequent discharge.

What interested the lawyer most, though, was the discussion Louise had overheard between the lieutenant and his visitor. "You say you don't know this man's name?"

"No."

"But you think he was a merchant?"

"Or a banker. He says to James he has a letter from the general with instructions to deposit funds to Burr's account."

"Hmm, that in itself is not incriminating. Wilkinson has his finger in so many pies it's a wonder he himself can keep all his schemes straight. He'll claim he thought he was investing in a legitimate enterprise. Or that he was merely setting Burr up to betray him."

Thoughtfully, Hay tapped the folded letters against his knee. "We must hope these documents yield some names. The fact that they were written in Wilkinson's own hand may provide the first incontrovertible proof of his role in the conspiracy. I'll get my team together tonight to help me decipher them. Where do you stay? I shall want to speak with you again once we've read through the letters."

"We've yet to find rooms," Daniel said, rising. "We'll send you word when we do."

"You'll not find rooms to let anywhere in Richmond. You must stay here. I'll speak with my hostess immediately. She'll be more than happy, I know, to accommodate you."

Charlotte Durham echoed Hay's invitation. A petite woman with a mass of curly brown hair and bright, intelligent eyes, she swept into the parlor with a swish of silk skirts.

"But of course you must stay at Durham House! George says you've quite astounded him with the information you've brought. I'm agog to discover what it is, but know better than to ask. This trial has made lawyers of every one of us."

Noting the weary slump to his wife's shoulders, Daniel accepted the generous hospitality with a bow. The brunette looped an arm through Louise's and guided her into the hall toward the sweeping spiral staircase.

"George told me you've been traveling for some weeks. You must be quite weary. I'll send up hot water for a bath, shall I? And a tray of dinner, unless you should wish to come downstairs and sit at the table with the men while they eat their beefsteak and blue the air with their pipes."

The mere mention of red meat and the sweet, cloying scent of tobacco put a gray tinge to Louise's cheeks. "A bath would be most welcome," she said, "but I don't wish for a tray. I'm not at all hungry."

"As you like. Mr. Morgan, shall you join your wife, or the men at table?"

Unwilling to subject his wife to the uncertainties of her stomach once again, Daniel chose to dine with the men. "I'll take a plate downstairs, if it's no trouble."

"None at all. George, take Mr. Morgan into the dining room while I see to his wife."

When Daniel climbed the stairs some hours later and was shown to a guest chamber, he found a candle flickering on the dressing table and Louise sound asleep in a high, four-poster bed. She'd flung off the coverlet in deference to the hot August night. Her limbs gleamed faintly through the sheer lawn of a borrowed nightdress.

Blessing Charlotte Durham for more than the hearty beefsteak, rich port and fragrant tobacco he'd just been treated to, Daniel shed his clothes and poured fresh water into the washbowl. He would have preferred a hot bath and a razor to scrape away his beard, but made do with a thorough scrubbing. His skin and hair damp after their toweling, he blew out the candle and eased down beside Louise.

While his eyes adjusted to the gloom, his mind roamed. The talk at the dinner table had centered on the Burr conspiracy. George Hay had excused himself and hurried off to confer with his team of prosecutors, but the rest of the men present were as familiar with the convoluted politics and legalisms involved as Hay himself. While they weren't yet privy to how Daniel figured into the situation or what startling information he'd brought, they were more than willing to share their opinions on the progress of the trial.

Those opinions had Daniel wondering once again if he'd done right by dragging Louise all the way to Richmond. As young Irving had hinted earlier, this whole sorry affair was sounding more and more about politics than treason.

Maybe Hay was right to question Daniel's motives in coming forward. Maybe he *did* want revenge on the Wilkinsons as much as Jefferson apparently did on Burr. Maybe he'd risked Louise's safety just to be the instrument of the father's downfall and the son's disgrace.

Christ! Was he really so small, so bitter? With a little grunt, he dragged his arm over his eyes. The abrupt movement brought a groggy murmur from the woman next to him.

"Daniel?"

He lowered his arm. "I didn't mean to wake you. Go back to sleep."

Ignoring his quiet order, she flopped onto her side and propped her head up with one hand. "You smell of pipe smoke and soap."

His thoughts about the trial fled instantly before the worry she might start retching again. "Does the smoke make you feel ill?"

"Strangely, it makes me hungry."

"You had no supper. Shall I go downstairs and raid the kitchens?"

"I don't speak of food. It is you I hunger for." Her hair draped to one side like a river of dark silk as she trailed her fingers down the damp curves of his chest. "I think I would like to know how it feels to lie under you on this so-soft bed instead of on a rough blanket or the thin, flea-ridden straw mattress of an inn."

Thinking of the child in her belly, Daniel smiled lazily. "How about you lie *atop* me in this so-soft bed?"

Sliding an arm under her hips, he set her astride

his thighs. She wiggled to free her nightdress from under her knees, then fumbled with the ribbons at the lace-trimmed neck and tugged the billowing folds over her head.

Daniel's eyes had adjusted to the gloom well enough by now to see every shadowed line and smooth, sinuous curve. The dark nipples tipping her breasts drew him like the call of a siren. He played with the buds, teasing them into points before curving a hand around her neck to draw her down and replace his hands with his tongue and teeth. Arching her back to give him freer access, she let him suckle and tease until her breath came in quick pants.

"Wait," she gasped when his fingers found the folds of hot, wet flesh between her thighs. "I am too eager!"

Laughter rumbled up from Daniel's chest. "Didn't Henri teach you a wife can never be too eager?"

"Ha! You will think otherwise if I find my pleasure too quickly and have no strength left to bring you to yours."

The rumble of laughter faded. Bringing his hands up, Daniel slid them into the thick curtain of her hair and stilled her wiggling movements.

"You bring me to pleasure a hundred times a day, Louise Therese. Each time I look into your eyes, I see the blue skies of Osage Country. Each time you speak, I hear the ripple of a clear mountain stream. You're like the land that bred you. Wild and untamed and free."

She cocked her head. "Did you find it so beautiful, the land of the Osage?"

"When I stood on that ridge with Henri, I thought it more beautiful than any other place on earth. And," he admitted wryly, "more savage."

Taking the corner of her lower lip between her teeth, she considered his words.

"Well," she murmured after a moment, "if it is wild and untamed that thrills you—"

A quick roll brought her off his hips and onto her side. This time, though, they lay head to foot and her mouth closed on his hot, rigid flesh. She slid her lips over the head and danced her tongue down the engorged veins, but it was the way she used her teeth that soon had Daniel grunting.

The stinging little nips were torture enough. She followed them with long, sucking kisses, slathering washes with her tongue and the rake of her nails under his heavy, aching sac. Daniel stood it for as long as he could. Pleasure was shooting through him when he wrapped a fist around her calf, dragged her leg over his shoulder and buried his face in the wet heat between her thighs.

Mere moments later she went taut. Her every muscle strained, then shuddered. A ragged groan ripped from the back of her throat. Daniel tasted the salty froth of her pleasure mere seconds before he spilled his seed into her mouth.

He had no idea how long they lay entangled before he found the strength to disengage and pull her up beside him. She was breathing slow and deep almost before her head found a comfortable nest in the hollow between his neck and shoulder.

Daniel should have followed her right into sleep. His mind was as exhausted as his body. Tucking her head more snugly in the crook of his shoulder, he stared up into the darkness and once more tried to discern his reasons for insisting they come to Richmond.

The clock in the hall outside their chamber had bonged twelve times before he gave up the attempt to sort through his feelings about the Wilkinsons, father and son. All he could do now was wait to see what tomorrow would bring.

25

The summons from Chief Justice John Marshall arrived while the Durhams and their guests were still at breakfast.

George Hay had warned Daniel and Louise to expect it. He and his team had spent most of the night deciphering the letters from Wilkinson to his son. While they found nothing to pinpoint the general as the one who'd conceived of the traitorous scheme to wrest the territory west of the Mississippi from both U.S. and Spanish control, the letters contained enough ambiguous references to raise serious questions about Wilkinson's loudly proclaimed innocence. Coupled with Louise's testimony, they could prove the last nail in the general's coffin.

Louise, at least, looked presentable for an appearance in court. She'd fully recovered from her illness of the previous day. Either that or their strenuous pleasure of the night before had put a bloom in her cheeks. Charlotte Durham had helped matters by sending a maid to press the wrinkles from the lilac gown and help dress her hair into a fashionable coronet.

Thomas Durham had offered Daniel the loan of a shirt, trousers and a blue superfine frock coat lavishly adorned with brass buttons. The fawn-colored trousers rose a bit high at the ankle but otherwise fit well enough. The shirt and jacket, however, cut into Daniel's armpits and threatened to burst at the shoulder seams with the slightest movement. He made do instead with a shirt of unbleached muslin purchased with a handful of coppers from the Durham's giant of a stable hand. The same accommodating servant also provided a coat of plain black cloth.

"I'd order the carriage brought around," Durham said with an apologetic smile for Louise, "but the streets are so clogged these days with vehicles of every sort, it's quicker to walk. Would you mind? It's only two blocks to the Virginia House of Delegates, where the trial's being held."

"I've walked much farther than two blocks," she assured him. "I will tell you sometime of the weeks I trekked down the Arkansaw with Daniel and his men."

"I should like very much to hear of it." Tucking Louise's arm in his, he escorted her from the dining room. "Perhaps you and your husband will extend your visit to Richmond and stay with Charlotte and me after the trial."

"I thank you, but we have not yet decided what we do after the trial." She flashed a look over her shoulder. "Daniel and I will speak of it later. After we talk with this man, Marshall."

The Virginia House of Delegates crowned a high hill crisscrossed with gullies and overgrown with vines. As Thomas Durham explained to Louise, that talented Virginia native and amateur architect Thomas Jefferson had modeled the building after a Greek temple called the Parthenon. Louise had no idea what a Greek was, much less a Parthenon, but the soaring columns and high, pointed cornices of the temple pleased her eye.

Huge crowds had pitched tents on the sloping grounds of the house. Most of them, it seemed, were lined up at the entrance to the building. Thomas Durham negotiated his charges past the eager spectators and gained access through a side door, where George Hay met them. Although it was still early morning, the lawyer's face shone with sweat and his starched linen stock had already wilted. A whole team of colleagues surrounded him as he greeted Louise and Daniel with nervous relief.

"Marshall's waiting for you in a side chamber," he informed them. "I should warn you he's a bit perturbed with this sudden presentation of new evidence so late in the trial. Come this way, if you will."

He led them down a hallway filled with imposing marble statuary and milling crowds. The bystanders parted to let them pass, some good-naturedly, some muttering beneath their breath. Daniel kept a firm grip on Louise's elbow so as not to lose her to the jostling throng.

When she came to a dead halt, he almost trod on her heels. "Louise, are you—?"

His concern she'd taken ill again fled when he followed the direction of her narrow-eyed glared and locked gazes with Major General Wilkinson.

Openmouthed in astonishment, the short, rotund officer gaped at them. "Morgan! What do you do here? You and Madame Chartier?"

The man's utter stupefaction afforded Daniel a fierce satisfaction. All those weeks of hard travel had been worth the effort. He and Louise had arrived in Richmond ahead of any frantic messages from Lieutenant Wilkinson to his father.

"We've come to lay information before Mr. Marshall," he answered flatly.

Wilkinson's face lost every vestige of color. His glance slewed wildly from Daniel to Louise before fixing on George Hay.

"You damned cur! Have you stooped so low in your efforts to blacken my name that you must drag my son's affianced bride into matters she knows nothing about?"

Bristling, Hay opened his mouth.

Daniel cut off the prosecutor's reply with a chop of his hand. His eyes as cold as the ice that had coated the Arkansaw, he set the general straight. "Madame Chartier is no longer affianced to your son. She's my wife."

Thrown off balance by the unexpected news, Wilkinson recoiled.

Daniel took grim pleasure in sending him back another step. "I regret we can't linger to exchange further pleasantries at this moment," he said. "Chief Justice Marshall awaits us."

To give him credit, the general didn't cower. He drew himself up to his full height, which left him well short of the other men, and curled his lip in haughty disdain.

"Marshall wants so badly to exonerate his old friend, Burr, I doubt that he will listen to lies spun by an uneducated half-breed and a man who left his first wife to die by fire."

Daniel's hands fisted.

Satisfied that he'd struck a raw nerve, the general pinned Hay with a hard stare. "Are you sure you don't need to seek guidance from the president before you introduce these people to Marshall?"

The sarcastic reminder that he danced to Jefferson's tune brought a flush to the attorney's cheeks. "I'm well aware the president holds you in some regard for exposing Colonel Burr's perfidy," Hay said stiffly. "Let us hope his esteem does not prove to be misplaced."

"Let us hope," Wilkinson mocked.

"Damned banty-cock," the attorney muttered as he herded his charges down the hall. "I'd like nothing more than to see him painted with the same tar as Burr."

Daniel gave him a considering glance. "You walk

a fine line here, my friend. Jefferson may not be best pleased if you go against his wishes regarding the general."

"The president directed me to try this case to the best of my abilities. That's what I intend to do."

Impatiently, he rapped his knuckles against a door set between two life-size marble statues. Just as impatiently, the door was yanked open from the inside. A tall, spare figure with a thick head of dark hair glared at the prosecutor from under beetling brows.

"You took your time getting them here, Mr. Hay. We're due to reconvene at ten o'clock."

"I'm aware of that, sir." Ushering Daniel and Louise inside the small chamber, Hay closed the door. "May I present Mr. Daniel Morgan and his wife, Louise Therese Chartier Morgan?"

Lifting her chin, Louise answered the chief justice's glower with a cool smile. "Among my mother's people, I am known as Wah-shi-tu."

Her composure took some of the starch from Marshall's rigid spine. He unbent enough to return her thin smile and gesture her to a seat.

"I read the letters Mr. Hay brought to me this morning. Now I would like to hear from your own lips what you know of General Wilkinson's involvement in the Burr conspiracy."

Seating herself, Louise smoothed the folds of her gown. Daniel took a stand behind her, one hand resting lightly on her shoulder.

"I know only what I hear," she stated calmly. "A

man comes to see James in his quarters in New Orleans—''

"The James she refers to is the general's second son," Hay interjected. "James Biddle Wilkinson."

Marshall's thick brows snapped together. "Do you think me a fool? I know to whom she refers. If you wish for me to allow you to call her into court, please refrain from further commentary until asked."

Hay's mouth tightened at the tongue-lashing, but he obeyed the curt injunction.

Once again Louise related what she'd heard the night of the flogging. Hands clasped behind his back, Marshall listened intently. Daniel studied him with the same intensity.

This was the man who'd determined that a charge of high treason required two eyewitnesses to an overt act against the nation. The controversial ruling had allowed Burr to narrowly escape indictment on that charge and left him facing only the lesser charge of conspiring against a nation friendly to the United States.

Would Marshall now allow General Wilkinson to evade justice to save his friend? Or did he truly agree with Burr's attorneys, who asserted that Jefferson had trumped up these absurd charges against his old political foe?

Daniel glanced about the chamber, struck by the enormity of events that had brought him to this place, at this time.

With this remarkable woman.

As she finished her brief recitation, Daniel tightened his grip on her shoulder. She'd traveled more than a thousand miles with him, engaged in a battle she cared nothing about, had done herself and him proud. Whatever Marshall decided, Daniel knew at that moment he was right to have followed his conscience.

He hadn't come to Richmond for revenge. He didn't really care whether Wilkinson was brought down or not. He'd done his duty as he saw it and ended his fourteen years of service to his country with honor.

Completely at peace with himself for the first time since Elizabeth's death, he felt little more than a brief stab of disappointment when Marshall shook his head.

"I cannot allow her to testify."

Hay surged forward, looking as though the top of his head might blow off. Marshall stopped him with an impatient wave of one hand.

"Save your dramatics for the courtroom, George. You know as well as I do she presents only hearsay evidence. You would not have brought her to me if you were convinced her testimony would stand."

"Damn it, John, you have to consider what she says in the context of those letters to Lieutenant Wilkinson. His father all but states his desire to set up his own kingdom, using Mrs. Morgan's monies to pay for the arms and supplies lost when his plans with Burr failed."

"Listen to your words, man! Wilkinson *all but states* his desire. Unfortunately, he *doesn't* come out and state it. Nor does an overheard conversation between his son and an unknown individual provide admissible evidence of conspiracy to commit treason.''

To Daniel's surprise, Marshall sounded every bit as frustrated as George Hay. The chief justice caught his assessing look and shrugged.

''I will admit I have no great liking for the general. He doesn't know fact from fantasy and changes his story every time he takes the stand. It would give me considerable pleasure to hold the strutting cock accountable for his actions, but to do so I must have hard evidence, not hearsay. I'm sorry you've come all this way for naught, sir. And you, ma'am.''

''We did what we thought we had to,'' Daniel answered. ''We'll leave you now to get on with matters.''

''Where do you go?'' Hay asked. ''In case I need to reach you,'' he added with a dark look at his colleague.

Turning, Louise arched a brow. ''Where *do* we go?''

''Damned if I know,'' her husband replied, grinning.

''Me, I think we should go back to Osage Country.''

Surprise blanked Daniel's face. He stared at her nonplussed until he recalled their brief exchange of the previous night. Before he could assure her he had no desire to take her back to a country and a culture where she felt unwelcome, Marshall bowed over her hand.

"I hear your country is quite beautiful, madam. I wish you a safe journey home."

"It *is* beautiful," she agreed. "And it is above all things foolish to think the Osage will share it with the Choctaw and Cherokee."

"I beg your pardon?"

"This plan to move the eastern tribes off their lands is most absurd."

"Ah, you speak of the proposed Indian Removal Act." Slowly, Marshall nodded. "As it happens, ma'am, I agree with you. The act is not only absurd, but an abrogation of treaties concluded in good faith by any number of legal representatives of the United States."

"I know not this abrogation, but I know this. If other tribes come to Osage Country, my uncle's warriors will sharpen their spears and wives will weep for their dead husbands. You must tell the Great Father, Jefferson, what I say when next you speak with him."

"I promise you I shall. The Indian Removal Act is only one of the areas where Mr. Jefferson and I disagree, but it is one of the most serious."

Satisfied, Louise dipped her head in a brisk nod and left the judge's chamber. Daniel and George Hay followed her into the crowded hall. A quick sweep of the crowd showed no sign of General Wilkinson. Daniel sincerely hoped the man had gone to ground and was stewing in his own sweat, but couldn't work up a real heat about the matter one way or another. He had other, more urgent matters on his mind at the moment.

He waited while George Hay thanked them both sincerely for coming forward and delivering the letters.

"I promise you this won't be the end of things with Wilkinson. We have our eye on him. We'll catch him in a trap of his own making later, if not sooner."

Daniel nodded, impatient now to take Louise away from the tangled web of politics and debate he'd dragged her into. Hay thanked them again, begged them to let him know their direction when they decided on it and hurried off to don his robe and wig.

Daniel didn't breathe easy until he'd gotten Louise out of the House of Delegates. They picked their way through the tents and gullies to the street below, and stood for a moment in the hot August sun. After being driven by military orders for so many years and by a sense of urgency these past months, it felt strange to have no immediate task or goal. Strange and unsettling, almost as though a great weight had been lifted from his back and he didn't quite know how to walk upright without it.

"We'd best collect our gear from Durham House and the horses from the tavern yard," he said, rolling his shoulders to adjust to this odd sensation of freedom.

"And then?" Louise asked, not moving. Sunlight glinted on the shining coronet of her hair and dusted her cheeks with a coppery hue. She stood straight and proud, a slight figure in a lavender day gown, but no man could walk past without turning for a second look.

Daniel's strange, rootless feeling faded. He'd shed a lifetime of burdens, had lost a wife of ten years and the company of his military brothers, but he'd found something more precious than he'd ever dared dream of.

"I'm thinking we might take ship like you talked about in New Orleans," he said slowly. "Go to France to look up your father or your husband's people. Or we might go down to Texas. 'Tejas,' as the Mexicans call it. I hear their government is offering land to settlers. I could stake a claim and get us a cabin built before winter sets in, so you could start building a nest for the baby."

She tilted her head, considering the matter. "Does this Texas you speak of have green mountains?"

"It's got a few hills."

"Does it have great rivers filled with beaver and otter and fish?"

"Well, there's the Rio Grande and the Red, which I hear is muddy and flat."

"Does it have high ridges peaked with snow and prairies that stretch as far as an eagle can fly?"

"Not prairies, exactly. More like dusty plains."

"Then, me, I do not wish to go to this Texas. I think we should return to Osage Country."

"You said you weren't happy there, that you

didn't feel welcome. Why go back where you're not wanted?''

"I'm not welcome in my uncle's lodge," she corrected. "Nor among the Quapaw. But neither do I wish to sail to France and live among strangers."

Lifting her hands, she cupped his cheeks. "Like you, I have no family to go to, no home to return to. We are both between worlds now, so we must make our own. You are my husband, my mate. Where you go, I go. Where we roll out our blankets and put our heads down is home."

The streets around them were filled with people and noisy with the rattle of wagons and the *clip-clop* of carriage horses, yet Daniel could hear the mountains and prairies and rippling rivers calling to him. He was no farmer, had never felt the urge to stumble along behind a mule and carve up the land with a plow. He'd been trained as a marksman, had been taught to use a compass and circumferentor, could navigate uncharted rivers—skills Louise apparently appreciated as much or more than Daniel himself.

"Change comes to the land where the rivers run and the eagles fly," she said, a troubled look in her eyes. "It is in the wind here, in the talk of presidents and generals. The Pawnee and Osage and Wichita will feel these changes, be caught up in them. Perhaps— Perhaps it is meant for us to go back, to be part of whatever happens. Perhaps that's why you trek down the Arkansaw and I travel to New Orleans and Richmond. We each learn different ways and now we must take that knowledge back to share with others. If settlers move into Osage Country and try to claim the land, or the Cherokee and Choctaw come, perhaps we can somehow keep the rivers from running red with blood.''

Daniel suspected it would take more than good intentions and knowledge of each other's ways to stop the inexorable tide of westward movement and the violent clashes that would result. But he, like Louise, was ready to be part of whatever came.

''All right,'' he agreed with a smile that went deep into his heart. ''We'll go back to the land where the rivers run and the eagles fly.''

Epilogue

October, 1808
Along a bend of the Arkansaw River

They stood on the high ridge where Daniel had buried Henri Chartier. Animals had scattered some of the stones covering his grave, but enough remained to mark the spot.

Louise stood at the small mound for some moments, murmuring the prayers for Henri that she'd not had a chance to sing two years ago. Daniel moved to the edge of the escarpment to give her privacy and propped a boot on a rocky outcropping. Above him, hawks circled in a sky so blue it hurt to look at it. Below, forests of pine and oak, flaming red and orange and gold, spilled down to the Arkansaw.

They'd climbed the ridge not solely for Louise to say her farewells to Henri. Daniel wanted to scout out the strange carvings in stone that Chartier had told him about, the marks supposedly left by Vikings. He intended to fix their location with the circumferentor and include them in the survey he'd been hired to perform for the United States government in anticipation of establishing a fort and moving troops into the region.

At this point, he didn't know if the troops were intended for defense against the Spanish or for peacekeeping. The issue of the Indian Removal Act had yet to be decided. One of the chiefs, John Ross of the Cherokees, had threatened to challenge the proposed act in the highest court in the land. If the challenge reached John Marshall's court, Louise was sure that would be the end of it.

In the meantime, Daniel and his wife had carved a place for themselves in the wilderness. The monies Henri had left her—which Bernard Thibodeaux had refused to surrender for use by a traitorous general and his son—had gone into a sound-timbered house and a trading post. The trading post was prospering, and Louise had plans for a school to teach not only their bright-eyed, inquisitive son, but any Osage, Wichita, Caddo, French or American children who cared to attend.

The house, the baby and the business kept them both busy and happy, but it was the charter from the government to survey the land that gave them the chance to roam. They'd traveled south as far as the wide, muddy Red River. North to the plains of the Kansaw and Pawnee, where the buffalo herds were so thick they formed a vast, brown sea. West until the hills flattened and the sky rolled on forever. But this— This place of majesty and savage beauty would forever remain branded on Daniel's soul.

As would the woman he'd found here.

Her prayers finished, she came to stand beside him. They didn't touch. They didn't need to. They were one with each other and with the land they'd made their home.

Author's Note

Daniel and Louise are complete figments of my imagination, but many of the other characters in this book were very real.

Lieutenant James Biddle Wilkinson did lead an expedition down the Arkansaw during the winter of 1806/07—the first official U.S. exploration of the land that would eventually become Oklahoma. The lieutenant never quite recovered his health after the arduous journey. He was appointed a captain in 1808 and asked to lead another expedition, but declined, pleading "a lingering nervous disorder." He died at Dauphin Island, Alabama, in 1813.

His father, Major General James Wilkinson, had to be one of the greatest scoundrels in U.S. history. He escaped being convicted of treason, as did Burr, but was eventually court-martialed by order of President Madison for his role in the conspiracy. Amazingly, he was acquitted. After leading a disastrous campaign against the British during the War of 1812, the general was again tried and acquitted, but his army career had *finally* ended. He spent his last years in Mexico, where he died in 1825 from the effects of smoking opium. Not until almost a century later did researchers going through archives seized in Havana during the Spanish-American War find documents indicating Wilkinson had sold information for decades to the Spanish government as Secret Agent #13.

You might also be interested to know that Washington Irving, author of *Rip Van Winkle* and *The Legend of Sleepy Hollow,* made good on his wish to visit the American West. He spent several years rambling and wrote wildly popular books set in the West, including *A Tour on the Prairies* (1835) and *The Adventures of Captain Bonneville* (1837).

By then, the wilderness Irving traveled through had officially become known as Indian Territory. Congress passed the Indian Removal Act in 1830 despite vigorous objection from many parties. While some Native Americans began a voluntary relocation to new homes, others resisted and took their case to the courts.

Watch for the next book in this series, *The Untamed,* coming from MIRA Books in 2004. The story opens some years after the passage of the act, when the land that eventually became Oklahoma was still a vast wilderness, and a scheming adventuress from England adds a new chapter to an ancient legend.